Rowland Evans Robinson

Sam Lovel's Camps

Uncle Lisha's friends under bark and canvas, A sequel to Uncl Lisha's shop

Rowland Evans Robinson

Sam Lovel's Camps
Uncle Lisha's friends under bark and canvas, A sequel to Uncl Lisha's shop

ISBN/EAN: 9783337422738

Printed in Europe, USA, Canada, Australia, Japan

Cover: Foto ©Andreas Hilbeck / pixelio.de

More available books at **www.hansebooks.com**

Sam Lovel's Camps.

Uncle Lisha's Friends
UNDER BARK AND CANVAS.

A Sequel to Uncle Lisha's Shop

BY

ROWLAND E. ROBINSON.

FOURTH EDITION.

NEW YORK:

FOREST AND STREAM PUBLISHING CO.

1896.

TO

MY WIFE

THIS BOOK IS AFFECTIONATELY
INSCRIBED.

AN EXPLANATORY NOTE.

THE Yankee is everywhere, and everywhere is heard his nasal drawl asking a question or answering one. But it is a sign that the manner of his speech is changing that to some readers of " Uncle Lisha's Shop" who are unacquainted with a dialect once common in Vermont, and as yet by no means uncommon in portions of the State, the meaning of some words and phrases used by the old cobbler and his neighbors has not been clear. For the benefit of such readers of this volume it may not be amiss to explain at the outset some forms of speech that are least likely to be understood by them.

" Julluk " is a shortening of just like ; " god daown," " pud daown," " led daown," " sod daown," and the like, are got down, put down, let down, sat down, with the last letter of the first word changed to d. " Luftu" and " lufted tu " are queer corruptions of love to and loved to. " Callate," sometimes " carc'late," is to intend or plan, not to compute. When a thing is sold it is " sol'." The " heft " of a thing is its weight and also the greater part of it, and to " heft it " is to try its weight by lifting. The word hold occurs in different forms in one sentence, when you are bidden to " take a holt an' hol' on." " Hayth " means height, the " hayth o' land," the highest land in a certain section of country ; the term was often applied in former times to the Green Mountain range. Creature has slight differences of pronunciation according to its application. A very poor or wretched person is a " poor, mis'able creetur," a wild blade, a " tarnal crittur," a bad man, a " weeked crittur" ; and a bull, when not a " toro," is as politely called a " cruttur," the " tts " scarcely sounded. " Mongst 'em " signifies other persons beside the one or more named ; as, " John Doe an' mongst 'em." To " shool" is to wander aimlessly ; to " flurrup " to move in a lively, erratic manner. A " heater piece " is a triangular piece of land, shaped like a heater or flat-iron. The " square room " is the best room or parlor. A " linter " is a lean-to, a single-roofed building set against a larger one.

When a Yankee " dums " or " darns " persons or things, he is not to be understood as cursing them ; church members in good standing do so without scandal as they mildly swear " by gosh" and " by gum" and "swan," " swow;" " snum," " snore" and " vum."

The Canadian who learns English of the Yankee often outdoes his teacher in that twisting of the vowels which, no doubt brought over in the Mayflower, became so marked a characteristic of New England speech. Some words are very difficult for him to master, but finally he gets the better of most, and no longer says " jimrubbit " for India-rubber, or " nowse " for noise. But stove is his shibboleth. To the day of his death he calls it " stofe," and the generation that follows him can speak it no otherwise.

ROWLAND E. ROBINSON.

FERRISBURGH, VT., January, 1889.

CONTENTS.

—•••—

THE CAMP ON THE SLANG.

—

THE CAMP ON THE LAKE.

SAM LOVEL'S CAMPS.

I.

UNDER THE HEMLOCKS.

BESIDE a low-banked water-way among the reddish-gray trunks of great hemlocks, there stood, one day in the third month of a year, half a long lifetime ago, a shanty of freshly riven slabs with the upper ends slanted together in the form of an A tent. In front of it a fire smouldered, the slow smoke climbing through the branches that waved their green spray and nodded their slender-stemmed cones in the rising current of warm vapor. A few muskrat skins, stretched on osier bows, hung drying near by on slim poles placed in the crotches of stakes, and two canoes, one a light birch, the other a dugout, lay bottom upward on the bank awaiting the day of use. The shanty was luxuriously bedded with marsh hay and fragrant twigs of hemlock, overlaid with blankets and buffalo skins, and stretching out into the light were two pairs of feet, one clad in stout boots, the other in moccasins. Four legs faded away in the dusky interior, till, beyond the knees, the eye was puzzled to follow them.

Presently the boots began to stir and then the owner became dimly visible sitting up on his couch.   When he had
crawled out and scraped a coal from the ashes into his
pipe, and having got it satisfactorily alight, stood up and
looked at the cloud-flecked sky and out on the ice-bound
stream, the tall, wiry form, and quiet, good-humored,
bearded and weather-browned face of Sam Lovel were fully
revealed.   He half turned toward the shanty, and lightly
touched one of the moccasins with his foot.   " Hello,
Antwine !" he called, " be ye goin' to sleep all day ?"

The moccasins moved a little, and a sleepy voice in beyond said : " Hein ?   What was be de matter ?"

" Git up an' light yer pipe, an' then le's go an' see ye
spear a mushrat as you've ben tellin' on.   Come !" and
Sam vigorously poked the moccasins till they were drawn
into shadow, then reappeared, and Antoine Basette came
hitching after them into the light and sat rubbing his eyes
as he said : " Bah gosh ! Sam, Ah dunno 'f Ah won't keel
you, Ah dunno 'f Ah an't !   You spile 'em up de bes'
dream Ah never smell all ma laf tam* !   Onion bilin' in
keetly, patack roast in ashins, bull pawt fryin' in paan,
moosrat toast on coal !   Oh ! bah gosh ! jes' Ah tryin'
mek off ma min' de fus' one Ah'll heat nex', you'll hol-
leh ' Aantwine ! ' an' dey all gone off.   Ah'll pooty mad,
me !" and he shook his head and smote his fists above it ;
but the broad grin that followed gave the lie to these angry
demonstrations.

" Wal, I swan, it is too bad, Antwine, seein' 't we hain't
hed nothin' so fur but pork an' dry bread.   But we'll
make up for 't bimeby.   Lemme see ; your onion smell

---

* This is Canuck for time.

must ha' ben the skunk 't ye ketched in yer mink trap las' night. The pertater smell I d'know where ye got, erless 'twas a last year's one. The bull paout smell is in the futur', an' the mushrat smell is consid'able present, but not 's much 's I wish 'twas. But light yer pipe an' git yer mushrat prod, an' le's go an' see ye use it,'' and Sam sang from the ballad of '' Brave Wolf'' these encouraging lines :

"Chee-er up your hearts, young men,
  Let naw-thing fright you ;
  Be a—w—v a galliant mind,
  Let tha-a-at delight you !"

So the Canadian got his black pipe ablast, and taking a one-tined spear and an axe from the shanty, announced his readiness to start.

They went out through the sere rushes, flags and sedges that lay lopped by the winds and snows of many a winter storm, over the frozen marsh, to where the channel of the '' Slang'' wound clearly defined under the snow and ice, like the street of an aboriginal village, with here and there set beside it the huts of the muskrats. Away from the un-wooded eastern bank stretched the wide, flat fields of the Champlain Valley, yet dazzling white with the slowly melting snows of the persistent northern winter, though in places the pall was rent where the knolls and southerly banks of the tawny earth had come to the surface again, and zigzag lines of fences cropped out above the drifts. A mile back the gray and dark green hills arose, and along the eastern horizon ran the hazy wall of the Green Mountains, topped with the shining towers of Mansfield and Camel's Hump. Westward from the standpoint of Sam and his companion an uninterrupted forest of hemlocks and tall pines seemed to reach to where the Adirondacks' scarred steeps gleamed through their veil of haze. Over the landscape bent a warm-tinted sky with fleeces of white cloud drifting slowly across it before a gentle southern breeze. The tempered air, a tinge of purple in the gray of the water maples' spray, the caw of returning crows, and the long resonant roll of the woodpeckers' drum-beat gave unmistakable signs of the coming of spring—yet many days off, but surely coming.

The fall after Uncle Lisha's departure to his new home in the West, Sam had taken the old man's advice into serious consideration, and finally for various reasons concluding to follow it, he bargained for the making of a lot of traps and took Antoine as partner and instructor as well, for Sam had not much experience in trapping muskrats, those fur-bearers being not at all plenty in the rapid, weedless streams of the hill country, where all his hunting and trapping had until now been done. Long before sleighing gave any sign of failing they had their boats, traps, and provisions hauled down to the trapping ground, built their rude but cosy shelter that was for some weeks to be their home, and were now waiting for the opening of small-craft navigation, when they would begin trapping in earnest. They had set a few traps in the muskrat houses, chopping out a small opening to the bed, whereon the trap was set, and the covering carefully replaced. From the houses so taken possession of rose the tally sticks, to which the trap chains were fastened, like miniature flagstaffs. To one not so marked Antoine now led the way. "Go steel naow, Sam," he said in a low voice as they drew near it; "not mek it no more nowse as leetly mouses. Naow. Ah m's goin' stroke it raght in dar!" and carefully laying down his axe, he drove the spear into the centre of the rough cone of flags, mud, and sedges, a little below the top and on the south side.

"Dah, seh, Sam, ant Ah tol' you? Ah'll gat she! Ah'll feel of it heem weegle! Ant you'll see?" cried the delighted Frenchman, and when he quit his hold on the spear staff Sam saw that it was violently shaken. Antoine now chopped into the house and took out a muskrat writhing in agony and biting at the cruel spear that impaled him. The half-savage Canuck was in no haste to despatch him, but Sam dealt the poor brute a kick in the head that ended his misery at once.

"What for you do dat, Sam? You wait mineet you see dat leetly dev' faght lak a coss! Have it some funs!"

"There, Antwine," said Sam, with an expression of strong disgust upon his face, "you needn't prod no more on 'em on my 'caount."

"Hein?" cried Antoine in astonishment, "what for Ah don't, Sam?"

"Wal, it's too durn'd savage. The's too much Injin 'baout that for me."

"Ant you want it moosrat? Don't dat goode way git heem, an't it? Ah'll git forty, prob'ly twenty so, in one day! You s'pose he an't lak it jus' well as be ketch in traap, hein? Pool off his laig all day, bambye heat him off, den 'goo' by, Sam,' he say! He feel bad, you feel bad, ant de bose of it no good, an't it? Bah gosh, Sam, you'll got foolish motion in you' head, seh!"

"Wal, I s'pose I hev, but I can't help it. I know trappin' is onhuman business the best way you c'n fix it, a-ketchin' critters by the' laigs an' lettin' on 'em suffer, but the' don't seem no other way o' gittin' some on 'em.

A deadfall, 'at knocks the life aout on 'em fust dab, is the only human trap the' is, but they hain't wuth shucks for mushrat. But when you come to set for mushrat in the water, they draound quick an' I guess don't mind it much, bein' they're so uster the water. We'll wait a spell an' git 'em that way."

Further discussion was stopped by the shouts of a man who was coming toward them over the ice at the top of his speed.

" Hello there ! What in thunder ye duin' on ?" and as he came up to them, breathless with unwonted haste— for he was short and fat, built, as Sam thought, more for sitting than running—he panted out gustily : " What in thunder an' guns be ye duin' on, ketchin' my mush- rats ? Clear aout, ye cussed thieves, an' le' my mushrats alone."

" Is this raly one o' your mushrats ?" Sam asked, picking up the animal and examining it closely ; " I don't see no ear mark ner brand on 't, but if it's yourn, 'prove prop'ty, pay charges an' take it away."

" Wal," said the new-comer, seating himself on the muskrat house and wiping his hot face with his coat-sleeve, " you don't b'long here ; you ha' no business here ! These is aour rats !"

" Oh, aour rats," said Sam quietly ; " yes, they be aour mushrats—when we git 'em, not afore. You take your sheer, an' I'll take mine, 'f we c'n git 'em. And I'm a-goin' to git mine 'f I know haow."

" I tell ye," the man reiterated hotly, " ye don't b'long here ; ye ha' no business here ! Thunder an' guns ! you're durn'd putty fellers, hain't ye ?"

" Don't b'long here ? I'm a V'monter, an' live in this

caounty, an' was borned and raised in it. Who give ye these mushrats ? D' you own this 'ere ma'sh ?''

No, the visitor admitted that he did not own the marsh, but he lived near it, and he and two or three other residents had always trapped in Little Otter and the two Slangs, "and the trappin' here b'longed to 'em."

"Haow many traps do the hull caboodle on ye set ?" Sam asked ; and after reckoning in his head and on his fingers, the man said, "'Baout hund'ed an' fifty."

"A hund'ed an' fifty traps on all these miles o' ma'sh ! Wal, I guess what we've got won't make no great diffunce wi' ye. So don't fret yer gizzard, my friend. The's room 'nough for all on us, an' we'd like to live friendly wi' you fellers, but anyway, we're goin' to trap here a spell."

"Who gin ye leave to camp over yunder ?" the man asked, waving his hand toward the shanty.

"The man 'at owns it," Sam answered shortly. "I do' know why in Sam Hill I never thought to ask you— but then, you see, I hed not hed the pleasure o' your 'quaintaince till jes' naow. Be you willin' ?''

"Humph !" grunted the aggrieved trapper. "Camp an' be cussed ! Trap and be darned ! Ye won't make much aouten on it, see 'f ye du !" and he went his way in no better humor than he had come.

When he was at a safe distance, Antoine, till now a very silent partner, shook his fists at his broad back, seized himself by the seat of his trousers and apparently lifted himself off the ice in a rapid series of short leaps, and cried in a tone that he was sure would not be heard by the retreating foe, " Hey ! bah gosh ! Ah wan' leek you, seh !" Then turning to Sam and throwing down his cap, " Ah dunno what for Ah ant tink for leek dat man when he here.''

"Wal, Antwine," said Sam, with a quiet smile, "I du."

Then they went back to the camp, and Antoine skinned the rat from chin to tail, and stretched the pelt on a bow of "nanny bush," fastening it in place by upward cuts through the skin and into the wood at the nether ends of the bow. Then they made their tea, frizzled their slices of salt pork over the coals, and ate their rude but well-relished supper. After a long smoke they turned into their robes and blankets.

Once when Sam arose to replenish the fire and take a quiet midnight smoke, he thought he heard the sound of axe strokes out on the moonlit marsh, but he saw nothing and thought then no more of it. But next morning when they went abroad he and his comrade found every muskrat house chopped down and uninhabitable, and the few traps they had set were thrown out upon the ice. Their unpleasant acquaintance of the day before, and his partners, had done their night's work thoroughly. The muskrats had retreated to their burrows in the banks, and there could be no more trapping nor spearing in the ruined houses. Antoine pranced and tore his hair, and made threats of terrible vengeance. Sam said, "Wal, arter all, 'twas kinder neighborly in 'em not to steal aour traps. We'll wait an' start 'long o' the rest on 'em when the ice goes aout."

II.

THE PASSING OF WINTER.

Sam and his partner lounged about camp waiting for the opening of the water, and there was not much to break the dull monotony of those days of waiting. For the most part there was little to do but cook and eat the simple fare, and sit by the camp-fire trimming muskrat bows and tally sticks. Now and then a chopper would stop at the shanty to light his pipe, and if a Yankee, to ask no end of questions; or if a Canadian, to jabber with Antoine till Sam was driven almost wild with the incessant jargon so unintelligible to him. A mile down the creek a party of lumbermen were building a raft of logs upon the ice, and often to pass the time away Sam and Antoine would visit them, and being expert axemen, help them make " knock downs" while they chatted and joked.

One day Sam was hunting about camp for something, and Antoine asked, " What you look see, Sam ?"

" I'm a-lookin' for a mushrat carkiss. I seen where a mink's ben gallopin' 'raound, an' I want some bait for a trap."

" Wal naow, seh, Sam, you goin' b'lieved what Ah'll tol' you. 'T ant no use for settlin' bait for minks to heat naow. He'll goin' sparkin' dis tam year, an' he ant cares no more for heat as you does w'en you'll goin' sparkin'.

Set you trap in road where he'll goin' see *hees* Mamselle
Hudleh, Sam, den you'll ketched it."

"Like 's not you're pretty nigh right, Antwine," Sam
said, laughing, "but he might be comin' hum hungry
arter his sparkin'.   I've knowed of such cases ;" and having found a bait of odorous muskrat flesh he hung it over
a moss-covered trap in a hollow log, and next morning
brought in the lithe slender fellow whose brown coat of fur
became so fashionable and valuable in after years, though
then worth no more than the muskrat's.

Once they went coon hunting in the great woods, and
after a half day's wallowing through the soft, deep snow,
tracked three coons to a big hollow pine stub, and chopping it down, took out five residents and visitors, whose
pelts made a showy if not a rich addition to their slender
display of peltry.

Along the winter roadway of ice, now made the most of
by teamsters while it lasted, frequent loads of logs and
wood or empty returning sleds came and went, crunching
in and out of sight and hearing.   To the eastward beyond
the wide fields, from where the smoke of farm house chim-
neys drifted upward, came sounds of busy life : the "jing-
jong" of old-fashioned "Boston" sleigh bells faring to and
fro on the highway, the steady thud of flails in barns, the
lowing of cows and the bawling of calves, the cackle of
hens and the challenge of chanticleer ; at noon the shouts
of schoolboys and the mellow blasts of the conch-shells
sounding for dinner.   To the westward were the woods,
their primeval solitude almost undisturbed, their silence
only broken by the strokes of a far-off axe, followed by the
dull boom of the falling tree.   At night the gloomy, cryptic
aisles resounded with the solemn notes of the great horned

owls, and once or twice the trappers heard there the wild caterwauling of a lynx. So forty years ago the narrow Slang was the dividing line between broad fields that had long been cleared and cultivated and a thousand acres of ancient forest.

In this way the days passed, while the snow slowly melted off the fields and the ice slowly rotted. More tawny knolls cropped out in pasture and meadow, gray streaks of ice came to the surface along the creek and Slang, and in the woods the snow sunk lower and lower its winter litter of twigs, shards of bark and slender evergreen leaves, till here and there a hummock brown with last year's fallen leafage, or a mouldering log bright with ever-verdant moss, came to the checkered sunlight again.

Cold nights and cold days were not infrequent, when the saturated snow was crusted hard enough to bear a horse, and a roaring fire was needed at the shanty front to keep the trappers warmed into anything like comfort. But after each "cold snap" the south wind blew warmer than before, more crows came sagging heavily along on it from their winter exile, the woodpeckers sounded oftener their cheery roll, bluebirds and the first robin came, a phebe called sharply for his mate and found flies enough in sunny nooks to keep him busy while he awaited her coming, and a dusky chorus of blackbirds gurgled out a medley of song from the tops of the maples, while the tardy spring drew nearer.

In these warmer days, hollow, unearthly moans and roars, rising at times almost to a yell, were heard along the lake, at first faintly from afar, then nearer, till every jagged steep of Split-Rock Mountain echoed with the wild voices, then fading away to a humming murmur in the distance. It

was as if some tormented demon was fleeing over the ice,
or a phantom host of the Waubanakee was rushing in swift,
superhuman haste along the ancient war-path of the dead
nations.   It was the booming of the lake, a sound strange
and almost appalling to Sam, who, till now, had never
heard it.

At last a great rain came with a strong southerly wind,
and the two made quick work of the snow melting, and
the brooks poured down their yellow floods till the sluggish
current of the Slang was stirred.   The ice, for some days
unsafe to venture upon, was now honey-combed, and presently was only a mass of loose, slender, upright spires of
crystal, undulating when disturbed in long, smooth swells,
and tinkling a faint chime as if a million fairy bells were
knolling its downfall.   Watery patches began to show here
and there on the marshes, great flocks of geese journeying
northward harrowed the gray sky, and ducks in pairs and
droves came whistling down and splashed into the open
water to feed and rest.

Then one morning, when Sam and his companion
crawled out of the shanty, they beheld the long wished-for
sight of marshes clear of ice, and after a hasty breakfast
they launched the birch and dugout and loaded them with
the traps already strung on the tally sticks, and each with
axe and gun they set forth to coast the low shores.   The
boats kept close together, the pine leading the birch, for
Antoine was now to take the part of instructor.   Scanning
every half-submerged log they passed, he soon stopped his
craft alongside a fallen limbless tree whose roots still clung
to the bank, while its trunk slanted with a gentle incline
into the turbid water.   Abundant sign about the water-line
showed that the long-imprisoned muskrats had already

made the most of their newly gained liberty to swim with heads above water.

"Dah seh, Sam, you see he been here, lot of it, an' prob'ly he'll comin' 'gin. Naow, chawp nawtch in de lawg, so," and with half a dozen strokes of his axe he cut a neat notch in the log just below the water-line, wide enough to hold a trap when set. It was a pine, well preserved, and the chips and notch were bright and fresh. "Naow you see, w'en de nawtch mek it too shone, you wan' put it on some weed, mud, sometings," and he overlaid the cut with a thin layer of sodden water weeds. "Moosrat he ant very cunny, but he lak see ting where he been look kan 'o usual." Then he drove the tally pole firmly into the soft bottom, and set the trap in the notch with no covering but the two inches of muddy water that rippled over it in the light breeze.

"Dah," he said, as he resumed his paddle, "if de water ant rose or don't fell, you as' dat trap to-morrah mornin', he tol' you, moosrat!"

At the next promising place Antoine superintended the setting of a trap by Sam, and pronounced it, "Pooty well do, for *bee*-gin." So they fared on through the marshes' floating weeds and bristly thickets of button bush, now over the submerged shore among the trunks and sprouts of willows, water maples and ash that bordered it. Often they were startled by the sudden splash and flutter of frightened wood ducks that arose before them and went squeaking away to some undisturbed retreat. Great flocks of the more wary dusky ducks swam safely far out from shore, but at the approach of the boats they too took wing with a tremendous uproar of splashing and quacking. More than once they surprised some strange water-fowl whose like they had never seen before, some resting wayfarer on that great thoroughfare between northern and southern seas. Sam's eyes ranged wider than those of Antoine, who was looking only for places where traps might be set. The tall Yankee laid down his paddle, took up his gun, and after a second's aim at a brown lump that made a scarcely perceptible motion on an insular stump, fired. The lump disappeared at the report of the gun, and close beside the stump the legs of a dying muskrat pawed the air.

"Hoorah for hoorah!" Antoine cheered, as Sam picked up his game. "Nev' min', Ah show it to you to-naght 'baout sun gone daown haow shoot moosrat! Yas, seh! Call it raght up, clear 'cross Slang, seh, you see?"

"All right," Sam said, "I wanter see you do it. D'ye shake a dish o' corn at 'em an' holler 'caday!' or whistle 'em up as ye would a dawg, er haow?"

"Nev' min', Ah show you, Ah tol' you truth, jes same always Ah do."

Sam got two or three more shots, and then they set the traps they had in their boats on logs, bogs, and the ruins of houses where the rats had come to feed on the succulent roots of underwater growth they had reft and set afloat, and the afternoon was well worn away when they went home to the shanty. Then they had a hearty supper, a part of which was the roasted bodies of two of the muskrats Sam had shot, and which he, much against his prejudices, was forced to confess were an agreeable change from salt pork. When the shadows of the tall trees touched the eastern shore of the Slang the trappers took their guns and went thither in their canoes, which they ran ashore, and there sat in waiting for the game to appear. The fires of the sunset glowed in the western rim of the clear sky, and their mirrored counterfeit shone as brightly in the quiet water below the black reflections of hemlocks and pines and the fine tracery of the water maples' graceful limbs. Presently a shining wake cut the shadows as a muskrat came up from the entrance of his burrow and cruised swiftly along the western shore, whining out a call to his lady love. As Sam watched the point of the lengthening streak of gold and listened to the plaintive impatient voice, so like the whimpering cry of a young puppy, he was startled to hear it repeated close beside him. As he turned cautiously in his seat, cocking his gun, he saw nothing but Antoine with his lips pressed firmly together blowing his breath out between them with what seemed a painful effort, for he was very red in the face and his eyes were bulging from their sockets. But his simulation of the muskrat's call was perfect, and the little swimmer at once shaped his course toward him. The treacherous call was kept up till the poor fool was within four rods of the muzzle of Antoine's musket, which then belched forth its fatal charge. "Dah!" said the Canuck, as he picked up the riddled muskrat, "Ah guess hees hole folks ant be worry for heem be aout sparkin' naghts some more, don't it? Bah gosh, ant Ah tol' you Ah'll call it, hein?"

Shining wakes streaked the darkening water in all directions, and Antoine called half a dozen more deluded victims to their doom before the gloaming thickened to the mirk, and gun-sights were no longer to be seen. As they wended homeward, guided by the faint light of their low camp-fire, Sam swore, " By the gret horn spoon, I wish 't I hed the ol' Ore Bed here ! It 'ould be fun to pop them swimmin' mushrats with it." (The Ore Bed was an ancient rifle owned by him, bearing a township fame for its shooting qualities, and owing its name to the many pounds of iron in its barrel.)   " I wish 't I hed it here !''

" Wal, Ah dunno—prob'ly 'f hole Bahtlett don't usin' hees big hoxens you can sen' lett' an' get heem drawed it daown here ; but Ah dunno, sleighin' all gone naow,'' said Antoine, as the canoe bottoms scraped the landing at the shanty.

As Sam lay on the buffalo skins smoking, between whiffs he practised the muskrat call that Antoine had taught him till he became so proficient that his tutor called sleepily from his bed, " Dah, Sam, you betteh stop you foolishin', fore fus' you know moosrat come an' bit aff you nose off.''

III.

NEWS FROM DANVIS.

THE quiet water shone like a broad floor of silver in the early light, when the canoes left the landing next morning and began to crinkle the reflections of banks and trees and reddening sky. The few new-come robins sang their loud " Cheer up !" here and there a blackbird called " shooglee !" from the shores, and the loud nasal " quank ! quank ! quank !" of the dusky duck resounded from distant swampy coves, as Sam took his course up stream where the fewer traps were set, while Antoine coasted down stream along the flat cape that lies between the Slang and Little Otter.

Each made frequent stops to examine the traps, some of which were undisturbed ; but the greater number were off the places they had been set on and out of sight under water. Such, when fished up with the trap hook, brought with them a drowned muskrat, his soft fur plastered to his body by long soaking, and his scaly tail curved like a cimeter ; or a foot, the ransom a captive had paid for his freedom ; or, as valuable as this to the trapper, but not so satisfying to his pride of skill, the sprung trap's jaws full of sodden weeds. In one Sam found a wood duck, his bright eyes wild with pain and fright. He eased the jaws carefully from the leg, which was not broken, and after admiring his beautiful prisoner's gay spring attire, while perhaps there was a little debate between a soft heart and a

pork-surfeited stomach, he said, " Wal, I ll be darned if
you ain't the harnsomest creetur 'at ever I see—too harnsome to kill in col' blood ! Good-by, an' keep off 'm
all lawgs this time o' year," and he tossed the bird gently
aloft. As it went whistling and squeaking out of sight between tree trunks and branches with twists as dexterous as
a woodcock's among the alders, Sam said after a long
breath, " Wal, Sam Lovel, like 's not you're a dummed
ol' chickin-hearted fool ! *I* shouldn't wonder."

Once in the still, sunny forenoon he stopped a moment
to listen to a voice that came from far across the water,
shouting something that was meant for the song of " Old
King Cole." " Humph !" he grunted as he sent his
boat forward again. " As Joel Bartlett's Irishman said when
he heard the ol' man tryin' to sing when he thought the'
wa'n't nobody in hearin', ' If that bees singin', cryin' bees
mournful ! ' " Then clear and tuneful the long-drawn
cadences of an old Canadian song came echoing along the
woody shores.   " That's Antwine," Sam remarked.
" Suthin' like singin', only it's the tune the ' ol' caow
died on.' 'F he only hed some words, 'n' hed 'em sot to
a white folkses' tune, Antwine c'ld sing." The song
stopped as suddenly as if the singer had heard this dispar-
aging criticism.

A little after noon he had made the rounds of his traps
and was back at camp, where shortly afterward the Canadian appeared with a cloud of gloom shadowing his usually
cheerful face, the more unaccountable that a goodly pile
of muskrats lay in the bow of his canoe. After dinner, as
they were skinning their catch, Antoine unburdened himself, breaking out suddenly after a long silence, " Bah
gosh ! seh, Ah'll see dat mans to day what come mek it

sass on de ice dat tam, you rembler. Bah gosh! he'll bruse me all up, wus Ah never was 'fore, seh.''

"Bruised ye, Antwine? Why, I don't see no marks on yer face. Did he kick ye, er what?"

"Oh, no na-no, no! He ant tawch me. He 'fraid for know better 'n dat. He bruse me wid his maouths; he call me more as forty Canuck! Tief! Peasoup! Evreeting he mos' can't tink of it! He bruse you, too; call it you 'Gum Chaw.' He tol' me, 'Haow much gum tek it for keep dat long chap 'live all day?' He askit me we settlin' trap where he b'long to it. We tief! Oh, Ah can' tol' all of it. If it ant for one ting, Ah come pooty near leek heem, Ah b'lieve so, seh!''

"What was't saved the poor creetur's hide, Antwine?'' Sam asked, as he tossed the last disrobed muskrat on to the gory heap of carcases.

"Wal, seh, Ah tol' you,'' Antoine replied, waving his bloody knife impressively, "Ah'll be so mad Ah'll 'fraid 'f Ah'll beegin Ah ant never stop 'fore Ah'll keel heem all dead! Den Ah be hang, jus' for littly ting lak dat! Den who goin' tek' care of it Ursule an' all dat chillens, hein? No, seh; Ah ant goin' dirty dat nasky Bastonien* wid ma finger. You wan' hear it talk, sing, too, bah gosh, dat mek you laff't at it; can' sing more as pigs—you go dat way to-morreh, Ah go todder way—— Oh, Sam, too,'' he cried, suddenly remembering an important bit of news, "peekrils beegin play! Ah'll see tree, four of it! If he

---

* NOTE.—I have no idea how this word, Canuck for Yankee, is spelled. The Abenakis of St. Francis call a Yankee "Pastoniak.' Probably both words mean a Bostonian.

be good day to-morrah, we have it some fun shoot it, an'
more of it heat it.   You'll see any?''

"Wal," said Sam, considering, "I did see wakes of
tew three fish a-skivin' away f'm the shore, but I do' know
what they was."

"Dat peekrils, Ah bet you head!" and he discoursed
at length on the spoit of pickerel shooting, while they
stretched the skins of the twenty five or more rats their
traps had yielded and hung them to dry on poles.   As they
lounged about the camp waiting for the evening shooting,
they heard a loud call on the opposite shore a little above
a cove where two brooks contributed their waters to the
Slang, and the long-drawn-out call, "Sa—am—will! An
—twine!" was presently followed by the dolorous howl of
a dog.   "If that hain't ol' Drive's hoot, I never heard it,"
cried Sam, his heart beats quickening at the old familiar
voice, "an' I'll bate that 'ere 's Peltier a-hollerin'!" and
running down to the landing he stooped and pulled the
bushes aside, and peering out saw the unmistakable, lank,
clothes-out growing form of his young neighbor, and sitting
close beside him on the clayey bank Drive, with uplifted
muzzle and ears drooping to his elbows, while his sonorous
voice awakened lowland echoes that it had never stirred till
now.

"All right, Peltier!" Sam answered, "I'll be over
arter ye torights," and called back to Antoine as he set
the dugout afloat, "I'll take your canew, it's stiddier 'n
mine," and in five minutes the craft ran its nose up among
the floating rushes at Pelatiah's feet.

"I swan! I never thought o' seein' you here yit awhile,
but I'm almighty glad to," said Sam heartily, as he stepped ashore and grasped the hand that was stretched out to

him a half foot beyond the shrinking coat sleeve. "An' you too, you blessed ol' cuss," as he bent down and patted the jubilant hound's hooped sides with resounding slaps, and pulled his long silken ears, while he looked into the face whose furrowed, sorrowful lines were lighted with an unwonted sunshine of joy. "What on airth brung you here? Can't you git along 'thaout me, ye durned ol' critter, hey? Come, Peltier," cutting short the hound's caresses, "git right in wi' your duds, if you've fetched any, an' we'll go over to the pallis an' git supper 'fore the roas' beef an' turkey an' things gits cold. Git in here, Drive, an' lay daown." And Pelatiah stumbled up the bank, turning toward his friend a puzzled face as he went, and returned with a great half-filled carpet bag of once gorgeous but now faded colors, which he handed to Sam, and then made another trip, bringing down this time the famous old Ore Bed. Sam's eyes shone with delight when he saw the ponderous piece, its long octagonal barrel cased to the muzzle in the "curly maple" stock, its trimmings, hooked heel plate, and patchbox of brass that glistened like gold where hand or shoulder had brightened them with wear.

"Jest ezackly what I was a-wishin' for yist'd'y," he said as he laid the cherished weapon in the canoe, pillowing it on the carpet bag. "How come ye to think o' bringin' on 't? But there! I'll bate you never brung a bullit ner moulds ner lead, 'n' 'tain't no more use 'n a club."

"Wall, naow, I did," Pelatiah drawled, combing out his words through a broad grin, "'n' the hull three on 'em 's in the v'lise."

"Good boy!" Sam said approvingly; "naow git right in an' squa' daown right there, an' set still, for this 'ere ol' holler lawg hain't quite so stiddy 's the scaow on the

mill-paund." That ancient square-built vessel, as incapable
of capsizing as of speed, was the only craft Pelatiah had
ever boarded till now, and he took his allotted place in the
canoe with no little trepidation, the obedient hound
crouching trembling and whimpering behind him. Grasping either gunwale with a firm grip he pulled lustily on the
one which dipped the lower to right the long narrow boat
as she backed careening from the shore. " Le' go the
sides an' set still," said Sam sharply, as he headed her for
the shanty, " erless ye wanter spill the hull caboodle on us
int' the drink !" And Pelatiah minded, not even speaking, and scarcely breathing till he felt the land under foot
again. Then regarding the Slang and letting out his pent-
up breath with a great sigh of relief, " Whoofh ! I swan to
man, this is the goldarndest pawnd 't ever I see ! I be
durned 'f 'tain't wussen crossin' the 'Tlantic Ocean !"
Then turning toward the shanty he saw the array of drying
muskrat skins. " Gosh all fishhooks ! Where d'ye git
sech a snarl o' stockin's ?"

" Dat coats, Peltiet," Antoine answered, now approaching and greeting the visitor, " moosrat coats. We'll trow
'way all hees stockin'. Haow you do pooty well, seh ?
Bah gosh ! Ah'll glad of it ! Haow pooty well all de
folkses up Danvis was, hein ? Ma waf he pooty well, too,
an' all de chillens ? Ah'll glad dat !" he ran on,
while Pelatiah nodded the answers that his slow speech
was allowed no time to give. " Wal, seh, Ah'll wan' see
it pooty bad me. Ah'll tink great many of ma waf an'
chillens."

" Well ye may," said Sam, hauling up the canoe ; " the's
a great many on 'em to think on. Haow many young
uns hev ye got, Antwine ?"

" Bah gosh, Sam, Ah dunno for sartin. Ah'll ant be home for mos' four week 'go ! You'll have askit Peltiet !"

" I wa'n't there more'n half 'n haour, 'n' 1 didn't hev time to count 'em, so I can't tell ye," said Pelatiah, fore-stalling the question.

" Wal, never mind naow, we'll take 'count o' stock some other time. Le's ha' some supper 'n' then go a-shootin'. I wanter be borin' holes in some o' them mush-rats' heads with th' ol' Ore Bed. Antwine, cook some o' them ma'sh rabbits, so 's 't Peltier c'n try 'em," Sam said, winking hard and covertly at the Canadian.

" Maash rrrabbeet ?" he said, with staring eyes. " Ooh ! yas !" as he slowly comprehended, " Ah'll got some dat all save up," and slipping behind the shanty, he soon reappeared with three pairs of small, nicely dressed hindquarters of dark-colored meat.

Presently they were sizzling in the frying pan, and their savory odor was pleasant to Pelatiah's nostrils, as to his ears were the bubbling of the potato kettle swung on its pole over the fire and the simmer of the teapot on the out-skirts of the coals. Then when the repast was spread on and about the slab that served, as far as it went, as a table, and the three seated themselves on blocks around it, Sam said as a sort of grace before meat : " The man 'at finds fault wi' this meal o' victuals is, like Uncle Lisher's cus-tomer, too durn'd p'tic'lar. A feller," he explained, as he helped himself to a potato and began to peel it with his jack-knife—for now that they could be kept in the shanty without freezing they had potatoes—" a feller come to Uncle Lisher onct for a pair o' right an' left boots. He wa'n't useter makin' nothin' but straight boots, an' when the feller come to try 'em on, lo an' behol' ! they was both made for one foot ! The feller begin to objeck some to takin' 'on 'em, an' Uncle Lisher he hollered so 's 't you c'ld a heard him half a mild, ' Good airth an' seas, man, you're too durn'd p'tic'lar ! ' ''

" Hounh !" Pelatiah snorted, " I hain't a-findin' no fault wi' your roas' beef an' turkey, by a jug full. This 'ere ma'sh rabbit is complete eatin'. I never hearn tell on 'em afore. It's darker meated and kinder juicier 'n whaot aour rabbits be. Turn white in winter, du they ?''

" No,'' Sam said, soberly, while Antoine was choking with suppressed laughter and cursing " dat sacré bone rabbit Ah'll swaller in ma troat.'' " No, they're diff'ent f'm aour rabbits in c'nsid'able many ways. They're pussier 'n' clumsier, 'n' some longer tailed 'n' shorter eared 'n what aourn be, 'n' they hant turrible wet places so 's 't ye can't hunt 'em wi' dawgs, and to my notion they be better eatin', as you say ;'' and Sam began on another quarter. " We'll show you haow we git 'em 'fore you go hum. An' speakin' o' hum, what's the news ? Everybody toll'able well ?''

" The' wa'n't nobody sick,'' as Pelatiah knowed on. " Hial Hamner hed a caow die, though—best one 't he hed. 'N' ol' Gran'sir Hill, he's kinder peaked this spring, though not to say sick. Braggin' wuss 'n ever 'baout what him 'n' Eth'n Allen done tu Ti. 'n' crosser 'n a bear wi' a sore head, M'ri Hill says.''

" All hands busy a-sugarin', I s'pose ? Putty middlin' good sugar year, judgin' f'm the weather here—frosty nights 'n' warm days for quite a spell naow.''

" Yes, sir ; hed two three o' the goldarndest runs 't ever ye see. Couldn't scasely git away, hed to most run away, sap run so, but the' was father, 'n' Jethro, 'n' 'Niram 'n' 'mongst 'em to tend to 't, 'n' so I come. Sugar an' surrup ! I mos' forgot !'' and he scrambled over to his carpet bag, and unlocking it, drew forth from its depths two quart bottles and a cylindrical package wrapped in a newspaper. '' Them's for you, Samwill,'' and diving again into the recesses of the bag, he came up with a larger package that diffused a garlicky odor as he tossed it to Antoine, '' Here's suthin' your womern sent ye.''

'' Onion !'' Antoine shouted, tearing open the paper and biting one of the hot little shallots as a boy would an apple. '`Dey can' be no better in dis worl'.''

'' Why,'' said Sam, uncorking one of the bottles, '' this 'ere 's maple sweet !'' and then as he unrolled the package a dozen little scalloped cakes of sugar tumbled out on to the slab. '' Much obleeged to ye, Peltier, for rememb'rin' on us this way.''

'' Hoh ! Ye needn't thank me for 't. Them 'ere 'lasses an' sugar didn't come aouten no trees o' aourn. The fact o' the business is, you're beholden to trees, an' things, 'at growed on the Pur'n't'n place, Samwill,'' and Pelatiah leered and winked, while Sam's sunburned face grew redder with blushes.

'' Wal, 'f we've goddone eatin' le's git ready 'n' go shootin' mushrat,'' he said ; '' I'm spilin' to pint the ol' Ore Bed at 'em. Haow 'd ye come to bring it, Peltier ? Didn't hear me a-wishin' for it, did ye ?''

'' I wish to gracious I hedn't thought on't ner ondertook ! My arms 'n' shoulders aches wuss 'n rheumatiz, a luggin' the pleggid ol' ton o' iron clearn f'm V'gennes daown here ! But, ye see, I couldn't get no gun nowheres—tried to borrer more'n twenty-five ; but they was all a goin' to use 'em, er they was aout o' kilter, er suthin' !

Then your folks said haow 't I might take the Ore Bed ;
thought I wouldn't, I s'pose. They didn't know what a
durn'd fool I was, 'n' I didn't, nuther ; but I du naow,"
and he rubbed his bruised shoulders and perhaps wondered
as he stroked his aching arms if the weight of the gun
had drawn them a little further beyond the protection of
the short coat-sleeves.

"Wal, I'm sorry ye hed such a job a-gettin' it here,"
Sam said ; "but naow, Peltier, every mushrat I shoot with
it you shall hev, an' every one 't you shoot with my shotgun, tu. Come, let's be off!"

So they went to the other side of the Slang, where
Pelatiah, armed with Sam's shotgun, was set ashore at a
likely place, the others stationing themselves in the canoes
near him. It was the young man's luck to have the first
shot. A muskrat broke the surface not far from him and
swam steadily past, while Pelatiah, with a thumping of the
heart that made his gun muzzle wobble, after a long aim
fired. When he craned his neck, expecting to see the dead
or struggling animal, there was only a boil of water en-
compassed with widening rings of little waves.

"You shot over him," said Sam in a low voice ; "you
wanter sight an inch below the water-line an' a leetle speck
ahead when they're swimmin' acrost ye."

Just then the uninjured rat came up fifteen rods to his
right, swimming straight away. The ponderous barrel
was slowly raised and cracked out its sharp report at the
very instant the small mark was covered, and the muskrat
floated dead, gently tossed on the wavelets of his own wake.
Sam soon had an opportunity to practise his newly acquired art. A rat struck out from a point above with the
evident intention of crossing to the west side, where per-

haps he had an appointment with some furry beauty of his race. If so, he was a faithless fellow, for Sam had hardly begun to sound the call before he turned and swam toward the siren voice, till the Ore Bed spat out at him its thin streak of fire, and he rolled over, feebly kicking his last with a bullet in his silly little brain.

"There's tew for ye, Peltier," Sam said, as he got his gun on end and began to reload it. "Let 'em lay where they be till we git through ; they're deader 'n hay."

Antoine had a couple of successful shots and a miss that set him to cursing, in turn, his gun, powder, and shot, and the muskrat who had been so impolite as not to receive his charge. Then Sam called one within short range of Pelatiah, who, carefully following the instructions given him, blazed away. The water boiled again when the muskrat had disappeared, and after watching the spot with mingled hope and disappointment till the troubled waters became quiet, and the last ripple washed the bank at his feet, the latter expression took full possession of his chop-fallen visage. "I can't hit nothin' !" he said, in a tone so melancholy that it was almost a wail. "I can't hit nothin', an', I won't try agin—be durned if I du !" Just then a dark object popped suddenly to the surface and lay motionless in the centre of the circling ripples. The boy could scarcely believe his eyes when he saw that it was the muskrat, "dead as a hommer," as he presently proclaimed. When they picked up the rat half an hour later, they found his jaws full of bottom weeds that he had grasped in his death struggle, and that had held him down till the buoyancy of his dead body loosened them.

It was now grown so dark, that looking toward the other shore, one could not make out where trees and banks left off and their reflections began, save when the ripples of a wake, breaking on the shore, caught a glint of the dying daylight, and divided the upper gloom and its mirrored double with a crinkled line of silver. Then they went to the "pallis," as Sam had named it, and reviving the feeble fire with an armful of wood, sat chatting of home, trapping, and hunting, till Sam remarked, "Wal, 's Uncle Lisher uster say, it's high time all honest folks was abed."

IV.

COLD WATER QUENCHES VALOR.

WHEN Sam, the earliest riser of the three tenants of the camp, crept abroad next morning the daylight pervaded a misty landscape. Close by the camp the silvery gray surface of the Slang was visible, then faded off into a dull white lake of fog that had for its further shore the dun upland fields and jutting capes of wooded hills. Out of it scattered trees arose with apparently unstable rootage, and roofs of barns like stranded hulks. The hemlocks dripped a slow patter of condensed mist, and the bottoms of the overturned canoes were beaded so thick with it that they looked as if sheathed with a coating of pearls. The light air from the south, so faint that it scarcely bent the columns of rising vapor, was soft with the breath of spring, and the voices of many birds uprose to welcome the beautiful day—the gurgle of blackbirds, the flicker's cackle, the robin's clear but jerky notes. the long-drawn whistle of the meadow lark away in the foggy fields, the trill of the song sparrow, and the joyous warble of the purple finch. A crow on a tree-top began to call his friends to breakfast with him on the heap of skinned muskrats that the trappers had left at proper distance from camp, and reminded Sam that it was time to make preparations for his own and his companions' breakfast. He raked a few live coals out of the heart of the ashes, and placing them be-

side the back-log, laid some " fat" pine shavings and sliv-
ers upon them, and after some lusty blowing got a blaze
started.   When he began to cut the wood to feed the fire,
the noise of the axe aroused Antoine, who came out on all
fours from his lair in such a half asleep and blinking condition that Sam was reminded of some hibernating aminal
taking its first look at awakening nature.   He said nothing till Sam hung the potato kettle over the fire, and claw-
ing a dozen potatoes out of the grimy bag they were stored
in, began to peel them.   " What you goin' call dat dinny
you mek it wen you git him do, suppy or breakfis, Ah
dunno, me ?"

   " Supper, I guess, 'f you don't flax 'raound a leetle
mite 'n' help.   Wake up 'n' get some ma'sh rabbits ready
'fore Peltier gits his eyes open 'nough to see what kind of
a critter the hindquarters growed on.   'T 'ould spile his
appetite t' eat if he knowed they was mushrats when they
was livin'."

   " Bah gosh !" Antoine grumbled as he shuffled away to
prepare the meat,   " Ah'll rudder sleep as git up in a
naght for heat !   Ah'll jes' beegin have it some funs
dreamin', you'll wek it me all up wid you hole ax —pluck !
pluck !"

   " High time to be a-stirrin', Antwine," Sam said
cheerfully.   " Traps to go 'raound to, an' then the fish
shootin' you've ben a tellin' on.   It's goin' to be the neatest day 'at ever was !"

   " Wal, Ah don' care for me," Antoine said, becoming
reconciled to the loss of his matutinal nap as he realized
what promise the morning gave.   " Guess he be pooty
good 'nough day — w'en he come."

   Pelatiah was called when the water was drained out of

the potato kettle and the frying pan was taken off the coals and set upon the slab beside it. Kneeling on the shore to wash his face and hands as the others had done already, he asked, turning his dripping visage toward them with an expression of disgust upon it, " Wha' d'ye du for suthin to drink ? This 'ere water hain't fit ! I hain't hed a decent drink o' water sen I come off 'm the hills. This 'ere stuff 'raound here don't hit nowheres !''

" Julluk me,'' Sam answered, " when I fust com' daown here. The well water an' sech didn't squench my thirst no more 'n it 'ould to open my maouth an' let the moon shine into 't. It's hard, all on 't ; you can't suds a pint on 't with a barrel o' soap ! But I'm a-gittin' use to 't an' the's a brook back here 'at dreens the snow aoutin the woods that you'll find toll'able satisfyin' 'f you drink tew three pailfuls on 't. Me 'n' Antwine goes over once a day reg'lar an' fills up. Draw up !'' he continued, seating himself beside the slab, '' draw up, Peltier, an' make yerself tu hum an' help yerself. The' might be better, an' the' is wus. You've got to wait an' eat to the secont table, Drive, 'f you *be* comp'ny,'' and the hound, who had been wistfully regarding the setting of the table, crept into the shanty and curled down on a buffalo skin, and watched the progress of the meal out of the corners of his eyes.

When they were ready to start, Sam down stream, Antoine up stream, leaving Pelatiah to wander at his will along the safe and stable shore, the sun was rising above the mist and glorifying it, transmuting the gray vapor into a long sun-glade of floating gold that stretched from the hills to them. The night had been such a mild and dark one as the muskrats delight to go abroad in upon their affairs, and Sam found in his traps many a poor fellow

whose wooings and nightly wandering had been ended forever since the last sunset. He was pushing his canoe
among the trees and water brush that stood ankle deep in
the shallow water, when he heard another boat scraping
the bushes along its course, the rubbing of the setting pole
on its side, and presently the form of a man appeared gliding over the water, upheld by some invisible buoyant
agency, which was revealed when a light skiff emerged from
a thicket of button bushes. Sam at once recognized the
occupant of the little craft as the one who had made such
a vigorous protest against their trapping here, and the salutation that he received left him in no doubt that this was
Antoine's reviler.

"Hello, Gum Chawer! Praowlin' 'raound on my
trappin' graound yit, be ye?" the man shouted, as if Sam
had been a mile away. "Say, hain't ye got a chaw o'
gum to give a feller this mornin'?"

"Yes," Sam answered very quietly, turning the canoe
toward the skiff; "tew on 'em 'f ye want."

When the gunwales of the two boats touched, the stout
man regarded the tall mountaineer with a puzzled half grin,
for there was a queer look in Sam's eyes, not quite in keeping with his apparently friendly movements. They came
abreast, and Sam rose to his feet, let go his hold of the paddle with his right hand, fronted the quarrelsome pre-emptor
of the marshes, and quick as thought dealt him a sounding fisticuff full in the face, knocking him sprawling over-
board and nearly capsizing his skiff. The fallen foeman
floundered to his feet in the hip-deep water, and sputtering
out mixed oaths and water, splashed toward his antagonist, who was balancing himself in the canoe, that rocked
violently from the recoil of his blow.

" If you come anigh me," Sam said, raising his paddle
for a two handed stroke, " I'll knock ye gally west !" and
the man halted, doubting whether it was better to incur
the execution of so dire a threat, or to retreat. " Naow,"
Sam continued, seeing that his enemy showed little dispo-
sition to renew his hostilities, " 'f you've got what gum
you wanter chaw tu-day, wade ashore an' I'll shove yer
boat tu ye."

The cold water had well-nigh quenched his valor, if not
his anger, and after a moment's hesitation and one more
look at the still upraised paddle, the man turned sullenly
and swashed his way slowly to the nearest land. The vic-
tor in this little naval encounter, seeing the vanquished
crew safely landed, set about getting the water-logged craft
into port, and with no little trouble accomplished it.

" Naow," he said, as if advising an unfortunate and mis-
guided friend, " if I was you, I'd empty the water aouten
my boat 'n' my boots 'n' my gun, 'n' wring aout my
close, 'n' go up to aour shanty 'n' build up a good fire
'n' dry aout. 'N' then, 'f I was you, I'd kinder 'tend tu
my own consarns, an' not be tu sassy tu folks 'at's a-
'tendin' tu theirn."

To this hospitable offer and wholesome advice the soaked
trapper made no reply, but sat down on a log and attempted to pull off his boots. They were as perverse as wet
boots ever were, and yielded no more to the owner's des-
perate tugs than to the accompanying contortions of his
visage, his grunts, and explosive curses.

" Gi' me a holt on em'," Sam said, stepping ashore,
and without waiting for one of them to be held forth,
seized the nearest stubborn boot and began pulling at it.
The unhappy wearer slid off his seat, his backbone grated

over the log, and he grasped wildly for some anchorage on
sedges, brush, and saplings, while his body ploughed a broad
black furrow in the mat of last year's leaves, and yet he
said not a word.

" Wal !" Sam puffed, stopping while both took breath,
" it does stick onaccaountable !   If ye won't kick, I'll give
ye a bootjack ?"

The man shook his head, and Sam turning his back to
him took the boot between his legs, grasping it at heel and
toe while the other set the free foot against him, and after
a short struggle the boot came off, and in the same way its
mate soon followed it.

" There, I guess you c'n git the rest o' your duds off
alone, an' 's mebby you're kinder modest, I'll clear aout."
Sam stepped into his canoe and pushed off.   His recently
aggressive acquaintance, still sitting on the ground and
beginning to fumble at his buttons, looked after him and
said at last : " Wal, I swear ! you're the curiest cuss ever
I see ; but I guess you're white.   I do' know as I can say
that I'm much 'bleeged tu ye—but you can trap an' be
darned for all I care."

" I'm a-goin' to trap," Sam said, and went his way.
He made the round of his traps, and at noon was at camp,
where he found Antoine returned and getting dinner.
Pelatiah soon came in triumphantly bearing by the gills a
huge uncouth fish with a wide mouth, eyes like a pig's,
coarse yellowish-brown scales, and a rounded caudal fin
that looked as if it had been trimmed to match the contour
of the thick clumsy tail.   Holding up his prize at arm's
length for them to admire, he said, " Wha' d'ye think o'
that for a mornin's work ?" then laying it down tenderly
and kneeling before it, " Supper 'n' breafus' ! wish I'd

a-brung it hum time ernough for dinner. My maouth is a-waterin' for a taste on 't. Oh, 'f I hain't hed fun alive ! I was a-pokin' 'long the bank over yunder, 'n' I seen a big wake scootin' off, 'n' then I seen him 'baout twenty feet off a-moggin' 'long kinder easy, 's 'f he didn't care a darn for all creation—an', sir, I drawed up 'n' let 'im hev, ker-bim ! an' he rolled tother side up 'n' lay just as still ! 'N' I was a-lookin' 'raound for a pole or suthin' tu claw him tow-waid me, an', sir, he begin to wriggle 'n' flop, 'n' I just dropped my gun 'n' in arter him clean up to my crotch, an', sir, I got him, 'n' ain't he an ol' sollaker ? I wish tu gracious," bending over the fish and caressingly arranging the fins—" I wish tu gracious I'd ha' brung him time enough ; wouldn't we ha' hed a dinner !"

" You ant wan' be sorry for dat, Peltiet," Antoine said, with suppressed laughter twinkling in his eyes and almost bursting out all over his face ; " he be jus' good for dinny nex' week as las' week, prob'ly better. Ah dunno 'f he ant he don' be no wusser, sartin."

" What kind of a durned critter is it, Antwine ?" Sam asked, after examining it closely ; " I never see no sech a fish !"

" Feesh !" cried the Canadian. " Dat ting don't feesh ! Dat *bow-fins.*"

" Why, Antwine," Pelatiah asked, the happiness fading out of his face, " hain't he good tu eat ?"

" Heat !" he said with disgust. " Bah gosh ! he don't no more good for heat you was ! No, sch, no more as you boot. Ah dunno what he was be mek for only feel up de water. You was bring heem here for heat ? Oh, Peltiet ! dat too fun for me !" and he laughed loud and long.

" Wal," Pelatiah said with a sigh of resignation, as the visions of glory and feasts vanished, " I hed fun a-gittin' on him, an' he is a reg'lar ol' sollaker, anyway."

" Come," said Sam, " le's eat an' be off, an' see 'f we can't git a fish 'at Antwine 'll 'prove on—a mud turkle, f'r instance—he eats them riptiles !"

" Mud turkey !" the Canadian said, stopping halfway from the fire to the slab with the smoking frying pan in his left hand and raising his right impressively, " Bah gosh ! seh, you give it me mud turkey, Ah show you some soups mek you wish dis worl' was big mud turkey, an' de sky was tip over for one big kittly for bile heem in, an' you was sit on aidge an' heat dem soup wid moon for spoon, more as tousan' year ! yes, seh !"

Then they fell to, and contenting themselves with such fare as they had, were soon ready to set forth.

V.

SHOOTING PICKEREL.

Sam and Antoine were to embark in the log canoe, while Pelatiah, still mistrusting the treacherous deep, was to hunt along shore, following the directions of the experienced Canadian. But first he pulled off his trousers and socks, which he wrung out and hung by the fire. Considering the chances of another bath, he debated a little whether he would not better go forth bare-legged, but at last concluded, for the sake of seemliness and convenience, to put on a pair of trousers that he hauled out of the depths of the carpet-bag.

The sun shone with almost summer-like fervor on the flat, wooded shore and clear, still shallows, where every sodden leaf and weed and sunken stick upon the bottom was revealed. The first frogs were sunning themselves on the fringe of floating and stranded last year's rushes that bordered the water, and on every side their crackling pur arose, as continuous, if not as loud, as the thronging blackbirds' incessant clamor, a medley of sweet and harsh notes, like the gurgle of brooks and the slow drip of water into echoing pools, with the grating and clatter and sharp click of pebbles tossed upon rocks. As Pelatiah slowly walked along the shore, at almost every step a frog startled him, scurrying over the weeds with spasmodic leaps and splashing into the water. Then a shadow flitted before him, and looking up, he saw a great hawk wheeling in a wide circle overhead, his wings golden brown with the sunlight shining through them.

"A hen hawk 's better'n nothin' tu show," he said, cocking his gun, and taking a slow upright aim. He was standing almost in the water with his back toward it, and the hawk's course tending behind him, he was leaning backward to the utmost of his balance when he fired, and the recoil of the gun set him down with a sudden splash that awed all the neighboring frogs into silence. After scrambling to his feet he cast a quick glance about him while the returning pellets of shot were yet raining down, to see if any one had witnessed his mishap, then one in search of the hawk. The bird was still circling undisturbed in a great upward spiral, and becoming a fleck of brown against the blue. "Wet agin ! an' not so much as a bow fin tu show for 't ! I might ha' knowed better'n tu shot. I couldn't hit a tew-storey haouse a-flyin'. But I kep' my gun dry, 'n' who cares ? That 'ere hen hawk don't, sartin.'' So embracing the nearest tree, he emptied the water out of his boots, then reloaded his gun and went forward. The wetting of his nether parts being now accomplished and not to be dreaded, he was no longer "cat-footed," but waded slowly and cautiously to every likely looking place, resembling, as he craned his long neck and scanned the water near him, some enormous heron seeking his prey. A slight commotion of the surface attracted his attention, and warily approaching the spot, he saw the back fin and tail of some large fish gently moving. "Bow-fin or no bow fin, I'll try ye," he whispered to himself, and remembering Antoine's last injunction to shoot at a fish "way under where he was," he blazed away.

Before the boil of the water had subsided he saw the white bellies of two motionless fish shining out of the bubbles and disturbed sediment, and splashing to them he plunged his arm in to the elbow and seized the largest, and tucking it under his left arm, grabbed the other. Just then he saw another that had been stunned by his shot, feebly writhing its fins and evidently gathering wits and strength for a speedy departure. How to secure it with one fish in his right hand, his gun in his left, and another fish hugged under that arm was a question that he speedily solved by seizing his right-hand fish by the tail with his teeth. But the free fish, the largest of the three, had now recovered, and as he reached for it, slipped through his fingers, and with a great surge disappeared, leaving only its slime in his grasp. After one longing, regretful look, he waded ashore with his prizes, and depositing them at a safe distance from the water, sat down upon a log and gloated over them, stretching them to their fullest length, arranging their fins, then turning them over, then "hefting" them separately and together. They were of about five pounds weight each, and most undeniably pickerel, the fish of all that the mountaineer prizes most, in spite of his intimate acquaintance with the clean, gamy, beautiful, and toothsome trout of his native streams and ponds. His admiration of this shark of the lowland fresh waters has spoiled the trout fishing in many a mountain lakelet, where the survival, not of the fittest, but of the biggest, the hungriest, and most fecund has been proved by the introduction of this alien.

In possession of the largest pickerel he had ever seen, and that of his own taking, Pelatiah had never felt more completely happy. If the day had been cold, the glow of pride and happiness would have kept the wet clothes from chilling him ; in the genial sunshine of this most perfect of early spring days, he scarcely felt that his boots were full of water, that he was soaked and sodden to the waist. He heard, but only noticed as a pleasant accompaniment to his inward song of thanksgiving, the frequent roll of the partridges' muffled drums far and near in the woods ; hardly wondered what unseasonable game Drive had afoot where he was making the woods resound with lazy echoes of his sonorous voice. Guns were booming all along the shores—the thin report of rifles spitting out their light charges, the bellow of muskets belching out their four fingers of powder, tow wads, and " double B's," and giving one's shoulder a sympathetic twinge as he thought how the shooter's must be aching—all proclaimed that it was a sad day for the pickerel that had come on to Little Otter's marshes to spawn. Probably not one man of the fifty who were hunting them there had a thought of what the fish were there for, or would have cared if he had. There were too many pickerel, and always would be. There could be no exhaustion of the supply of them nor of any other fish. Any proposition to protect fish and game of any kind, to prescribe any method of taking, to limit the season of killing, would have been thought an attempt to introduce hated Old World laws and customs. Hunting and fishing were the privileges of every freeborn American ; to use or abuse whenever, wherever, and however he was disposed. And he could not live long enough to see the end of it, for why should there not always be fish and game as innumerable in all these unnumbered acres of water and marsh and woods ? Alas ! why not ?

A nearer shot, that seemed the familiar voice of the

" Ore Bed," caused Pelatiah to peer among the tree trunks in its direction, and he saw the log canoe not far away and one of its crew taking something from the water with a sheen of scales and drip of sparkling drops   At first he had a mind to hail them, learn their luck and proclaim his own, but on second thought he felt that there would be more glory in surprising them on their return to camp with the actual, unimpeachable proof of his success. So after watching them out of sight, he cut the brightest blood-red osier twig he could find and strung his fish upon it, though with the feeling that a silver cord would more befit their worth and beauty. Then he reloaded his gun with a most generous charge in consideration of its recent good service, and went on in search of new conquests, his boots chuckling at every step in their lining of water, as if they, too, were rejoicing in his triumph. He soon saw where a fish was " playing " at some little distance from the shore, and working carefully toward it under cover of an insular stump, he gained that coigne of vantage, and stood with unstable footing on its roots when he saw the fish within short range and fired at it. The recoil of the heavy charge pushed him a step backward, his foot caught in a root, and over he toppled at full length with a gasping grunt and a splash that drove an upward shower of water drops into the lower branches of the trees. He hardly waited to regain his feet before he scrambled to the place where he had last seen the fish. And there it was, motionless, belly up and bigger than those he had on his string! He thought as he slipped the osier through the gills and viciously toothed great jaws that he had suffered none too much for such a reward, that he would rather have been put to soak in the Slang for an hour than to have lost it. When he became fully possessed with the sense of his exploit, he could not withhold a triumphant yell, so discordant and so unlike any voice the distant shooters had ever heard, that a report soon after became current of "a painter a-hengin' 'raound in the Slang woods."

His gun was wet now, and he had only wet tow to swab it with, and though the powder was dry in his horn, the little paper box of caps with a lot of foreign lingo printed on the green cover around the prominent letters " G. D." (which some took to be abbreviated profanity) was satu-rated almost to pulpiness. But he must try once more, and so he wrung out a handful of tow and swabbed the gun from complete wetness to moderate dampness, poured in a handful of powder and rammed down upon it a wad that needed no chewing to moisten it, emptied in his last charge of shot, wadded that, and placed a forlorn hope of a cap that he had blown the water out of on the nipple, in which not a grain of powder showed. " Nothin' like try-in'," Pelatiah said hopefully, and, mooring his fish in a safe puddle, he went to where a great mossy log reached far out into inviting waters. He worked his way with careful steps along it, crouching under overhanging branches that he steadied himself by, and looking sharply on either side. A basking turtle slipped off the outer end, and the splash of his sudden immersion startled a fish, that came with a great arrowy wake a little out from and paral-lel with the log. Watching the point of it, Pelatiah saw in the amber shallows the great savage head and long blotched sides of one of the monster pickerel of the marshes, slowing up just against him. His heart almost stood still as he put his gun to his yet aching shoulder. Whispering

to it inwardly, " You won't sarve me sech a dummed caper
agin," he leaned far forward to counterbalance the expected recoil and pulled the trigger with might and main.
The striker fell on the wet cap with a dull, flat click, and
too late aware of a misfire to recover his balance, he went
sprawling into the water, the gun slanting breech up with
the muzzle stuck a foot deep in the soft bottom. The
frightened fish made almost as great a commotion in getting out of the dangerous precinct, at the first dash nearly
stranding itself on the weedy slope of the shore, then
struggling well afloat again, making a wild dash through a
tangle of bushes that made their tops shiver along his course,
then surging into the open water and departing with a
wake like a boat's. Pelatiah got upon his feet, and, pulling his gun out of the mud, waded ashore. " The's one
goldarned comfort 'baout it," he said aloud, as he turned
and sadly surveyed the yet troubled waters, " the' wa'n't
nobuddy seen me a-kerwollopin' in there like a fool, 'n'
I don't care !"

" Waal," said a nasal voice not three rods away, " that
'ere was a consid'able of a splotteration-ah !" There was
a kind of grunt at the end of the speaker's sentence, as if
his overcharge of words kicked.

Turning his astonished and abashed face, the young fellow saw a tall raw-boned man regarding him with a grin,
whether serious or mirthful, it was hard to decide.
" That 'ere was an all termutable big pick'ril-ah. I wish
t' land o' massy I'd ha' got here fust-ah ! I'd ha' got
him, an' you'd ha' lost him-ah ! But that's allus my
pleggy durned luck—somebody er 'nother a-gittin' in
'head on me an' a takin' the bread right outen my
mouth-ah !"

"Kinder seems 's 'ough we'd both on us lost him," Pelatiah said, picking up his string of fish and making ready to depart. The late comer strode to him, and snatching the string from his hand and holding it close to his nose, slowly turned the fish one way and another, as he critically examined them.

"Honh! waal," with a half-contemptuous snort, "you've had sorter half-way decent luck-ah. Them's middlin' decent sized fish — wuth carr'in' hum 'f you ha'n't had no fish t' eat this year-ah." Pelatiah was beginning to hate him. "But-ah," returning the fish to the owner as if they were worth no further notice, "you've got a' orfle sozzlin' tu pay for what you got an' ha'n't got-ah, an' you'd orter go right straight hum an' git some dry close on 'f you've got any-ah. It is driffle onhealthy a-gittin' wet so wi' your close on-ah. Like 's not you'll have the rheumatiz—er chills—mebby it'll set ye inter fev'n'aag'; shouldn't wonder a mite-ah. Naow, take it in summer, 'n' I luffter onstrip an' go in under the dam 't the Holler an' shaower off 'n' then take a head dive int' the pawnd, 'n' turn the circ'lation o' the blood tother way—it makes a feller feel so neat-ah! But this traipsin' 'raound in your wet close is tur'ble bad-ah! I wouldn't git wet 's you be for four dollars 'n' seventy-five cents ah! Where 'baouts du ye live when you're t' hum, anyway?"

"Up tu Danvis," Pelatiah answered.

"Tu Dan-vis!" the man exclaimed; "you don't say so? It's as much as twenty mild off-ah! Waal, 'f you've got tu go clearn away there 'ith yer wet close on, you'll hafter hoof it tarnal smart t' git hum 'fore you're sick, 'n' ye can't lug them fish 'n' yer gun-ah. You'll wanter

keep yer gun, I s'pose, though 'tain't much to look at,
but I'll take yer fish 'f you don't wanter heave 'em away-
ah!''

Pelatiah would as cheerfully have given him his heart as
those precious fish. " 'Bleeged tu ye ; they're little bits
o' fellers, 'n' I guess I c'n kerry 'em," he said rather
sarcastically, declining the generous offur, " fur 's I'm
goin'. I got some folks a-campin' up yunder," nodding
in the direction of the " pallis.''

" O-ah !'' with a tone of disappointment. " Waal,
you'd better go an' dry off 's soon 's ye can-ah. I didn't
come a-huntin'," glancing at the ancient musket he held
in his hand, " I come a-lookin' arter some rhuts 't I want-
ah. My womern she's a fee-male doctor, messmericle.
My brother, Job, Junyer, he gives her the in-flew-ence 'n'
puts her to sleep. 'N' then she can look right inter yer
insides an' read 'em just like a book-ah. Terms, half a
dollar for examernation, one dollar for proscription, cash
on delivery-ah. Sleepin' Sairy, probably you've hearn
tell on her.''

Pelatiah was obliged to confess that he had never heard
of this supernaturally gifted woman, and turning away went
toward camp as his new acquaintance muttered something
about " onenlighted critters.'' Casting a look behind, he
saw him walking carefully out along a log, with his gun at
a ready, and wondered what kind of roots he could be in
search of. Pelatiah's heart was not entirely regenerate, and
perhaps just then nothing would have gladdened it more
than to have seen the disparager of his luck make a " splot-
teration'' such as he had suffered.

Arrived at camp, he made a complete change of raiment,
and was toasting himself in great contentment by the re-

plenished fire when, late in the afternoon, his companions
returned.   He had thought of dressing his fish, but it
seemed too bad to take even a scale from them before his
friends had seen them in their entireness.   How he wished
that he might display them on the store steps at Danvis
and tell the story of their capture, with judicious omis-
sions, to the admiring audience of evening loungers.   His
pride was somewhat brought down when he saw the dozen
or more big fellows that Sam and Antoine tossed out of
the canoe, but still he felt that he had done well, for a
boy, and his friends gave him generous praise.

Antoine dragged a slab to the water's edge, and seating
himself a-straddle of it, slapped a large fish upon it in
front of himself, which he forthwith set about cleaning,
while Sam and Pelatiah squatted close by and watched the
process.   "You wan' scratch it, scratch it, dem peekrils
great many," he instructed them out of the shower of scales
he set flying.   "Den w'en you'll pull off all hees shell off
of it, you wan' wash heem plenty—wash an' scratch—so!"
and he doused the scaled fish in the water, scraping it with
his knife and washing it, over and over again, till the skin
was quite white and free from a suspicion of slime.
"Somebody he ant' more as half scratch off peekril clean
'nough, den he cook it, an' he ant tas' good of it, den
he'll said, ' dat peekrils, he don't fit for be decent!'   Bah
gosh! Ah show you, me!"   Then he split the fish down
the back, cut off the head, took out what he called the
"inroads," washed it again, and cut it into convenient
pieces for the frying pan.   When he had tried the fat out
of a couple of slices of salt pork and set the fish to hissing
in the pan with the bubbling accompaniment of the potato
kettle, an odor so savory pervaded the atmosphere of the

camp that it made the mouths of the hungry men water, and the minutes of waiting for supper seem like slow hours of starvation. The fragrance of it was wafted to the nostrils of a wood-chopper half a mile away, and so aroused the sacred rage of hunger within him, that he was forced to shoulder his axe and go home to an early supper.

Antoine set the potato kettle on the board, and lifting the frying pan from the coals, with his hat for a holder, set it there also and announced supper. " Goo'by, M'sieu Cochon ; goo'by, M'sieu Mash Rabbeet ; how you was pooty well, M'sieu Peckril ? Ah'll very glad for see you to-day, seh ! Hoorah, boys !" The bag of dry bread was brought out, and then the three fell to work in a silence that was broken only by grunts and sighs of satisfaction, the sputtering out of fish bones, and the clatter of the few implements of onslaught. At the end of it Antoine said, as he prepared a charge for his pipe : " Wal, seh, boy, 'f Ah always feel jes' Ah was naow, Ah ant never heat no more ! He ant cos' much for mah boards den, don't it, Sam ?"

" I expeck," Sam answered, searching for a grass stalk to clear his pipe-stem. " 'at it's some wi' you as 't was wi Brother Foot tu the prayer-meetin', ' Brethren and sisters,' says he, ' as I feel naow, I wouldn't take the hull world for the feelin's 'at I feel ! But, brethren and sisters, I don't allers feel jes' 's I feel naow !' "

The sky had become overcast with curdly clouds except a strip along the horizon, which at sunset was a broad belt of orange-red fire glowing between the dark gray clouds and the blue-black bastions of the Adirondacks and the frayed fringe of sombre woods ; and nearer than the shadows of these, the brimming expanse of unruffled water glowed with the same intense color. When the trappers crept into their nest, the night was dark and starless ; a chill breath of northerly air was sighing in the hemlocks, and the great owls were hooting a dolorous warning of coming storm. Listening to them, Sam remarked as he made his final yawn under the blankets, " Not much fun nor profit for us fellers to-morrer, so the aowls sez."

VI.

THE next day's dawn came with slow reluctance to dimly light a dismal landscape, over which had come one of those disheartening changes so frequent in our northern latitude that it seems strange they are not expected as in the common course of nature, rather than wondered at and spiritually rebelled against. The succession of the seasons had apparently been turned backward in the gloom and mystery of one night, and where yesterday spring was jubilantly triumphant over the reconquest of her realms, winter was reigning again. Snow had been falling for an hour or more, driven by the north wind in a long slant from the leaden sky to the earth, whitening the dun fields and turning the brown and green woodlands to spectral gray, till the trees looked like ghosts of the slain embodiment of spring. The sluggish waves of the Slang beat with a sullen wash on the wind-swept shores, but in the sheltered coves a seal of leaden ice was set upon them. The wild ducks, happy and content in any weather that gave them open water, were splashing and diving and breasting the black flood, but the land birds were in sorry plight. They huddled in the thickets for shelter, and if one attempted to pipe a song, its thin, half-frozen notes added no cheer to the day, but rather made it the more dreary.

When Sam awoke with a dull sense of changed weather

in his bones, and sat up in his bed to look abroad, the picture set in the triangular frame of the shanty front, a pointed bit of gray sky above white fields and black water, with a foreground of snow-laden bushes, the blackened stakes, cross pole and brands of the dead camp-fire, was so utterly cheerless, that only the desire of companionship, ever craved by misery, impelled him to arouse his comrades. The hound came stretching and yawning forth, and after a sorrowful look abroad and a sniff of the damp air gave a dolorous whine, crept back to his dark corner to comfort himself with forgetfulness of the outside world. While Pelatiah suffered in silence, with unworded wishes for the comfortable warmth of the kitchen stove at home, Antoine loudly denounced the meteorological change. "Ah'll never see so many kin' wedder in litly while all ma life tam! What for he ant jus' well be sprim wen he'll get all ready, jus' well as jomp raght back in midlin of winters? Bah gosh, Ah dunno, me! Wal, Ah don' care, Ah s'pose we'll got have it some fire on aour stofe, ant it?" and getting himself together he began a search, axe in hand, for some dry kindling. Chipping away the weather-beaten outside of an old stump, he soon got at its yellow heart, and with shavings and splinters of it presently had a cheerful blaze lapping the snow and dampness off the back-log. Breakfast was hardly in preparation when the snow turned to more dreary rain, that came pelting down with a dull patter, freezing as it fell. All hands turned cooks and made frequent rapid dashes from the shanty's shelter to the sputtering fire, one encouraging its feeble efforts with a punch or a morsel of dry fuel, another giving the frying fish a turn or a shake, another snatching out of the veil of smoke a hurried glance at the pot that was fully possessed of the proverbial perverseness of watched pots, and stood long on the order of its boiling.

When at last patience was exhausted and hunger would no longer be temporized with, they made a sally and brought in the half-cooked rations. The potatoes seemed to be suffering an epidemic ossification of the heart, for every one had a "bone in it," and the fish, except the outside and thinner parts, was raw. Antoine's onions did strong and excellent service in helping out the sorry meal. and when it was got through with the little party settled down to making the best of the discomfort of a rainy day in camp. They related the events of yesterday; what befell Pelatiah has already been told in the last chapter, and so he told it to his companions with but few eliminations, for he felt no unwillingness now to let them enjoy the fun of his mishaps, and he with pride set forth to the fullest extent the dimensions of the big fish that he had lost, a monster that somehow seemed to belong to him almost as completely as if he had captured him—as the big fish lost by all of us who go a-fishing are yet ours. Is it by right of discovery that we hold a sort of claim on them?

Sam and Antoine had not gone far on their cruise the day before when, as they rounded the point between the Slang and the creek and floated slowly over the sunny, wooded shallows, a party of "playing" pickerel was sighted by the Canadian, who was paddling. Two or three lusty fellows had the upper tips of their tails and dorsal fins above water, now gently moving them, now splashing about in a spasmodic flurry, then disappearing for a minute, then breaking the surface in another place near by. Antoine got the canoe close to them without alarming them, and Sam fired into the thick of the group. The Ore Bed's big

bullet made the water boil and set half a dozen swift, arrowy wakes flying off in different directions ; but that was
all.   Not one silvery, upturned belly gleamed out of the
settling sediment, and Antoine broke forth in lamentations
and reproaches.   "Oh, sacré ton sac !   Oh, bah gosh !
da's too bad.   Oh, you'll shoot all over it !   Ant Ah tol'
you more as fo' honded tousan tam, wen you'll shot at
peekril you ant want shot at it, hein ?   You'll want shot
at it where he'll ant look so 'f he was !   Way onder where
you'll see it !   You don't can't rembler dat, hein ?   Bah
gosh !   wen Ah'll rip-proach you up to some more of it, 'f
you ant did more better as you was dat tam, Ah'll goin'
shoot masef !"

"Wal, Antwine," Sam said with a shamefaced little
laugh, "I never shot at one afore, 'n' 'f I don't du better
next time you ' reproach ' me up tu some fish, you shell
do the shootin'.   *Re*-proach !   Oh, golly ! wal, I'll be
durn'd 'f I s'posed you'd lugged any o' Solon Briggs's big
words all the way daown here !"   and moistening a patch
he rammed a bullet down the long barrel, making the
grimaces that one who drives home the ball in a muzzle-
loading rifle always does, as if his own interior was suffering the leaden invasion.

"Wal, Ah don't care, Sam, Ah'll hit dat words 'baout
so close you'll hit dat peekrils, ant it ?"

"Cluster, Antwine, cluster, you knocked the head right
off on 't !"

And so with restored good-humor they went on till another bunch of fish was sighted and got near to, when Sam,
aiming well under, "onhitched."   Four good-sized pickerel, some hit, some only stunned, rolled bellies up and
were got in board before they had thought of moving a

fin. In such murderous fashion, approved by custom like many another quite as bad, they got all the fish they cared for, and met with no mischance worse than one or two misfires. When they were homeward bound and both paddling without change of places, as they rounded a broad patch of button bushes they came suddenly upon Sam's late adversary, poling his skiff slowly along and looking for fish with his gun lying in front of him. His face still bore the imprint of Sam's fist, but he bestowed upon them a friendly grin, and hailed them with "What luck?"

"Tol'able," Sam answered, "What's yourn?"

"The cussedest luck 'at ever you see," was the reply. "My blasted ol' gun 's missed twict when I had all-killin' good chances, an' one big one 't I rolled up got away 'fore I c'ld git a holt on him. S'pose 'f I didn't want one so con-demn bad, I'd a-got a boat-load. My folks is sick [in Yankee parlance one's "folks" means his wife]. No appetite t' eat, 'n' nothin' 'll du but a fish, an' I swear! I can't git so much as a punkin seed!"

"Wal," Sam said, picking up a good fish by the gills, "we've got more'n we c'n use 'fore they spile; take this t' yer folks."

"Why, naow," said the man, poling his skiff a stroke nearer, "if 'twan't jist as 't is, I wouldn't think on it, but if you *kin* spare it jest as well as not, I 'ld be a thaousan' times 'bleeged tu ye, 'cause Seusan, she—but," stopping his craft, "I do' want no more o' yer cussed gum!"

"All right," Sam answered with a laugh, "we hain't a-peddlin' gum to-day. Haul up an' git yer fish." And tossing it into the skiff, he paddled away, while the recipient of the gift thanked him a "thaousan' times" and profanely remarked in conclusion, "You *air* the curiest

man ever I see, I swear! Say," he shouted after them,
"you c'n come here 'n' trap an' be durned a thousan'
years!"

While Sam was pondering as he paddled whether this
long lease of privilege pertained to trapping or perdition,
Antoine interrupted his meditations with the question,
"What you s'pose mek dat mans so good nachel, Sam?
What you s'pose he'll got matter wid his face of it? Look
lak he strak someboddy wid it, ant it!"

"Oh, like 'nough he knocked it agin a tree or suthin'
pokin' 'raound here 'mongst this 'ere trash. An' he's get
over bein' mad 'cause he's faound out 't we're harmless
kinder creeturs."

"Dat all you'll know 'baout it, Sam?" with a crafty,
inquiring glance as he leaned sidewise to get a look at his
companion's face. "What mek it got so clever so quick
aft' he'll bruse bose of it so hard? Hein?"

"Oh, thunder in the winter! no, I d' know nothin'
'baout the man. Mebby he's ben tu a prayer meetin' 'n'
'xperenced a change o' heart."

"What he'll meant he ant want some gaum, hein?"

"Hain't a-hankerin' arter it, I s'pose. What in time
du we care 's long 's he behaves hisself? Let 'im go."

After several minutes of silent paddling Antoine asked
in a low, earnest voice, "Sam, 'f Ah'll tol' you sometings, you ant never tol' someboddy long 's you leeve, you
hope to dead fus'?"

"Wal," Sam answered with deliberation, "I do' know,
Antwine; 'f you ben a-stealin' suthin' or a killin' some-
b'dy, I don't wanter hev ye tell me on 't; but 'f it's some
little thing 't ain't very weeked I ha' no 'bjections to
promisin' an' a-hearin' on 't."

" Oh, no-no-no-no !   Ah ant never steal notings, an'
Ah ant never keel someboddy sin Papineau war ; not quat ;
come pooty near dough dis tam, but Ah ant keel it, do it
some good.   You ant tol' of it ?"

" No, I won't tell ; ease your mind, Antwine."

" Wal, seh, Sam," with slow impressiveness, " what
hail dat man his face of it, what mak' heem be so good
nachel, Ah'll goin' tol' you, seh.   Ah'll leek it dat man
tudder day !"

" You licked him ?   Why, you hain't seen 'im 'fore
sen the day 'at you was tellin' me haow he sassed ye ; an'
you said then 'at you didn't tech him, nor wouldn't.
Why didn't you tell me 'baout your lickin' him then ?"

" Wal, seh, Ah'll tol' you, Sam.   You see, Ah was
'fraid Ah'll keel him, Ah'll leek it so hard.   Naow Ah'll
fin' aout he ant be dead, Ah don' care for tol' you.   Oh !
bah gosh ! Ah'll mos' keel it.   Ah'll keek it on hees face
wid ma fis' where you'll see it.   Ah'll strak it wid ma
foots where you ant see it.   Ah'll paoun' it, Ah'll mek it
hollah, ' Oh, don't hurt me some more.'   Ah'll be so scaie
all dat naght for 'fraid he'll dead.   Ah ant mos' sleep
any, seh !   Yas, ant you hear it me tombly an' grunt,
hein ?"

Sam was shaking, but as Antoine could not see his
face, he thought his agitation was perhaps caused by
horror at the recital of the terrific combat.   Warming with
the Falstaffian tale, he shook out a " B-o-o-o-h-h-h !"
from his pursed lips, and shouted, " Oh !   Bah gosh !
Ah'll paoun' it, Ah'll jomp top heem of it !   You ant
b'lieve it, you come 'long to me, Ah'll show you where
Ah'll knock de barks off de tree wid heem, an' de bloods
an' skins an' hairs all scratter 'raoun' de giaoun' !"

Sam was no longer able to contain the fulness of laughter that oppressed him.

"What you lafft at, Sam?" Antoine demanded sternly.

"Oh, dear me, suz! Antwine, I can't help a-laughin' to think what a wollopin' you give that man, an' a slattin' the graound with him, an' barkin' trees with him! What a massy it is you didn't kill the poor creeter!"

"Wal, Ah tol' you, Ah'll feel pooty glad for dat, me. Ah'll ant wan' be hang for it. Say, Sam, you s'pose prob'ly dat fellar sue me up to law for leek heem so hard, hein?"

"Wal, no, I don't hardly b'lieve he will, Antwine. I guess he's hed all he wants on ye."

"Wal, Ah guess so."

"Come to think on 't naow, I seen him the next day arter you give him sech a whalin', an' I never noticed 'at the' was a thing the matter of him. Cur'us, wa'n't it?"

"You'll see it nex' day?" Antoine asked anxiously. "Wal, bah gosh! Ah dunno 'i he ant show it; prob'ly hees faces ant got tam yet for swellin' up an' git blue an' black, ant it?"

"I shouldn't wonder a mite 'f that was it, Antwine."

This dismal day Antoine swore Pelatiah to secrecy, and enlivened an hour with the acted story of his great fight, that began at this relation to assume in his mind the reality of an actual occurrence. Often after their return to Danvis the doughty champion recounted this exploit to half credulous audiences, and though Sam, when a listener, seemed sometimes to laugh in the wrong place, he never let fall a word to cast a shadow of doubt on its truthfulness.

Antoine proposed to concoct a chowder, which he promised them should furnish a dinner so good as to make amends for the badness of their breakfast.

"Dey ant on'y but jes' one ting was better as feesh, an' dat was be feesh wen he be cook in chowdy, 'cep' mud turkey." So putting on a heavy coat he took the kettle to the shore and spent so much time there in washing it that he came back with a shell of frozen rain upon his garments, such as loaded all the branches with its dull glitter, cracking and clattering with every sway of the wind, and crunching under foot on the iced mat of last year's herbage. Pork, fish, potatoes, crackers, and onions furnished all the requisites for a chowder, a dinner all in one pot, and one that needed no constant tending, therefore well suited to the conditions of a roofless kitchen in a stormy day. When it was set to seething over the now well-established fire, they sat in the shelter of the shanty front, the elders smoking frequent pipes, Pelatiah solacing himself with spruce gum.

"Samwill," he said after much speechless if not quite silent rumination, and a long look out into the cheerless, icy woods, with no sign of life in them but one red squirrel chipping a cone on a hemlock limb, and too much depressed in spirit to utter one saucy snicker or defiant chir, "Samwill, I sh'ld think the' 'ld be bears, an' painters, an'—an' annymills in these 'ere woods. They're big 'nough, seems 's 'ough."

"Don't 'pear to be much in 'em bigger 'n coons," Sam answered; "we thought we heard a lynk oncte or twicte, but mebby 't wa'n't nothin'. Like 's not the's a painter a-travellin' through 'em oncte 'n a while praowlin' back an' to, but I ha'n't seen no signs on 'em."

"Tell us 'baout that painter 't you killed, Samwill,"

said Pelatiah, starting up with a sudden interest ; " I never
heard ye, though I've kinder hearn tell on 't."

" Oh, the' wa'n't nothin' 'baout it, only I happened
to shoot him."

" Wal, Samwill, tell 'baout it, won't ye?"

" Wal," Sam said, looking abstractedly into the fire
while he slowly filled his pipe out of a nearly-spent blue
paper of Greer's or Lorillard's " Long smoking," " the'
wa'n't no painter huntin' 'baout it, only a happen-so.   I
was a bee huntin', in September it was, 'n' his hide wa'n't
wuth fo'pence only to look at, 'n' I'd got some bees to
workin' in a little lunsome clearin' 'way up 'n under Tater
Hill, 'n' lined 'em int' the woods, 'n' reckoned I'd got
putty nigh the tree, 'n' I was saunderin' 'long lookin'
caref'l at every tree 'at hed a sign of a hole in it, when I
seen a shake of a big limb of a great maple, 'n' then I seen
the critter scrouched onto it clus to the body 'n' a-lookin'
right at me.   I'd left the Ore Bed back in the clearin'
much as ten rods off 'long wi' my bee box, 'n' my hat sot
mighty light on top o' my head as I backed off, slower, I
guess, 'n' I'll go to my own fun'al.   Soon as I got him
aout o' my sight—though I don't s'pose I was aout o'
his'n—I made durn few tracks to the ol' gun, I tell ye,
'n' then come back slow 'n' caref'l.   There he sot
scrouched daown jest where I left him, an' his durned
yaller eyes right on me 's if he hedn't never took 'em off,
'n' mebby he hedn't.   When I got in 'baout six rods, I
drawed a bead right betwixt 'em 'n' onhitched.   He didn't
jump, but kinder sagged daown ont' the limb 'n' turned
under it 'n' le' go fust one foot 'n' then 'nother, 'n' arter
hangin' by the last bunch o' claws for a minute, come
daown, kerflop.   He clawed 'n' flurupped 'n' graowled

julluk any durned waounded cat, 'n' I stood back 'n'
gin him the floor. But his senses was all knocked aouten
on him, an' he didn't know 'nough to git to me 'f he
wanted tu. I hussled 'nother charge int' the Ore Bed
tol'able spry, but 't wa'n't needed—he was deader 'n hay
'fore I got the cap on. An'," said Sam, after a pause in
which he refilled his pipe, " I faound the bee tree not tew
rods furder on, an' tew weeks arter I took it up an' got a
hund'ed paounds o' the neatest honey 't I ever see."
And he seemed to feel quite as much satisfaction in the
recollection of finding the bountiful supply of wild honey
as in the killing of the great cat.

" By gol !" said Pelatiah, letting out his long-held
breath in a great sigh, " I sh'd thought you'd a ben scairt !"

" Wal, no," Sam said, still thinking of the bees, " I
hain't feared o' bees ; they never sting me none tu speak
on."

" Dat mek me tink," said Antoine, coming in from a
brief inspection of the chowder, and nursing a coal that he
had scooped out of the ashes in his pipe bowl, " mek me
tink one tam me ma brudder-law keel one dat panter in
Canada. We was go huntin' for deer. Ah guess so, an'
da was leetly mite snow on de graoun'. Wal seh, we'll
see it track, we ant know what he was be, an' we'll folla
dat, oh, long, long tam. Bamby he'll go in hole in rock.
leetly laidge, you know, 'baout tree, fo', prob'ly seex
tam big dis shantee was. Wal, seh, boy, Ah'll left it ma
brudder-law for watch dat holes, an' Ah'll go 'raoun' back
side laidge see all what Ah'll see Ah'll look veree
caffly, an' what you tink Ah'll fin' it ? Leetly crack
in rock 'baout so wide ma tree finger of it, an' dat panter
hees tail steek oif of it 'baout so long ma arm, prob'ly,

where he'll push hind fust in dat holes. An' he'll weegly hees tail so,'' waving his forefinger slowly. "Wal, Ah'll tink for spell what Ah do. Den Ah'll go cut off strong steek so big half ma wris' and two foots long. Den Ah'll tek hol' dat tails an' tied knot in him, verce caffly, den Ah'll run steek t'rough an' pull knot hard! Oh, bah gosh! you'll oughty hear dat panters yaller an' holla! Wus as fo' honded tousan' cat! Yes, seh! Oh, he'll hugly, Ah tol' you! but he can' help it, he can' gat it loose 'less he pull up hees tails off. Wal, seh, Ah'll lafft at it, Ah can' help it, mos' Ah'll split off ma side. Den Ah'll go 'raoun' ma brudder-law, an' he'll be scare mos' dead, an' goin' runned way. Ah'll tol' heem, Ah goin' in dat holes shoot dat panters. 'Oh, gosh!' he'll ax me, 'he tore you dead more as forty piece!' Ah'll say, 'Ah so good man Ah'll don't 'fraid me.' Den Ah'll crawl in dat holes an' Ah'll shoot it, boom! raght 'tween hees head! An' bamby pooty soon he ant yaller some more, be all still as mices. Den Ah'll come off de holes an' Ah'll tol' ma brudder-law he'll crawl in an' pull off dat panters. He'll pooty 'fraid for go, but bamby he go. He touch hol' of it, he can' pull it cause hees tail tie, but he ant know. 'Bah gosh!' he say, 'dat panters more heavy as two ton! Ah can' pull it!' Den Ah'll go 'raoun' an' taked off dat steek, an' holla 'pull!' an' ma brudder-law pull more harder he can—boom! he go tumbly on hees back, dat panters on top of it! Oh! 'f he ant scare, ma brudder-law. Yas seh! Wal, seh, boy," after a pause during which no one spoke, "'f you ant mek b'lieve dat stories you go Canada 'long to me Ah show you de steek. Ma brudder-law he'll saved it. Ah ant never tol' you stories so true lak dat, seh!''

"I ha' no daoubt o' that, Antwine ; you couldn't tell a lie big 'nough to choke ye. Hain't that 'ere mux o' you:n 'baout done ? I'm a-gittin' wolfish."

After due examination the French cook pronounced the chowder ready to be served up, and it proved so toothsome that of the whole kettleful there was hardly enough left for Drive's supper.

Then with smoking and more story-telling they wore out the dreary day, and at nightfall the sky was brightening with the promise of a more cheerful morrow.

VII.

PELATIAH GOES VISITING.

THE bright and cloudless morning had a sharp chill in its breath, and the Slang was frozen from shore to shore, its waters smooth with ice of the regulation thickness of the first and last cold mornings of a year—namely, " as thick as window glass." Even in the wide expanse of Little Otter there was no open water but in streaks along the channel, marked by shimmering wavelets in their lines of blue and gold when the first rays of the sun shot across the landscape. All the hills and mountain ranges were hoary as they had been in midwinter, for snow had fallen on them while rain had fallen on the lowlands of the Champlain Valley. There could be no visiting of the traps before noon, for though the stout dugout—a shapelier craft, be it said, than Uncle Lisha had prophesied could be turned out by its builder's hand—might make its way unharmed through the ice, it would cost hard work, and the frail birch would be cut in shreds in making a passage through it. And so, when breakfast was cooked and eaten, and the slight task of washing the few dishes performed, there seemed not much but loafing to fill the forenoon with.

"We can't eat half o' them 'ere fish afore they spile," Sam remarked, after a long look at the hanging row of dressed pickerel ; "I wish 't some o' the folks up to

Danvis had t' other half. Say, Peltier, don't ye wanter take a walk an' see the country?''

"Honh! I swan, I'd know 'baout it,'' with a blank stare toward the far-off hills of his birthplace; "I do' know 's I raly wanter hoof it clearn ov' to Danvis t'day!''

"Danvis! Shaw! nob'dy wants ye tu. I was a-thinkin' mebby 't 'ould be a pious idee to take three four pickril up t' ol' Mister Bartlett, 'at gin us leave to camp here. A dreffle clever ol' gentleman he is, a forty-leventh cousin of Joels', an' a Quaker too, but t'other kind, Hicksite. He lives up there in that tew-story white haouse. 'Tain't more 'n a mild, 'n' we c'n set ye crost in Antwine's canew, er you c'n go 'raound 'f you'd druther. 'Tain't fur t' the head o' the Slang, er tu where you c'n cross on some lawgs. 'F you'd jes' livs not go an' take him a mess o' them fish I'd be 'bleeged tu ye. 'N' Antwine, we're e'en a most aouten terbarker 'n' crackers. S'posin' you set Peltier acrost, 'n' go 'long up t' the store 'n' git the staffs o' life? 'N' say, Peltier, the's an al-kill-in' slick gal up t' Mr. Bartlett's!''

Pelatiah's blushes shone through the sunburn of his honest face. "Oh, you git aout, Samwill!'' with a bash-ful guffaw; "I don't care nothin' 'baout no gals!'' Then, with quick forgetfulness of his denial of such weak-ness, as he looked down upon his worn and outgrown raiment, turning his arms this way and that to inspect their covering, "I do' wanter go a-lookin' 's I du, where the's any—any young folks!''

"Wal, Ah don' care for me,'' Antoine said, getting promptly to his feet, "Ah guess Ah'll lookin' well 'nough 's Ah do, an' Ah'll gat ma close all pref-fume for go see de gal. Ah'll carry dat feesh, an' Peltiet go store for de *pro*-vizhin.　Ah ant see homan so long ago Ah'll freegit what kan close he wore.　Come, hoorah boy!" He cut a forked twig from a water maple, and stringing four of the nicest fish upon it led the way to the landing, whither Pelatiah presently followed after hatchelling his towy locks with the sparsely toothed and only comb the camp afforded, and vainly attempting to pull his trousers down into neighborliness with his boots.　They launched the dugout, and boarding it, ploughed and broke their slow way to the farther shore, the ice crashing and tinkling and jingling along their course, and hissing in long fissures on either side.　When they had landed, Sam noted that after keeping together through the first field, Antoine diverged to the right in the direction of the store at the Corners, and Pelatiah to the left toward the big white house that shone among its gray locusts and against its dusky background of orchard.　With his pleased half laugh and muttered "jes' 's I 'xpected," came a faint sigh as he turned his eyes toward the white dome of Tater Hill, in whose morning shadow dwelt his buxom sweetheart.　There was some comforting promise in the ranks of drying muskrat skins that brought a contented expression to his face after he had cast a slow calculating glance upon them.　Then he gathered some turpentine from half a dozen boxed pines, and melting it with grease in a bullet ladle, set about salving his canoe, which had got a grievous wound from a hemlock snag.　He had the camp all to himself, for Drive had gone off hunting on his own account, and his earnest baying could be heard away upstream, mixed with the querulous whistle of the woodchuck he was besieging.　But Sam was never weighted with any feeling of loneliness in the companionship of the woods.　If, when among the patriarchal trees and their tribes of tenants and dependents, any sense of isolation made itself apparent, it was what he called "a good lonesome," and he enjoyed it to-day. Out of the woods came only its own voice and the voices of the wood folk : the sigh of the pines and hemlocks ; the thud of the partridges' drum-beat, beginning with measured strokes and ending in an ecstatic roll ; the soft cluck and whistle of the jay's love-song, intermitting with his more discordant cries ; the woodpecker's note of mating time, as if he was sharpening his bill with a steel for the battles love might cause ; and from far away, like the jingle of many discordant bells made almost melodious by distance, came the clamor of a convention of crows gathered to denounce some detested hawk or owl or fox. Near by a chipmonk clucked incessantly over his recent discovery of a new world wherein were sunlight and fresh air ; and Sam's neighbor, the red squirrel, was in high spirits with such sunshine after storm, and flung at him a shower of derisive jeers and snickers from the trunk of the great hemlock, where he clung with spasmodic jerks of feet and tail.

"You sassy little cuss !" said Sam, "what sorter names be them you're a-callin' on me ? I'm a dum'd good min' ter stop your chittereein' with a pill aouten the Ore Bed ! You'll be a suckin' aigs an' killin' young birds wus'n a weasel in less 'n a month, you little pirut ! But you're hevin' lots o' fun livin', 'n' I d' know 's they're my aigs 'n' birds, so jaw away." And Sam lit his pipe with a coal and continued the application of the plaster to the canoe bottom.

Now and then the ice fell along shore with sudden jingling crashes to the level of the falling water, and as the forenoon wore away and the shadows shortened it melted

apace where the sunshine fell full upon it, and open water
began to ripple and shimmer in the breeze, and there was
a prospect of making the round of the traps in the afternoon if Antoine returned in time. The rent in the canoe
was mended, and Sam lay taking a lazy smoke beside the
ashes, casting an occasional glance across the Slang for his
companions, when a slight wake attracted his attention, and
he saw a small, dark object swimming past. "Naow,
Mister Mushrat," he said, as he crawled into the shanty
and brought forth the Ore Bed, "don't ye know 't ain't
healthy for none o' your fam'ly 'raound here?" but as he
crept to the shore with his rifle cocked and at a ready, he
saw that the lithe, snake-like movements of the swimmer
were not those of the muskrat. "Ah, Mister Mink, beg
pardon an' make my manners," he said, speaking with the
spiteful crack of the rifle. The silent wake ended with the
spat of the ball, but before the first wavelet set the ice to
tinkling along the shore, the mink slid to the surface feebly
making the last struggles for his tenaciously held life.
"That trouble in yer head is too much for ye," Sam said,
as, after launching the birch, he picked up the yet writhing
animal and gave it a finishing whack on the gunwale of
the canoe, "you tough little cuss. What a hard-lifed critter an auter must be; julluk you, only cut tu a bigger
partern. By the gret horn spoon! I wish 't I could git a
crack at one on 'em jes' onct! 'N' the' hain't one left in
the hull o' these tew cricks they give the' names tu, I
s'pose. Ho, hum! Haow many year afore the' won't be
nothin' left, I wonder? Not till arter I'm a-sleepin' under
a blankit o' sods, I hope." As he sighed and cast the
vague yet scrutinizing glance of a hunter over water and
banks, and it was caught by something larger than mink or

muskrat swimming toward him, nothing was further from
his thoughts than the old adage, "The devil is nighest
when you're speakin' on him." "What's that 'ere ol'
fool of a haoun' dawg comin' hum by water for? An' it
col' 'nough to—Drive, you cussed ol' fool," beginning
under his breath to formulate a rebuke ; then as it became
apparent that the swimmer was not Drive nor any other
dog, quite holding his breath, he reached cautiously forward for the gun, which he was too experienced a woods-
man to let long accompany him uncharged. His nerves
vibrated with a slight tremor when the stock touched his
cheek, but at the right moment the long barrel hung firm
in his grip and the Ore Bed snapped out its sharp little
voice. "'F that hain't an auter the' hain't none !" said
Sam, looking anxiously over the vacant water as he arose
and began to reload the rifle. "An' I'll be dum'd 'f I
hain't missed him ! Hev I forgot haow to shoot jes' the
minute in my hull life 'at I'd orter shot the clustest?"
But now, a rod or more from where the beast had disappeared, it broke to the surface again in a wild, writhing,
flurrying struggle, like a great fish in its death throes ; and
Sam, having hastily but steadily finished the loading of his
gun, fired with instantaneous aim at the dark centre of the
widening circles of waves ; then, laying hold of his paddle,
with a few strokes sent his craft thither, and dealt the struggling otter a downright blow with the paddle's edge that
took all the fight and nearly all the life out of him. When
he lifted his prize inboard—the last otter ever killed in these
waters—Sam was as full of happiness as Pelatiah had been
over the capture of his big pickerel, but he raised no shout
of triumph ; he only heaved a great sigh of intense satisfaction and said, " Well, there ye be !"

Not long after Sam had gone ashore Antoine appeared on the eastern bank. The unsteadiness of his gait and the loudness of his voice showed that he had more than tasted the storekeeper's "old Medford," and Sam watched his embarkation with some anxiety; for though a soaking was not likely to injure him, crackers and tobacco would be the worse for it. But he got himself and his provisions safely afloat, and then, a few boats' lengths from shore, remembered Pelatiah, for whom he began to call : "Hey! Peltiet! where you was be? Come! Hey! Hoorah, boy! Mos' suppy ready. Bed tam for go sleep! Wal, you'll ant goin' come, va zu diab', go to dev'! On'stan' bose of it, hein?" Then, resuming his devious way, he lifted up his voice, sonorous and tuneful in spite of its drunken huskiness, in English song, after this wise :

"'Haow dear of ma heart was de screen of ma chilshood,
When fon' reggylecshin' bring him up of ma view,
De orchy, de middle hees deep tangly wil'wool,
An' hitch bee-love spot of ma infant, he's new '—

"What was nex' of it Ah freegit for rembler—oh, Ah know :

"'Hokeyhol' buckle, ha-ern bung buckle,
Hol' cover moss buckle, he'll hang up de well !'"

Having got the better of this to his complete satisfaction he fell to murdering the words of another cold-water song high in the popular favor of those days :

"'Oh den r r re-sagn dem r r ro-sy wahn,
Hitch smahlin son of a daugh-taa,
For he ant so good for de useful blood
As a col' of spahklin' wa-taa !'

"Whoop! Hoorah for hoorah! Where was you goin' for go, can-noe? Ant you'll know it way for shanty?

Prob'ly you'll get start for Danvit, ant it? Gat sail on woggin, do dat!'' He had become awaie at last that the canoe, after making some uncertain progress toward the desired port, was now headed for the eastein shore of the Slang. '' Here, Antwine, come here!'' Sam shouted, becoming anxious again concerning the fate of the crackers and tobacco ; then to himself : '' Hear that durn'd Canuck, drunker'n a bumble bee, an' a singin' temp'ance songs ! What sets folks allus to singin' them when they're full o' rum, an' ongodly sinners to shoutin' hymnes, I wonder ? Kinder ev'nin' things up, I s'pose. An' there comes Pel-tier ! If that durn'd fool ondertakes to bring him over, he'll draownd him, sartin. Peltier ! don't ye tech to come acrost till I come arter ye ! Come here, Antwine, wi' them crackers an' teibarker—I'm most starvin'.''

'' M'sieu Lovet, Ah'll been mek it *un petite voyage* for ma healthy ! Naow Ah'll goin' git Peltiet, seh,'' and he be-gan to shape his course to the best of his ability toward the waiting passenger.

'' Oh, come along here, Antwine,'' Sam called, coax-ingly, '' I've got suthin' to show ye !''

'' Bah gosh, M'sieu Lovet, Ah'll captins dis boats !'' Antoine answered, still paddling on his way with blunder-ing strokes. '' W'en Ah'll get ready come dar, Ah'll com-in' ; w'en Ah'll ant get ready, Ah'll don't comin' ! bah gosh feesh hooks ! On'stan' ?''

'' Look a-here, Antwine,'' said Sam, in a different tone, and at the same time launching the birch and stepping into it, '' you come ashore right straight off, er I'll come aout there an' knock ye gally west, an' tow ye ashore ! I've goddone a-foolin'.''

'' Oh, Sam, you'll ant gittin' mad, was it ! You ant

wan' leave you visity for roos' all naght on banks lak
geeses, don't it? Ah'll goin' git it, me."

"You come here!" Sam said sharply, as he pushed his
canoe afloat; and Antoine, turning the prow of the dugout
homeward, was soon alongside. "Oh, Sam," he whined
in maudlin tones as he tumbled ashore, "what you was
talk lak dat way for? You'll know Ah ant wan' faght wid
you, Sam. Dey ant fo' honded tousan' man could scairt
me, but Ah ant wan' leck ma frien' seh! Bah gosh,
no!" and he made an attempt to embrace Sam.

"All right," Sam said, putting him aside, "I must go
an' git Peltier. You look a' that 'ere annymil 'at I killed
whilst you was gone, an' then lay daown an' take a
snooze, for I know you're turrible tired with all 'at you've
underwent."

As Antoine balanced himself before the dead otter and
focussed his vague stare upon it, he was at first almost overcome with wonder. "What you call dat, Sam? Pant-
eis? Bears? No, he ant bears, he'll got some tails!
What he was be?"

"Auter," Sam answered.

"Oh, yas, otty, yas, what we'll call it *la loutre*, yas, yas.
Ah keel more as fave honded of it in Canada, some of it
more bigger as you was, but dis one so small Ah ant know
heem. Ah s'pose you'll feel pooty plump, Sam, prob'ly,
but he leetly fellar, not much bigger as minks was. What
for you ant let heem growed, Sam, hein?" But Sam was
half way across the Slang, and when he returned with Pelatiah the Canadian was snoring his way into the oblivious
interior of the land of Nod.

"You needn't git nothin' for me t' eat," Pelatiah said,
as Sam began preparations for a late dinner, "for they

made me eat dinner with 'em. Oh, my gol! a heap bigger 'n I c'ld see over, they piled ont' my plate! They
hedn't hed a fish this year, 'n' they was turrible 'bleeged
tu you, 'n' made me bring a hull ha' bushel o' apples,
signofiders an' gillflaowers, they be. I'm goin' to take
the bag hum sometime. An' they thee'd an' thaou'd me
jes' 'f I was a member 'mong Friends 's they say. 'N'
old Mister Bartlett he wanter know 'f I knowed any stiddy
feller 't wanter hire aout for six or eight mont's, an' fin'ly
sez he, ' does thee wanter?' S'pose aour folks 'ould let
me, Samwill, bein' 't I hain't come o' age, an' haow
much 'd I orter ast him? Say," without waiting for an
answer, "that gal hain't their darter, she's their hired
gal, but she's harnsome 'nough to be the Pres'dent's
darter. She's neater 'n any schoolmarm! Oh! 'f I wa'n't
'shamed o' my darn'd ol' ragged duds, an' me a stickin'
tew foot aouten both ends on 'em. Shouldn't s'pose she'd
ha' spoke tu me, but she ast me a hull lot o' questions
'baout my folks, an' kep' a-smilin' jes' 's clever! S'pose
she wouldn't look at me agin, would she, Samwill?"

"Can't tell ye, Peltier; the's no tellin' nothin' 'baout
what women folks 'll du or won't du," Sam answered,
rising and brushing from his tawny beard the crumbs of
the crackers wherewith he had made his dinner. " Wal,
I must be off an' tend to what traps I can, for that poor
creetur won't be no use to-day. Peltier, don't ye never
drink no sperits 'thaout ye raly need 'em, 'n' that'll be
mighty seldom. When huntin' an' fishin' an' trappin'
an' drinkin' goes together, the huntin' an' fishin' an' trappin' gits dreffle poorly 'tended tu, I tell ye. If he wakes
up ugly, you kinder saunder off an' let him work it off
alone by hisself, erless"—after a little consideration—

"you'd druther swat him side of the head tew three times an' make him behave hisself. If he thinks you're the least mite afeared on him, he'll be meaner 'n tunket, arter the way o' all his dum'd breed."

Giving this advice, Sam departed, and during his absence Pelatiah comforted himself with apples and gum and pleasant waking dreams.

The sun had gone down behind the woods and twilight was creeping over the landscape, and the evening air was vibrating with the ceaseless pur of the toads and the shrill chime of the Hyla's vesper bells, before the light dip of Sam's returning paddle was heard, followed presently by the swish of the canoe bottom on the matted drift of rushes. He had as little to show for his voyage as was to be expected after such an unpropitious night for trapping as the last had been, and he had not had time to visit and reset nearly all the traps as he might have done with Antoine's help, and so Sam was not in his pleasantest mood when he stalked into the firelight with his light burden of muskrats. "Hain't that durn'd peasouper come to his senses yit?" he said, pausing a moment to listen to Antoine's snores; "wish 't he'd crawled int' the Slang an' draownded hisself; but he couldn't—he hain't one o' the draowndin' kind. Wal, Peltier, le's ha' suthin' t' eat—reckoned you'd ha' got some supper ready 'fore naow."

"Wal," Pelatiah apologized, "I did think on't some 'n' I went so fur 's to cut some pork, but I was feared I'd spile it a-fryin' on 't; 'n' went so fur as to wash some 'taters, but I didn't know whether no to put 'em in hot water or col', 'n' the same wi' the tea, 'n' I didn't know whether no it took a han'ful for a drawin', er less, er more, 'n' so I didn't do nuthin' sca'sely, 'n' Antwine he hain't

done much only snort 'n' grunt. I'm sorry, but I guess
my 'cumilary edication has been sorter mislected,' as
Solon Briggs says. Cumilary! what in J'rus'lem does
that mean, s'pose?"

"Oh, wal," Sam said cheerily, "nev' mind, we'll ha'
suthin' to rights," and he soon had pork, fish, and potatoes cooked and ready. "I b'lieve I'll call aour sleepin'
pardner; he's hungry 'f he only knowed it. Antwine!"
Getting no response but a grunt, he dragged the Canadian
forth by the legs and shook him to such wakefulness that
he sat upright and stared blankly at the smoking slab.
"Bah gosh! where Ah'll was? Ah'll t'ought Ah was
keel in de Papineau war!"

"You'd orter ben," said Sam.

"Oh, Sam, no! Dis was gra' deal bettah for me. 'F
Ah'll dead, Ah can' heat, but naow Ah show you, me!"
And he did, while they ate their supper without much sauce
of conversation.

"Naow then, Antwine," Sam said, as they prepared to
turn in for the night, "I wanter tell ye one thing, 'f ye
git drunk agin whilst we're here, I'll give ye the almighti-
est hidin' 't ever you hed wi' the best blue beech gad I
c'n find--an' I know where the' 's some neat ones!"

"Me? Dronk! Oh, bah gosh! Ah'll ant never got
dronk ma laf tam fore, nor aftyward, nor dis tam. Ah
was tire, an' sah, Ah was nat'rally seek!"

"Wal," said Sam, "it'll be better for your health not to
hev no more sech fits o' sickness."

Then, lulled by the incessant, monotonous chorus of the
toads and frogs, they went to sleep.

VIII.

SPEARING BY JACKLIGHT.

AFTER the cold snap came a week of soft breathed days and dark, still, frostless nights, wherein the traps waylaid many a nightly wandering muskrat, and the trappers' harvest was rich

Some of the earliest comers of birds were beginning nest-building ; the wood-ducks had chosen their homes, and dusky ducks in pairs sought the remotest coves, while great flocks of their companions went on their way northward. The crows scorned now the once prized heap of muskrat carcasses, for they had entered into full possession of their ancient rights, and swaggered about the fields with an air of absolute ownership, and were evidently somewhat impatient that their tenants, the farmers, were so slow in beginning corn-planting.

More birds came from the south : re-inforcements of the dusky army of blackbirds, with flashing troops of redwings ; the main body of the robins joined the advance guard, and the thickets were more populous with slate-colored snow-birds, and noisy with their sharp metallic chirping ; and there were many arrivals of later comers. The highhole cackled and hammered again on his lofty perch : the white-throated sparrow called all day long for the ever-absent Mr. Peabody, and the wailing cry of the grass plover arose from meadows and upland pastures. Out of nooks of the marshes the booming of the bittern resounded over the watery level, a sound so strange to Pelatiah's ears that he asked, "Who be them fellers a-drivin' stakes in the ma'sh, an' what be they a-duin' on it for?" and was greatly astonished when told that it was only the voice of a bird, and entertained an uncomfortable suspicion that Sam was fooling him till one day when he stealthily stalked the sound and saw a "gob gudgeon" standing on a mass of marsh drift diligently pumping out his dolorous love-song. "Golly blue!" Pelatiah remarked, as, when he disclosed himself, the startled fowl sprang upon his awkward flight with a contemptuous parting salute, "his ol' pump needs primin' 'f that's all he's got for so much fuss!" By day and by night stranger outcries came from the marshes, weird laughter and wild yells, the voices of unknown water-fowl that were never seen.

The recurved lines of the water maple's branches began to glow with dots and clusters of scarlet, and the willows shone with catkins of silver and gold, caskets which held a treasure that all the bees of the region came to steal. The grass was greening in the swales and on the warmest slopes, and the farmers were ploughing in a dozen fields within sight and as many more within hearing, all shouting to their slow teams of oxen so vociferously that Pelatiah said, as he lounged on the bank in front of the shanty : "It's eq'l tu a lawgin' bee t' hum!" and as his thoughts ran homeward, led by these familiar sounds, "Darn it all! I s'pose I'd ort t' be t' hum a-helpin' aour folks, but I snum, I'd druther stay here!" and his gaze wandered across lots to the white house.

"Wal, we'll all go to rights, Peltier," said Sam ; "the trappin' 's 'baout done up—hain't got sca'sely nuthin' these

tew three nights—'n' I expec' the'll be a team arter us
'fore the end o' the week, 'n' then we'll pull up 'n' clear
aout.''

" Bah gosh !'' cried Antoine, " we'll ant go 'fore the
bull pawt was bit an' we'll ketch lot of it ! No sah !
De evelin was be gittin' warm, an' Ah'll know he was bit
pooty soon, prob'ly to-naght, prob'ly to-morreh naght,
Ah dun-no. Ah'll gat some hook an' lahne w'en Ah was
go store. Where Ah'll put dat ? Ah freegit, Ah'll be so
seek dat tam !'' and he began a hurried and excited search
among his disorderly effects for the missing tackle.
" Hoorah, here he was ! Naow, Sam, give me some bullet for mek sinkit an' Ah'll feex up for try to naght, 'f Ah
can fin' som' wum. Ah'll gat some pole-feesh more as
week 'go. Oh, Ah can ketch it if anyboddy can ketch.''
he bragged as he half hitched a hook on to the coarse
line. " Ah was preffick feeshymans.'' Then he split one
of the Ore Bed's big balls half in two and closed it on the
line, which he then rigged upon a pole that had had more
labor bestowed upon it in trimming and peeling than its
original worth seemed to have warranted, for it was top-
heavy and as crooked as an eel. Perhaps its owner considered this a virtue rather than a fault, and hoped that the
reflection of the contorted " hard hack'' might entice some
lonely eel to its companionship : and the eel was to him
what the trout and salmon are to the scientific angler.
Having his outfit arranged to his satisfaction he crossed the
Slang in the dugout to the cultivated fields beyond in quest
of earth worms, and Pelatiah accompanied him on his way
to return the borrowed bag, while the camp was left to the
keeping of Sam and his hound.

Sam busied himself with bundling up the dried peltry,

and Drive was as busy with ineffectual digging in the nearest muskrat burrow, which he did not abandon till long after the beleaguered rat had ploughed his way to safety toward the channel of the Slang with a sluggish, heavy, under-water wake faintly marking his furrow ; then, shaking and wiping some of the dirt from his long ears and sorrowful face, he sought more congenial pastime in chasing and being chased by a vixen who had begun housekeeping and the rearing of a family not far away. Once, rating this ancient enemy of her race with angry, gasping barks, she followed him so close to camp that Sam got a full view of her in her sorry and tattered faded-yellow garb of vulpine maternity, not twenty yards behind the slinking, shamefaced hound. "Good-arternoon, marm !" he said ; "'f 'twas in the fall o' the year, naow, yer tail 'ould be pintin' tow-wards that 'ere sneakin' ol' bundle o' kag hoops, an' the'd be a diff'ent style o' music in fashion ! Good-by, marm," as the vixen vanished behind the veil of hazy undergrowth ; " I wish ye good luck a raisin' yer fam'ly, an' 'ould like to make the hull of yer 'quaintances come November, an' ye git yer good close on. Oh, Drive ! hain't you a spunky dawg, a skulkin' hum with yer tail atween yer laigs afore a nasty little bitch fox not quarter 's big as you be !" as the hound came up to him and endeavored to explain the peculiarities of the situation with whimpers and more deeply corrugated brow, and quick, low-swung tail beats that shook all his lean anatomy. " A spunky ol' haoun' dawg you be ! But yer julluk me, an' I guess the most o' tew-legged he humerns. Lord ! I'd druther wrastle with a mad painter 'an to face a jawin' womern, I be durn'd if I hedn't ! If they won't take the spunk aouten a feller, he's tougher 'n a biled aowl !"

The sun was down, and the reflected gold of the western sky lay unbroken on the quiet water save where a skimming bank swallow touched it with the light dip of his wing, or a fish lazily rose to an insect that dimpled it as it fell exhausted in its too adventurous flight, before the returning dugout vexed the Slang into a thousand distortions of mirrored sky and shores.

Antoine's bait hunting had been successful, and he had an old teapot half full of angle-worms—an encouraging sign of future luck, he thought ; and supper was no sooner over than he betook himself to the bank with pole and teapot. He charged his hook with a bait that might entice the fullest-fed and most indifferent bullhead in all the Slang, and spitting on it for luck, sent it with a whistling overhead cast straight out from shore, where it and the heavy sinker plunged with a kerchug that again awoke the waves.   While he sat waiting with statuesque patience for a bite, his companions watched him with an interest at first quite intense, but which grew languid as Antoine's form became an undefined dark blur in the dusk and yet gave no sign that his patient waiting had been rewarded with even a nibble.

Then they saw the flicker of a feeble light just kindled away down stream on the farther shore.   Presently it grew from the volume of a candle flame to a brilliant blaze, and then began to slowly skirt the shore, attended by its glittering red dancing reflection, and revealing one figure, one side red with firelight, the other black with shadow, standing close behind it, and dimly suggesting another crouching a little farther away, with a paddle that gleamed for an instant at regular intervals as it was raised for a stroke, then faded into the gloom.   Then the light turned toward them, and yawing along its course came more swiftly down its

own shortening glade, growing larger and sending down
frequent showers of sparks on either side, each spark and
its double meeting at the water's surface and vanishing there
together. The square prow of a scow became visible, and
a man standing therein. wielding a spear that he made a
show of well-intended but ineffectual paddling with.

" Hillo, Danvis !" hailed the actual propelling power
in the stern.

" Hello, Lakefield," Sam answered, recognizing the
stentorian voice of his whilom enemy, and giving him in
return the name of his township.

" Wanter take a leetle turn up the Slang a-spearin' ?"

" Wal, I do' know," said Sam, rising and going toward
them as the scow surged through the floating sedges and
butted against the shore ; " I can't spear a fish ; never done
sech a thing in my life."

" Oh, you needn't du no spearin'. Jimmy 'll 'tend t'
that ; he's a ripper t' spear. You c'n help me paddle 'f
you're a minter, an' Jimmy 'll prod 'em. He's wus'n a
kingfisher ; hain't that so, Jimmy ?"

Jimmy, who seemed not much given to speech, answered
only with a grunt, and drew from his pocket a plug of tobacco, which, after slowly and thoughtfully turning in the
light of the jack in search of the most vulnerable corner,
he gnawed a quid from, and then extended toward Sam.
The friendly offering was declined with thanks and the explanation that Sam " didn't never chaw."

" Come on," urged the other occupant of the scow,
" an' ha' some fun an' git some fish f' yer breakfus. He
c'n go tew, 'f he wants t' see the fun. The's room
'nough," nodding toward Pelatiah.

" Feesh for breakfis !" cried Antoine, as he jerked a

bull-head out and landed it with a heavy thud on the bank
the pole and line's length behind him, where it protested
against the sudden change of elements with vigorous flapping of its tail and grinding of its jaws. " Bah gosh ! here
he'll was, dumn sight gre' deal better as peckrils was !
Ant you'll hear it grape hees toofs ? Dat 'cause he'll know
haow good he'll was w'en he'll be fry, an' he'll mad 'cause
he can't heat some of it heesef. Oh, he'll good wan !'
as, with the handiness of one who knows the trick, he
grasped the fish between the thorny pectorals and dorsal
and disengaged the hook ; " he'll humpy fellar. Dey's
more of it comin'. All hees ree-lashin' comin' breakfis.
You go spearin' you wan' to, Ah'll stay here an' tol' it
good evelin w'en he'll come.''

Sam and Pelatiah took their allotted places in the boat,
which resumed its slow and silent way over the submerged
marshes. The glaring light of the jack, fed at times from
a store of " fat" pine, out of the darkness conjured ghostly
forms of trees that seemed to stalk out from the shore to
meet them, then receded and vanished in the gloom behind
them. A muskrat in bootless quest of departed friends
halted on his course and lay for a moment with as little
motion as a drifting stick, regarding the unwonted floating
illumination of his haunts, then dived with a startling sudden splash. An owl flitted with noiseless flight like a
gigantic moth close to the glaring torch, and disappearing,
hooted out a cry of wonder or a hoarse laugh of derision
from the more congenial depths of night. Wood-ducks
sat on their roosts of prone trees with charmed gaze till the
falling sparks hissed close beside them before they sprang
fluttering away into the gloom, uttering wild squeaks of
fright. As the scow headed across a broad shallow, the in-

tent spearsman raised his spear, and as the craft was checked
in obedience to the motion, he made a quick thrust and
brought in a great pickerel, whose struggles were quickly
ended by a stamp of his captor's boot-heel.

"That's the sort, Jimmy," said his comrade in loud
approval. Jimmy only grunted, and a moment later hurled
his spear twice its length. As the boat came up to the
wriggling and waving shaft, he stooped, and picking it up,
boated a large fish. "Swago" he laconically catalogued
it, and stamped it into everlasting rest.

"That's the way Jimmy jerks 'em in," cried his friend
and patron. "When he runs his eye aout at 'em, they're
goners, you better b'lieve! I argy he does it by charmin'
on 'em with his good looks. You've noticed 'at he's on-
common harnsome."

"Onph!" Jimmy grunted, and after some slow rumination of his cud, speaking more at length than was his wont,
"Guess you hain't no gret to brag on that way, Joe, no
more 'n me. Folks calls him Time," addressing Sam and
indicating his comrade by a backward movement of his
head, "'cause he favors the pictur' o' Time in the primer."

"'Tend right tu yer spearin', Jimmy, an' don't tire yerself a talkin'," said Joe. And Jimmy raised his spear,
then arresting it in a half-delivered stroke, said with su-
preme contempt, "Cussed bowfin!" and the boat moved
on. Presently he poised his spear and announced, "Mud
turkle. Ol' buster. Shell I?"

"Let him hev!" shouted the commander of the expedition, and the spear went unerringly to its mark. Jimmy
grunted profusely as he lifted the sprawling monster inboard
partly by the spear and partly by a "tail holt." He was a
patriarch of the oozy depths, with the moss of many years

clinging to his broad shell, and was vicious in appearance and behavior.

"Cut off his cussed ol' head," said Joe, passing his open jack-knife forward, "an' let him c'mmence his nine days o' dyin' right off. Mebby you're the man 'at ketched my goslin's, you humbly ol' cuss! Haow d'ye like that kind o' sass yerself?" as Jimmy sawed away at the turtle's tough neck just below where the spear transfixed it, while the reptile clawed at the knife and hissed angrily. When he was decapitated and laid upon his back the boat moved on to new conquests, Jimmy taking many fine fish of various kinds before they reached the head of navigation, where a rude, low log bridge barred their farther way. As they skirted the left bank on their homeward cruise, Jimmy still alert for more victims, Joe said : "Jimmy's a cuss to spear, wus'n a kingfisher or a blue herrin', but he won't paddle er pole. Some says it's 'cause he's lazy, but I 'low it's on'y 'cause he don't like tu work !"

"Onph ! Lazy ! The' wa'n't nobody 't ever wasted the' breath a tellin' haow 't you was lazy," was Jimmy's only reply to the imputation.

When they reached the landing at the camp all went ashore and stretched their cramped legs, and found the warmth of the fire very comforting, for the dampness and chill of the spring night had crept into their bones.

IX.

BREAKING CAMP.

RADIANT in the light of the camp-fire they found Antoine rejoicing over a baker's dozen of bullpouts, which he was about skinning. The dressing of these fish was a revelation to Sam and Pelatiah, who had never before seen it done. One cut of the knife forward from behind the sharp-spined dorsal, a rip down the back, a snap of the backbone attended by a pistol-like pop of the bursting air bladder, and the fish was stripped, beheaded and disembowelled by another motion with a suddenness that made it and these two observers gape with astonishment.

Jimmy, after looking on a short time, drew forth and opened his knife, and after carefully licking from the blade the gummy morsels of tobacco adhering to it, sharpened it on his boot and picked up a bull head, which, with more cuts and a little less speed than Antoine used, he rid of its incumbrances of big head, skin, and entrails to the saving of some meat.

"Saves a mou'f'l er tew o' good meat," he remarked, displaying the dressed fish a moment before he cast it into the pan with the others. Then, wiping his knife on the ground, he shut it, returned it to his pocket, grunted and lapsed into his normal silence and slow rumination, making no response to Antoine's comment, "Ma way save tam, an' tam was worse more as meats. Mans dat know,

say tam was money, an' paoun' of money worse more as
paoun' of meats, don't it, hein?"

When they adjourned to the scow to divide the night's
catch of the spear, Antoine could not repress his admiration of the fine pickerel, and, more than all else, of the
great turtle. "Here, Peasoup," said Joe, heaving it
ashore, where it landed right side up and began an aimless
journey, perhaps in search of its head, " yer pardner says
you eat these 'ere overgrowed bugs. 'F you want it, take
it."

"Oh, bah gosh!" cried Antoine, heading off the ponderous present—if a headless thing can be headed off—and
hastening to tether it with a cord to a bush, " Ah'll veree
tousan' tam ob-laige to you, seh! More as Ah can tol' of
it. Ah'll took dat home an' fat up all my waf an' chillens
wid him, you see 'f Ah'll don't, Sam."

It was noticeable that while Joe treated Sam with a rude
deference and respect, toward Antoine he bore himself
with a half contemptuous condescension hardly comport-
ing with the mien of the conquered in the presence of the
conqueror; but when their visitors had departed Antoine
said, with a grin of great width and satisfaction, "Ant
you'll see haow good dat man's 'have itsef every sin Ah'll
leek it? Dat was de way for mek hugly mans be good,
you betteh b'lieve so!"

The next morning's round proved the spring crop of
muskrats so nearly exhausted that the traps were forthwith
taken up and strung in rusty dozens for transportation, and
the disused tally-sticks went drifting away to contribute
their mite of driftwood to various shores.

Late in the afternoon, while Antoine's comrades were
assisting him in the final vivisection of the turtle, a team

of horses came in sight hauling a lumbering wagon
slowly across the fields toward the farther shore of the
Slang.

"Hello!" cried Sam, "there comes aour baggidge
waggin. Who is 't a-drivin'? Jozeff Hill, I guess, b' the
dumplin' shape on him, an' the way he jounces 'raound
on the seat, toes jes' techin' the waggin bottom. Yes,
that's Jozeff," after an intent consideration of the approaching teamster, who presently could be heard bumping out
snatches of tuneless song mixed with broken words of en-
couragement and reproof to his team, as they passed across
the rough field.

> "'Odn Maadnsfield Maounting onct didn ndwell-ell,
> N-a likeli you ugh-th I-ee knowed full well-n.'

"Git up, ol' mare!

> "'Cur-d-nell Maaryit's onli sodn,
> N a-a-abaout the aage of twednti-wodn-n-n.'

"Go 'long, Jim, why don't ye, con ugh-sarn yer ol'
pictur'! er be ye goin' t'other way, you ol' snugent o' the
de-sarts!"

Sam went over in the dugout to meet him and helped
him to unharness the horses and shelter and feed them in
the shed of an untenanted barn that stood in the middle of
the field. Arriving at camp Joseph was cordially welcomed
by the others, and soon began to unladen himself of his
burden of neighborhood news, to hear which now would
remind one of the items of a country paper of to-day.
While his late dinner was cooking, and while he ate with
full enjoyment the fried pickerel, he told them that it had
been "a good sugarin' year—fust chop—wal, more 'n
midellin, anyway," and undertook to tell how many pounds

each neighbor had made, though, as usual, he was never quite sure which neighbor it was, nor of the number of pounds. Also, that "Hanner Ann Jones er her sister Huldy Jane was a-goin' to teach in their deestrick this summer; that Joel Bartlett an' 'mongst 'em seen a bear up on the side o' Hawg's Back—big one er little one, didn't know, but they seen tew—'n' Joel, he was a gittin' ready to fix up his haouse—er mabby 'twas his barn—'n' they was a-buildin' tew three new haousen for the work-men to the forge—goin' to du maricles, er more, to the forge this summer, fer iron hed riz, er was a goin' ter. His father's rheumatiz was wus—didn't know as they was raly wus, but he was a sufferin' more pain with 'em, seem 's 'ough, 'n' he hedn't no gret of an ap'tite t' eat much. Ol' Mist' Pur'nton he was toll'ble well this spring, an' Mis' Pur'nton she was smarter 'n a crickit, 'n' the hull fam'ly wus well, he b'lieved, though mabby some o' the younger feemale portion was a-gittin' sorter lunsome-—like 'nough, he didn't know." Then, wagging his head toward Pelatiah, without taking his eyes from the not quite un-fleshed bones of the bit of pickerel in his hand: " Pel-tier's folks is well, I b'lieve, though they be gittin' sorter oneasy 'baout his not comin' back hum; guess they kinder need him 'baout spring's work-—do' know 's they 'zactly need him, but they kinder want him, er think mabby he might 's well be t' hum, naow, er putty soon; 'n' An-twine's folks an' young uns is well an' hearty, an' was a polly vooin' like all git aout when I come along past airly this mornin'; I think they was; mabby 'twas the frawgs a bellerin' ov' t' the pawnd, but frawgs hain't a-bellerin' naow; I guess 'twas Antwine's fam'ly a polly vooin'."

Then, when he was relieved of the chief weight of his

gossip, he had as great a burden of questions to unload concerning the luck and adventures of the trappers.

As evening drew on they all began to gather a pile of wood to illuminate that night's bullpout fishing, which was to be the great final event of this spring's camp life. Antoine had provided plenty of bait and the angling outfit for his friends after the approved fashion of his own, except that possibly some of the poles were straighter than his; and at dusk they lighted their fire and began fishing. The fish were plenty, and blessed or cursed with good appetites, and one after another, with a sluggish, stubborn, downright pull for life and freedom, was torn from its watery hold and came walloping and creaking to land. To Sam, Joseph, and Pelatiah the unhooking of one was at first a rather perilous feat, and Pelatiah gave a bellow of pain when his finger was impaled by the horn of his first fish. "You wa'n't caffle, Peltiet," said Antoine, as the young fellow came to the fire, by turns sucking and inspecting the injured finger; "dem bullpawt he's bit pooty hard wid hees horn, Ah tol' you! Touch hol' of it jus' sam' lak Ah do, you t'umb an' fingler 'hind hees side horn, you palm you hand of it 'fore hees top horn—so. Den squeezle heem, haard!" and they all soon got the knack of it after the added lesson of some sorely punctured hands.

The generously fed fire sent up great tongues of flame licking at the gloom, and showered an upward rain of sparks into the branches that waved and tossed in the rising currents of warmed air. Across its dusky edged circle of light, as the fishermen went to and fro, fell elongated shadows of legs, here joined to the gloom as if that was some enormous beast of undefined ponderous form noiselessly circling about the fire, there stretched from where the distorted, shadowy bodies flitted like gigantic goblins among the spectral boles of great trees.   On the water side the poles and lines were defined against the darkness with seeming unreality, as if they were the angling gear of pis·catorial ghosts ; and when a plunging bait and sinker or a writhing outdrawn fish broke the water, and wavering shim-mers of reflected light started forth and vanished in the blank silence, it was as if they had broken on the intan-gible shores of the land of ghosts.   But by the cheerful, liv-ing fire there was life enough, and such sport as satisfied these jolly but most unscientific anglers.

By midnight they had sport and bull-heads enough to have satisfied greedier men than they were, and Antoine's highest hopes were realized in the catching of a great eel. To have heard him vituperate the unfortunate fish while he was unhooking it, one would hardly think he valued it so much.   " Oh, kanfoun' you, you hugly hol' brute snakes ! What for you ant lied steel an' let me steck you 'tween de necks, hein, you slaamy hol' coss ?   You'll ant fit for be decent, bah gosh, all feesh hook !   Saay, you'll goin' be dead littly, naow, hein ? you hol hugly !''

When he had stamped and stabbed it into a quiet ac-ceptance of fate, then with a sigh of satisfaction, " Bah gosh ! if ma hwoman don't happy to-morroh naght w'en he'll got hees husbin come home an' brought it bullpawt, an' mud turkey, an' heel, it don't no uses for try mek it happy in dis worl'.''

Next morning the sleepy occupants of the shanty awoke late, and even while Antoine was cooking the appetizing breakfast of fish, the others bestirred themselves in making ready for departure.   And when the breakfast had been made speedy way with, the canoes began to pass across the

Slang with cargoes of peltry and camp gear. By the middle of the forenoon the boats had made their last trips, and, with the baggage, were snugly stowed on board the wagon, the horses were hitched on, and the homeward journey began. All but Joseph Hill, who drove, trudged beside and behind the load through the greening fields that lay between the Slang and the highway. They were not very jolly as they set their faces toward their native hills, for who ever left a camp where few or many happy hours have been spent without a touch of regretful sadness? Even the hound seemed touched with this feeling, and sent wistful glances backward as he ranged the fields and snuffed the faint odors of last night's fox trails. As Sam cast a last look on the spot that had been his home for a month, a bittern's booming and the lazy quack of a dusky duck came from afar across the hazy marshes like friendly farewells, and the camp squirrel chattered from his favorite hemlock a not unkindly adieu. A wreath of smoke fluttered away from the dying camp-fire like a gauzy flag lowered and trailing on the ground.

Not many days passed before mink and skunk and woodchuck began boldly to visit the deserted shanty, and mouse and chipmunk took up their abode in it. Moss and lichens began to grow on the slowly rotting roof, blades of grass and weeds sprang up among the brands and ashes of the fireplace, and growth and decay began to obliterate the traces of human occupancy.

X.

A LETTER FROM UNCLE LISHA.

THE trappers tarried in Vergennes to dispose of their peltry, and succeeded in doing so on terms satisfactory to all concerned, after some lengthy bargaining with the hatter, whose shop was made conspicuous by a stuffed lynx set in its window.

After brief sight-seeing and the purchase of a few articles not to be found in the Danvis store, they resumed their homeward way. The road was long and rough, but almanac and sky promised them a moonlit night for what should remain of their journey after daylight had gone. Their shadows in the setting sun were moving far before them along the road in a grotesque silhouette when Joseph Hill gave the reins to Sam while he donned his "s'tout." When he had thrust himself, with a series of jerks, into that close-fitting, many-caped garment, he began his customary, uncertain search for pipe and tobacco.

"What in Sam Hill!" he ejaculated, as he brought up from the recesses of a pocket of his "gret cut" a soiled and travel-worn letter, and held it at half arm's length before his staring eyes. "What in Sam Hill! Oh, Samwill Lovel! 'f I hain't kerried this 'ere letter fur you all the way f'm Danvis an' so fur back, an' never thought tu give it tu ye! My sakes! I'm shameder 'n a licked dawg!

But the's one comfort, Huldy never writ it ; it's a furrin letter, f'm way off.''

Sam was assured of this when he saw the big, square letter addressed in a large, laborious hand :

" SAMMEWILL LOVE'L,

Danvis,

Sharlott Co.,

State of Vermont."

in haste."

He turned it over and over, studying the ill-written address and postmark and the dauby seal, puzzling himself to guess from whence it had come a long while before he thought of solving the riddle by the easiest way. Then he sniffed a familiar odor.

" By the gret horn spoon, boys, it's sealed wi' shoemaker's wax, an' it's f'm Uncle Lisher !''

" Why, sartinly,'' said Joseph, '' an' I rec'lect naow, 'at when Clapham tol' me the' was a letter for me tu kerry tu ye, he looked in the Liqrish draw, where he allus puts the L's, an' couldn't find it, and then he looked in the Sal'ratus draw, I b'lieve it was, where he puts the S's, er mebby 't was the Cinnerment draw, an' at last he faound it in the Shellac draw, said he put 't in there, 'cause he was feared 't 'ould make the liqrish taste. But why in Sam Hill I never thought tu give it tu ye jest beats me all holler. Seem's 'ough I'd ha' thought on't fust thing, but I b'lieve I be gettin' furgitful, erless I can't remember nothin'. I've tol' M'ri so tew three times. I b'lieve it's newrology er rhemmatiz, which I've hed 'em both.''

While Joseph was excusing and explaining his negligence, Sam was unsealing his letter with awkward care, and having got at its contents began to read. This was no easy task, for the jolting of the wagon would have made it difficult to follow the lines if the words had been plainly written in the blackest ink. But the letter had been begun with pale ink and a pen that either spluttered or refused to make any mark, till the writer's patience had been exhausted, and he had exchanged them for a hard lead-pencil, that in its normal condition left but faint trace of its progress over the paper, though it had evidently been weightily borne down upon. Then the chirographer had licked it, and produced somewhat more satisfactory results, which presently failing, he had softened his obdurate pencil with a more thorough moistening, and succeeded in bringing out two or three words in a strong though neutral tint. Then the lead would thirst by the wayside, perhaps in the middle of a word, and make but a shadowy record of its course, till again refreshed. The writer's moments of meditation, wherein he had pensively sucked his pencil, were marked by the exceeding distinctness of the following word.

Photography was unknown in those days, but the best instantaneous production of the camera could hardly have shown to Sam more vividly than this letter did the picture of his old friend with elbows sprawled over a table and feet hooked into the rungs of his chair, with intent, corrugated brow and mouth set into a hard circle, around which rim his tongue ran in accompaniment to the slow movement of his fingers, more laboriously engaged on his sheet of

foolscap, in the production of this letter, than he would
have been in the familiar task of cutting a side of sole
leather into soles and taps. If Sam's lips could not forbear a smile at the homely picture which his fancy wrought,
neither could his eye withhold a mistiness that made dim-
mer the scrawled words. Reading them to himself, while
his companions waited for what he should give them there-
of, they ran in this wise :

HEGALGAN, HEGALGAN Co.,
Wis. Feb. the 4th.

S. lovil respected frend.

i take my pen in hand to seet myself to rite thees fu lines to
let you no that i am wel whitch i hope this may find you the
saim, and all frends in danvis whitch godnose i wish to see and
was in for i do not addmire this boosted land of westconstant
none tue well not to deny but what it is most frutelle in abunder-
ant crops and game dear and wile tirkees prayry chickin like the
patter ridges to homb but larjer and so neumerrus whitch wood
sprise you to see and delite to hunt not to speke of fish in plenty
in the lake whitch shamplane is pudil and buffalow not fur to the
west thair paths and wollers remane and bones whitch was kill
by ingeans whitch they is plenty anuff but not danjerous and has
not skalp me tell josier hill nor bit by snaikes nor had feavnage
tell him but not this that i do not like the westconstant so mutch
as i ekspekt i shud and Jerusha my wif is not ruggid and cherk
tho she take grate comfurt with georges childerin 2 nise boys
and 2 nise gals whitch take tue her natterly as moste do that no
her as you no we are lonesum for the mowntins whitch this
countray is flattern a pancake. nor no woods to call woods nigh
to smel of a balsum a spruce a hemlok whitch our ize miss the
site and my noze whitch you no not small the smel now my
frend i want you to see joel hartlit and see if he will take what
he giv for the ole plase if he will bargin for it as if youself byin
i hav got anuff to pay up i will let you hav it on sheers me and
Jerusha to liv with you and hulda til we dy and you tacare of us
til we dy and you shal hav the plase then anser as soon as you

can and not say nuthing of this to noboddy but hulda whitch i hope you are marrid most happy your frend til deth

ELISHA PEGGS, p s

remember me to all inqirin frends as if namd what fun we will hav in the ole shop agin doos it look natteral or all run down jerusha sens her love to you and speshal hulda direk to Elisha Peggs in care of George Peggs Hegalgan hegalgan co. Wis."

Visions of a cosey home of his own arose before Sam as he read the letter to himself, and still as he read to his companions such portions as he might, there floated before his mind pleasant pictures of the future—the "house part" of the old couple's domicile again warmed to life, and a brighter life than it had ever known, the shop, with Uncle Lisha on his bench hammering merrily on his lap-stone, and the old visitors in their chosen places. For a moment it seemed almost a reality, then vanished like smoke in the wind, as he remembered how seldom happy dreams are realized.

The pale half moon grew silver bright in the darkening blue, high above clouds aflame with the sun's afterglow, and the clouds faded to pearly gray, and gray shadows grew black across the moonlit road and fields as the little party journeyed slowly homeward, still discoursing of the old friend so freshly brought to mind.

When they entered the hamlet it had betaken itself to its accustomed early sleep, and there was no sound of life in it but the thunderous beat of its heart, the great hammer of the forge, nor, except the lurid gleam of its fires, cast athwart the street through the wide doors, any light of life but the faint glimmer of a lamp in Hamner's bar-room, and another as faint in a quiet house, where it was guessed "someb'dy was sick or a sparkin'."

" Do' know raly which is the wust," Joseph Hill mused aloud ; " sparkin' is the most pleasantest, but it's full dangouser 'n most kinds o' sickness ; seem's 'ough 'twas, most allus." He sighed as he cast a longing backward glance to Hamner's dim beacon.

The drowsiness of the village was infectious, and for the next hour the travellers were only kept half awake by the jolting of the wagon, and gave up all attempts at conversation.

XI.

THE HOME RECEPTION.

When they came to the house of Sam's father, the men aroused themselves to unload his canoe and other effects and bade him good-night, "or mebby good-mornin'," Joseph said, unwilling to commit himself even in a parting salutation.

They went their way, and left him " on the chips," which were the only garniture of the untidy yard. Sam sighed as he turned from watching the departure of the wagon and cast a look over the house he called his home. Its nakedness and unthrift were as drearily apparent in the faint light of the clouded moon as in the glare of day. It had never looked homelike since his mother died, for the kindly touches of her brave but feeble hand had been quickly effaced by the shrew who, with unseemly haste, was installed in her place.

" If she'd lived," Sam said to himself, pitying his un-cared-for childhood, " mebby I'd ha' ben suthin' better'n a loafin', shifless, huntin', fishin' cretur. 'F I'd hed her an' a hum 'at was a hum ! But mebby it's better for her as 'tis ; the' wa'n't much comfort for her here, I guess," and he pitied her hard life more than his own. " Mebby a womern c'n du suthin' for me yit." Standing on the rotting step at the kitchen door he glanced upward and saw the old familiar oval plate of tin on the lintel with the word " Mutual " upon it, and remembered how when he was a boy and could first read it, it gave him a feeling of kinship with the world of Danvis, for there was not a well-to do farmer in the township that had not this seal of the insurance company set upon it. There was one over the door of the Purington homestead, and it made his heart beat quick to think that he would pass under it to morrow night. There was one at Joel Bartlett's, but not above the entrance, for Joel felt it borne in upon him that such a display of gilded letters would be entirely out of plainness, and had made the insurance agent nail the plate behind the kitchen door, where it was seldom seen. He must see Joel Bartlett to morrow and learn if there was any chance of buying back the old place.

He raised the latch of the unfastened door and pushed it open as quickly as its creaking hinges and sagged condition would let even him, who had learned so well its tell tale tricks. When he had closed it he listened a moment, but heard no sound that betokened the awakening of the in-mates. There were only the slow and squeaky ticking of the tall clock, the purring of the cat under the cold stove, the gnawing of a mouse somewhere in the woodwork, as mice had always been gnawing since he could remember sounds, and the gasping, intermittent snoring of his father, that used years ago to make his heart stand still as he lay listening in his lonely bed, wondering if the last explosive expiration was not final and he the most forlorn of orphans.

Taking from its box on the mantelpiece a home-made brimstone match, and lighting it with a coal raked from the ashes, he lighted the slender dip candle which he found in its accustomed place by the match-box, and as its feeble light illumined the kitchen's tidy discomfort, the bare walls, newly whitewashed, the few well scrubbed wooden-seated chairs, the big table, Sam comprehended at a glance, as he hung the Ore Bed on its hooks, that house-cleaning was over, and was thankful that his return was so well timed.

The slight sounds of his entrance had not awakened his stepmother; perhaps it was the light that aroused her, perhaps it was the clatter of Drive's toe nails as he sniffed an inventory of the room's contents, perhaps the rattle of her cherished crockery, when Sam explored the pantry shelves in search of something for himself and Drive to eat, but just then her voice flashed out sharply :

" Who's that ?"

" It's me," he answered, and asked, " haow be ye all ?"

" Me ! yis, an' high time 'at ' me ' come hum, I sh'd think !" she snarled in a sleepy voice ; " but I do' know 's the' was any p'tic'lar need o' sneakin' in in the dead o' night, when the's jes' 's many days 's the's nights ; awakin' up folks 'at hevs tu work stiddy, instid of shoolin' 'raound a-trappin', an' a huntin', an' a-thisin' an' a-thatin', so 's 'tain't work. Make thet 'ere pleggid haoun dawg lay daown, a-trompoosin' over my clean kitchin floor 'at I've scrubbed and scaoured half a day."

" Here, Drive," Sam said, as if he had not heard her tirade, " here's a col' johnny-cake, an' I'll d'vide wi' ye."

" O dear me, suz !" groaned Mrs. Lovel, " I wish 't the' wa'n't none o' them pleggid men in this livin' worl, erless I wish 't I was dead."

" Seein' 't the' so many more on 'em 'an the' is o' you, I'd take the cheapest way tu git clear on 'em 'f I was you, marm," said Sam, taking a mouthful of johnny-cake and dropping as generous a piece into Drive's alert jaws.

"I won't die tu please you," she snapped, smothering the last word in the blankets as she settled herself in the bed, whose sudden spiteful creak proclaimed that she would vouchsafe no further speech.

"She saitinly never done much tu," Sam said to himself, as he gave his dog the last morsel of their frugal supper.

His father, who had not deemed it prudent to appear earlier, now came forth, very quietly, a queer figure in a short red flannel shirt astilt on long bare legs, bringing to mind the old simile of a "shirt on a bean pole." While he scratched his side with a scant handful of flannel, he welcomed his son with a pleasant smile and a whispered,

"Wal, Samwill, haow air ye? Hed good luck, an' kep' well, hev ye?"

"Yes; an' be you well, father?" Sam answered and asked in a whisper, scanning the old man's weak, kindly face.

"Find suthin' t' eat? The's some pork an' beans in there some'eres," indicating the pantry by a sidewise nod. "Do' know where she put 'em. Hey, Drive, good ol' feller!" he whispered, stooping to pat the hound very softly. "You better keep middlin' still, ol' feller!" as Drive's friendly tail-beats smote chairs and wall. "Wal, I guess I'll be crawlin' back. She's putty nigh beat aout a-haouse cleanin', an' so be I."

Sam took Drive to his bed in the barn, and then sought his own in the cheerless kitchen chamber. Home was home after all, and he settled himself to sleep under the sloped ceiling with a sense of usage, if not of perfect content, in which there was a degree of comfort. In his dreams he was a boy again, and his mother's toilworn hand

caressed his weary head with the kindly, unforgotten touch
of the nights of long ago.

As soon as might be next day he sought an interview
with Joel Bartlett, and after much roundabout talk concerning weather and crop prospects broached the real object of his visit. He was not disappointed when Joel refused to dispose of the Uncle Lisher place at the price he
had given for it, for that was not the thrifty saint's way of
doing business. But when he offered an advance of fifty
dollars, then of seventy-five, and finally of a hundred dollars, and each offer was promptly refused with a declara-
tion that Joel " did not feel clear tu sell at no price likely
tu be gi'n him, bein' it come in so well with his own farm,
which it was onct a part on, the original tew hunderd acre
pitch drawed tu the right o' Hezekier Varney, which he in
some ways foolishly got red on," Sam turned away, his
heart heavy with hope deferred. Not yet, as he had per-
mitted himself to hope, was the door of a real home opening to Huldah and him.

That night the lovers built nothing so grand as a castle
in the air, only a snug log-house up among the cheaply
valued acres of woodland that Sam's small savings would
buy. Better that, they said, than going to the West, far
from kindred and old friends and the beloved Green
Mountains.

The neighbors remarked that " Sam Lovel hedn't never
took a holt so afore as he did in this spring's work."

But when the slack came after planting, the old wild
spirit laid hold of him. " I got tu go daown there a-fishin' jest oncte," was his answer to his sweetheart's opposing
arguments.

SAM LOVEL'S CAMPS.

THE CAMP ON THE LAKE.

I.

VOYAGE DOWN LITTLE OTTER.

FOLLOWING out a plan conceived during his spring cam
paign on the Slang, when he had been amazed at the numbers, size, and variety of fishes inhabiting Champlain
waters, Sam Lovel and some of his friends with a wagon-
load of camping outfit were one day slowly jolting down
the steep, winding road to the landing below the first falls
on Little Otter.

It was one of those lazy afternoons in June when all
nature basks in the new warmth and nothing seems better
to all things than to be still and enjoy laziness. The bull-
frogs sitting on the rafted logs at the mill tail only winked
their enjoyment of sunshine as they dozed beside their
voiceless brothers, the little turtles. A kingfisher sat motionless on a fishing-stake, apparently regardless of the
swarm of minnows poised beneath him. A big fish, finding himself floating too near the glassy surface, broke it
with a languid flap of his tail as he sought cooler depths,
the slow wavelets just stirring the young water weeds and
lapsing softly on the shores. High overhead a hen hawk

swung in a wide circle as slowly as swept the lazy drift of
silver clouds above him, and almost at rest upon the wing.
The voices of the birds were hushed ; the merry bobolinks
jangled only occasional snatches of song in the meadows,
where loitering strawberry-pickers lounged in the long
shadows of trees, and a wood pewee in the great elm over
the mill was the only one of the thousand singers that sang
continuously, and his sweet, pensive notes seemed like the
fragrance of flowers, more exhaled than sung. The per-
vading spirit of indolence had fallen upon mankind as
well. The miller lounged in the doorway of his mill with
no sign of his vocation but the dust on his garments, while
no sound was in the misty precincts but the drowsy murmur of the waste water dribbling from the flume ; and from
the wide portals of the sawmill only at rare intervals was
heard the creak of the sawgate, the swish of the saw eating
its way through the log, and the clink of the ratchet in the
rag wheel ; and the sawyer only moved from his jerky seat
on the log when it had brought him into dangerous prox-
imity to the saw, reluctantly, and wishing the log was
longer. Then he arose and leaned lazily against the lever
that sent the carriage on its backward course to its starting
place, and after due deliberation set the log up an inch
sidewise, dogged it in place with slow strokes, and when
he could think of no pretext for longer delaying, hoisted
the gate and set the squeak and swish and clink a going
again and fresh terebinthine and balsamic odors afloat on
the air. Women lolled in doorways with elbows on knees
looking intently at nothing, while children, too young to
be at school, were taking their afternoon nap. But the
curiosity of these good people was awakened and unwont-
edly stirred by the arrival of Sam's party, for a camping

outfit was an unusual sight in those days, when camping
was not in fashion with those who were considered quite
respectable. Only white vagabonds and bands of Canadian Indians who had not much better shelter at home
were supposed to live in shanties and tents for the pleasure
of it, even in the pleasantest weather. Perhaps the memory of the hardships of the pioneers, some of the younger
of whom were yet living, was not enough obliterated for
such primitive ways of life to seem at all desirable to their
descendants. At any rate, the folks about the falls wondered
to see such decent-looking men as these coming of their
own free will to take boat here to go to the lake for some
days of vagabondizing. This they signified their intention
of doing when the miller and the sawyer with moderate
haste drew near, with some others who suddenly emerged
from neighboring houses, rubbing the traces of recent
slumber from their eyes.

Sam inquired for the owner of a roomy boat to take
their effects to the mouth of the creek, and the miller looking at the sawyer, said, " Wal, there's ol' Uncle Tyler hes
got a tollable big scaow boat, an' hain't nothin' much t'
du. Mebby he'd take ye daown t' the san'bar. S'pose he
would, Sargent ?"

" Yaas, I sh' think like 'nough he would."

" Yes, he'll du it," the miller said very confidently now.
" Goin' fishin' ? Thought most likely ye was. Uncle
Tyler lives up yunder in that leetle haouse wi' the linter
on the west side on 't—that leetle heater piece is his'n, an'
there he is a-pokin' raound in his garding. There, he's
comin' daown t' see what's a goin' on—thought he would
—hain't nothin' else t' du. Most on us putty busy this
time o' year ; ha' no time tu be foolin' raound day-times."

"So I see," Sam said. "C'n we git someb'dy t' keep aour hosses a week er so?"

"Wal, Sargent's got a parstur handy," the miller replied, questioning the sawyer with his eyes.

"Jump?" Sargent asked.

"No, sir," Sam answered; "do' wantu, an' can't," which statement the subdued mien of the ancient and clumsy animals seemed to verify. So a bargain was made with the sawyer for their keep, and Uncle Tyler being now present, bestowing a slow, senile, lop-jawed stare impartially on each of the newcomers, negotiations were entered into with him. "They wantu hire yer boat tu take 'em daown tu the san'bar," the miller shouted with great distinctness, making it apparent that Uncle Tyler was hard of hearing. "Your boat! san'bar!" yet louder and pointing to the scow drawn up among the willows, and then down the creek.

"Ooo-h!" said Uncle Tyler, slowly looking them over again. "Where'd ye say ye come from?"

"Hain't said," Sam answered.

"Stanstead? Why, that's way up beyund Canerdy line! Hoss thieves up there!" Uncle Tyler said severely, turning the focus of his dull stare on to the horses.

"We—live—up—tu—Danvis," Sam proclaimed with slow and loud distinctness.

"Ooo-h! Danby?" said Uncle Tyler, "'way saouth o' here—Quaker taown. Haow come ye t' come 'way up here? Hain't Quakers, be ye?"

"Dan-*vis*," Sam roared.

"Oh, ooo-h, yis! Danvis, yis, yis, over here," and the old man pointed vaguely eastward. Sam nodded assent. "Yis, yis, Danvis," Uncle Tyler repeated; "Danvis;

got relations up there, er my ol' woman has ; 'maounts tu 'baout the same thing, gen'ally—name o' White—White by name but not by natur'—dark-complected folks ; know 'em ?"

Yes, Sam knew a family answering to that name and description.

" Yis, I guess I c'n take ye daown termorrer mornin', arter breakfus. Sh'll want a little suthin' fur't ; orter be workin' in my gardin—weeds jest a-bilin' up aouten the airth naow. S'pose yer willin' tu pay reson'ble ? Hev ye got any terbarker 'at's fit tu smoke ? I meant tu ha' sent up t' the store an' got me some, but I forgot it."

While the price of Uncle Tyler's prospective services was being fixed upon, and he was filling his pipe from Sam's blue paper of " long cut," Antoine returned from an inspection of the craft in the harbor, rejoicing as if he had met an old friend. " Say, Sam !" he cried, " you ant b'lieved it. Ah'll fan' dat sam' raf' we was helped it dem feller buil' las' spring ! Yas, sah ; bah gosh ! He'll got dat lett' on en' of log of it, feesh hook, an' hoxin's yoke !"

" J. B," Sam suggested.

" Yas ! yas ! Wal, seh, Sam, 'f Ah'll can' haire aout some boats, Ah'll goin' borried dat raf's an' pole heem daown de crik, hein ?"

" I guess, Antwine, 'at necessiation won't impel us tu sech ways o' navigation," said Solon Briggs, glad of an opportunity to let these proud lowlanders know that although he lived among the mountains, he was not to be outdone in the elegant use of their common language by any one in the lake region, " for Sammywell is a-negotiratin' with this elderly an-cient gentleman tu export us an' aour defects in a occupacious boat o' his'n."

When he had done Joseph Hill heaved a sigh of relief, and said aside to Sam, " Wal, I swan ! I begin tu be afeared 'at Solon 'ould git stuck, an' never git red of all that 'thout chokin' ! I'll be gol dum'd 'f his thrut hain't the size of a saw lawg ; not quite the size o' some o' these mebby," slowly measuring with his eye some of the largest logs piled in the mill yard, " but the size of a middlin'-sized, sorter sizerble saw lawg."

Arrangements were made with Uncle Tyler to take the most cumbersome of their baggage to the lake in his scow next morning, and accommodations for the night were found for the party at the miller's house. The remainder of the day was passed by them in comfortable lounging about the neighborhood of the mills, watching the boys catching rock bass at the foot of the rapids, themselves tak-ing a hand occasionally in the sport of capturing these vig-orous biters, and in informing themselves concerning a desirable camping ground, and the best places for fishing.

" You c'n fish anywheres 't the's water 'n' ketch suthin' 'nuther," said the miller, " but 'f you want a ri' daown good campin' place, arter you git beyund the Slab Hole, you turn int' the left, on the wes' side o' the crik, 'posite the san'bar, where the's a lot o' willers, an' you'll find the neatest place 't you ever see ! Ye needn't build ye no shanty, for the's rocks a-hangin' over 'at'll shelter ye, an' the's lots o' cedar browse tu make yer beds on, an' wood ! the Slab Hole's full on't—lawgs, an' slabs, an' sticks o' fo' foot wood, 'n' everything, f'm kin'lin' tu back lawgs. An' there ye be, right t' the lake, 'n' right t' the crick, an' Lewis Crik an' the scinin' graound not mor'n a quart' of a mild off !"

Uncle Tyler's appointed hour of departure, " arter

breakfus," came in good time, and the party was afloat
not long after sunrise. Sam and Antoine led the flotilla
in the birch and dugout, which had been transported from
Danvis on their wagon, and Uncle Tyler, Solon, and
Joseph were captain and crew of the scow. The old man
steered with a paddle, and struggled with his latest borrowed pipeful of damp plug tobacco, while each of the
others manned an oar and wrestled desperately with it, for
rowing was a new and painful experience for them. Now
they "caught crabs," and now they dug the bottom with
the oar blades, bringing up on them specimens of aquatic
plants that would have rejoiced the heart of a botanist ;
and they bumped their noses and their knees with the
handles, while the splashing of the water, the creaking and
thumping of the clumsy oars, and the grunting and puffing
of the rowers, intermingled with the directions of the
helmsman, delivered in the loud, unmodulated tone that
deaf persons are apt to use, made a confusion of sounds
most wonderful to hear. If the ancient mariner laid aside
his paddle for a moment to give his pipe its often-needed
lighting, Solon's oar was sure to be midway in or at the
beginning of a stroke, while Joseph's blade was pointing
at some quarter of the heavens between the zenith and the
horizon, and presently the scow was headed for the shore,
her bottom brushing over the young rushes and sedges of
the marsh. " For massy's sake ! didn't nary one on ye
never have a holt of a noar afore ?" he would shout, as with
lateral sweeps of his paddle he got the boat upon her course
again. " Don't dip so deep ! Keep the blades o' yer oars
jest onderneath the water—but ye got tu stick 'em in the
water ! ye can't row in the air !" as one of them skinned
the surface with his blade. " Oh, for massy's sake ! can't

ye hear nothin', er can't ye onderstan' nothin' ?'' The old
man's patience was almost exhausted, when his pipe, turning over in the unstable grip of his gums, emptied its now
well-fired contents upon his knee, unnoticed till it burned
through his trousers to his leg. "O massy! I thought I
smelt suthin' a-burnin' !" he cried, slapping wildly at the
smouldering fire. His pipe dropped and was shivered at his
feet, and just then Joseph missed a stroke into which he had
put much strength and good intention, and went sprawling
heels up in the bottom of the scow, while his oar blade
came down with a thud on Uncle Tyler's pate.

"Be ye tryin' ter kill me, er what be ye tryin' t' du ?
Breakin' my pipe, an' a-knockin' on me in the head, an'
a-burnin' on me up alive ! Gimme a holt o' them oars,
an' git aout o' that mighty quick !" crawling over the baggage toward them. "Lay daown—er git aout an' go
afoot ! I don't keer a dum mite which ! Ketch me
a-goin' a-bwutin' agin along o' a passel o' idjits 'at do'
know a noar f'm a pudd'n' stick ! Ye can't row a bwut
no more'n a goose c'n gobble !"

One bestowed himself in the bow, the other in the stern,
while the old man, as speechless with wrath as they were
with mortification, sent the boat forward with long, even
strokes that made the water surge under her broad bow.
The young lily pads danced madly on the waves of her
wake, and the little whirlpools that spun away from the oars
twisted into tangles the slender new leaves of wild rice and
engulfed fleets of water beetles.

The commotion on board the larger craft had caused
Sam and Antoine to cease paddling and wait to ascertain
the cause.

"What hail dat hol' can' hear not'ing man ?" Antoine

asked as they looked back. " He'll don't goin' t'row
Solem an' Zhozeff board over, ant it? Oh, bah gosh!
Ah'll bet you head Ah'll know what was de matter be!
Dey'll can't roar!"

" Wal, by the gret horn spoon! I sh'd think by the
saound 'at he c'ld roar 'nough for the hull three on
'em!" said Sam, as the steady rumble of Uncle Tyler's
angry bawling came over the water.

" Oh, Ah'll ant meant roar, a nowse! Ah'll meant
r-r-roar dat hol' boats wid r roar! Ant you'll on'stan',
hein? Ah'll ant never see langwizhe lak Angleesh,
me!"

" Wal, Antwine, I never did nuther—not as you speak
it." The scow seemed to be making fair progress now,
and they went on their way.

Solon, after long and intent study of the Tyler method
of handling the oars, at last said : " I du raly b'lieve,
Jozeff, 'at I hev got a clear an' intercate idee of the modus
upperdandy, as they say in Latin, an' 'at I c'ld naow,
arter a leetle practyse, expel this boat putty nigh as rapid
as what he does."

" Wal, it looks tollable easy, but I hain't faound it so—
that is, not so turrible easy," said Joseph.

" Naow, she's a goin'!" proclaimed Uncle Tyler, unconscious of their conversation, and sending a grim but
somewhat mollified glance fore and aft.

" She?" queried Solon, after scanning each distant
shore, " who's she? I don't discover no one of the
femaline sect nowheres."

" What she is a-goin'?" Joseph shouted at Uncle
Tyler.

" Hey? Oh, massy sakes alive! I never see such

dum'd ign'nt creeters. Why, this bwut is ' she.' It hain't
he, is it ?'' and the old man was obliged to quit rowing a
moment to unburden himself of wheezy laughter.

" That is a most cur'osity idee,'' Solon said, after some
consideration of the subject, '' a-speakin' of a onhumern,
onanimit boat as if it belonged tu any sect. I don't see
nothin' phillysoffycable in it ?''

" Wal,'' Joseph said, " I do' know. Mebby it's 'cause
if they take a notiern tu go, they're a goin', an' if they
don't, they hain't, erless a feller knows haow tu make
'em 'thaout lettin' on 'em think they're bein' made, which
it is a knack 'at few on us hes—er mebby it's 'cause they
take a feller jest where they're a minter—I do' know.''

" It proberbly deriginated someway aout o' their con-
trairiness. Haowevertheless, it 'pears tu me it 'ould be
more properer tu call 'em ' he,' bein' 'at they hev starns,
which men is spoke of frequent as the ' starn sect.' ''

" An' then there's the baows, tu. Women allus
curcheys.''

" That's the way to row a bwut ?'' Uncle Tyler said,
only knowing by the motion of their lips that they were
speaking, and imagining that they were expressing admiration of his skill.

" Goin' ahead looks easy 'nough,'' Joseph said, pondering, " but s'posin' a feller wanted ter hev him—no,
' she ' is what he calls the dum'd ol' thing—hev her go
t'other way, what's goin' ter be did then ? What d' yer
du when ye wanter back her ?'' loudly addressing the
ancient mariner.

" Hey ?'' he shouted, suddenly alert and resting on his
oars. " Want terbacker ? Course I du, but ye broke my
pipe, an' I can't smoke 'thaout you lem me have yourn,

an' I hain't got no terbacker ; meant tu sent up tu the store an' got me some yist'd'y, but I forgot it.''

Joseph began whittling a plug of tobacco, and filling his own pipe, handed it with flint and steel and a bit of punk to the old man, who, dropping his oars, at once set himself to lighting it. '' Ol' as he is, he hain't forgot haow tu suck,'' Joseph remarked in an ordinary tone as he watched him pulling at the pipe with resounding smacks. '' Don't ye see the sparks a-comin' aouten his ears ? I do' know as I see the sparks, ezackly, but I'm sartin I du the smoke.''

'' That's the way tu row a bwut !'' Uncle Tyler repeated when, having got his pipe in satisfactory blast, he resumed the oars and sent the scow snoring on its way. The sound of its progress was not unlike the heavy breathing of a sound sleeper, the long, grating squeak of the swivels simulating the indrawing of the breath, the gurgling swish of the water during the stroke, its exhalation. '' It's jest as ea-sy !''

'' I know it is,'' said Joseph, '' leastways, I think it is, tu look at it. I c'ld set an' look at ye duin' on't, an' never git the least mite tired ; an' I do' know but what I c'ld larn, jest a-settin' an' a-watchin' on ye. Anyways, I'm willin' tu try larnin' that way a spell. Golly blue !'' inspecting his palms, '' the's blisters on my han's bigger'n ac'rns, an' a dum sight tenderer ! That ol' dried-up crit- ter hain't juice 'nough in his hull carkiss tu make one sech blister. Mebby the' is in his hull carkiss, but the' hain't in his han's, I don't b'lieve. An' his back hes got jest the right hump for the business. Tell ye what, Solon, I b'lieve ol' folks is the fellers 'at is ezackly cal'lated for 't. If I was tu set here an' watch him till I git tu be as ol' as he is I shouldn't wonder 'f I could oar one o' these she

boats, but I do' know, it don't scasely seem, 's I feel
naow, as 'ough I keered 'baout tryin' much afore."

When the two canoes came to where the tributary East
Slang somewhat widened the slow current of Little Otter,
Sam pointed with his paddle to the low cape, now green
with water maples in full leaf, even now standing ankle-
deep in the still brown water, whose weedy surface dully
reflected their greenness and graceful ramage and the
flash of the starlings' wings that flitted among them.
"Up there, Antwine, is where we camped last spring, an'
hed fun. I wonder haow it looks naow 'at summer's
come, if the shanty 's standin', an' whether that 'ere little
squirrel sets there a-chitterreein' on that hemlock yit?
Dum'd 'f I don't gwup an' see haow it looks some day ;
lunsomer 'an it did then, I guess."

"Yas, sah ! Oh, 'f Ah'll ant have it good tam dere,
me ! An' dat de place you'll see dat crookit tree where
Ah'll leek dat mans. Ah'll bet you head you can fan' de
brark scrape off de tree yet, an' de ha'rs scratter 'raoun' —
prob'ly de blood all wash away 'fore naow."

"Most likely," Sam said.

The scow having now drawn near, they passed on together toward the lake. "I was a-cal'latin'," Uncle Tyler
said, addressing the fleet in general, but particularly his
crew, "for ter troll some comin' 'long, but you be so
okkerd ! I got a rig there an' posserbly you might hang
on to 't so 's t' snag a pickril," and reaching before him he
took up a short pole with many crooks in it for its length
whereon was wound a stout line which had a hook baited
with a piece of pork rind and a strip of red flannel.
While he kept the boat slowly moving he unwound thirty
feet or so of the line, and handing the pole to Joseph went

on at a leisurely stroke. "The' hain't no better trollin' graound in the hull crik 'an the' is atwixt the tew Slangs," he said, and as they neared the mouth of the South Slang Joseph returned jerk for jerk on the trailing line with a grunt thrown in. "What be I a-goin' t' du naow?" he asked in dire perplexity, though he set his teeth and held to the bending pole with a will; "I can't get him 'thin twenty foot on us wi' this dum'd little short pole."

"Gim me a holt on 't!" said Uncle Tyler, dropping his oars and rising to the occasion. Laying hold of the pole he drew the tip far behind him, and grasping the line hauled it in hand over hand with deliberate celerity, till the wide-mouthed pickerel came gaping alongside and was lifted on board by the hook, forgetting to resent his injuries till he dropped on the bottom of the scow, which he then belabored with strokes of his tail, while he snapped his ugly jaws. He was a slab-sided fellow, whose six pounds of weight were spanned by two feet and a half of length, but he was admired as a beautiful monster by Solon and Joseph, and almost as much by Sam and Antoine, who came alongside to look at him.

"Massy sake!" cried Uncle Tyler in wondering pity, "it does beat all natur' haow you folks does vally these 'ere goo'-for-nothin' pickril! I'd a gre' deal druther have a neel. Wait till ye git aholt of a fo' fi' paound pike, an' then you have a fish 'at's wuth a-havin'! Pickril!"

The trolling line was let out again as they went forward, and to keep it clear of the weeds Joseph now ventured to direct their course with commands, or rather friendly advice, which would have puzzled a strictly nautical man to obey or follow. "'F I was you I'd gee a lee-tle mite. Naow haw more 'n ye gee. Now oar the hardest wi' yer

north oar.   Guess ye'd better oar most wi' the saouth one
naow—guess it's the saouth one—do' know but what it's
the west one—lem me see," taking a look at the sun and
the eastern hills—" yes, oar the west one."

" Oh, go 'long wi' your tarnal geein' an' hawin', an'
your northin' an' saouthin' !" Uncle Tyler droned loudly.
His father had migrated to Vermont from the sea-coast, and
something of his salty flavor had been imparted to his son.
" This 'ere hain't a nox cart, it's a bwut, an' this side on
her is starb'd and that's larb'd er port.   When you're
a-wantin' on me tu pull this oar, holler ' starb'd ! ' an'
when you're a-wantin' on me tu pull t'other, holler
' port ! '   But I guess you'd better shet yer head alto-
gether.   Anyways, quit yer dum'd geein' and hawin', I
hain't a yoke o' oxen !"

Now came a heavy, dead pull on the line, and Joseph,
following the recent example of Uncle Tyler, laid the tip
of the pole forward, and snatching wildly at the line,
caught it at last and hauled it in with such haste and excitement that it was snarled in an almost inextricable
tangle about his feet and legs when the hook came alongside with a great burden of lily stems, and pads, and water
weed.   His look of disappointment when he saw his
worthless catch was not dispelled when he contemplated
the tangled confusion of the line, and he was not comforted by Uncle Tyler's assurance, " You've got a job 'at
'll last ye till ye git t' the lake, a onravlin' that 'ere line !
If you'd a-had it aout a-passin' the Saouth Slang, you'd a
got one !   The's allus a good one a-layin' there."

Now they were on the last reach of the channel, bending here in a long curve through the " wide ma'sh," as
Uncle Tyler informed them this portion of the stream was

called. Through the willowy gateway of the creek's mouth they could see the lake, the "Bay of the Vessels," with Garden Island, green and white with leaves and blossoms, set like a nosegay on its shining bosom, clasped in the rocky arm of Thompson's Point. They soon passed the "Slab Hole," a great drift of flood wood lying along the western shore, and presently landed among the willows at the place the miller had told them of. They found the shelter of rocks under the bluff, but decided to pitch their tent, for the overhanging ledge looked like a pokerish roof to sleep under.

The pickerel was dressed and fried for dinner, and even Uncle Tyler, despite his unfavorable opinion of pickerel, made way with a generous portion of it. The old man was paid for his services, and made preparations for his homeward voyage. He pushed his craft afloat and embarked, but presently came ashore again, and they returned to the landing to see what he had forgotten.

"I wish 't some on ye 'ld gim me a pipeful er tew o' terbacker. I'm a-goin' tu send right up t' the store an' git me some jest as soon as I git hum. I meant tu yiste'd'y, but I forgot it." For some minutes after he left them they could hear the smacking of his lips as he pulled at Joseph's pipe, and for half an hour longer the squeak, and clank, and surge of his laborious progress, while they busied themselves with the arrangement of the camp.

They had not finished pitching the tent before they were assailed by swarms of hungry mosquitoes, the constant warfare with which left them little time for peaceable labor, and soon made it apparent that there was no comfort nor rest for them in this place. Sam and Antoine made their way to the top of the rocky bluff, and finding their perse-

cutors much less numerous, the tent and camp equipments
were carried thither, and their temporary home established
among the cedars.   Northerly winds from the lake and
southerly winds from the cleared fields landward swept
their winged enemies away and filled the air with balsamic
fragrance that reminded them of Danvis woods, and
through the green masses of cedar boughs and meshes of
trunks and branches they caught glimpses of the blue lake
crinkled with gold and silver waves.   The thin soil and
the rocks were spread with a soft carpet and cushions of
fallen cedar leaves and moss set in various patterns of russet
and green, and about the bases of the rocks were springing
the young shoots of mountain fringe, ready to overrun
them with a graceful invasion of vine and flower.

   " Ah'll tol' you, boy !" cried Antoine, looking with
admiration on the carpeting of the tent floor, just finished
with his last armful of cedar twigs, " 'f he ant mek you
felt sleepy for jes' look at dat beds !   Oh, 'f we ant
took comfor' here !   An' don't dat neat fireplaces you'll
buil' dar?" inspecting the result of the others' labors
—a broad fireplace built of flat ledge stones.   " Jes' as
handle as stofe was ; yas, seh, more handle, 'cause you'll
don't got for hopen no door for put hwood, an' you'll
don't got for took off no gribble for brile you pot of
it !   Dat mek it all de hwomans in Danvit cry 'f he'll
see it !   Naow 'f we can honly jes' git some bullpawt,
dey ant notin more in dis worl' we'll as' for it !   But
Ah'll 'fred, me, we'll ant ketch it much dat kan', 'cause
de she one he'll settin' on hees aigg naow, Ah b'lieve, an'
de he one, he'll watch of it.   But Ah ll goin' try it.   Ant
you go 'long to me, some of it ?"

   Solon expressed a desire to test his " fishcatorial skill,"

and the two went down the bluff, and launching the dugout, paddled out to a convenient stake set in the further
edge of the channel. More than once as the narrow craft
lurched along its course and Solon grasped the gunwales,
he wished the broad and stable bottom of Uncle Tyler's
scow was beneath him, but he felt safer when the canoe
was made fast to the stake and the green weeds of the
marsh were within reach, though under them were six feet
of water and unfathomable mud.

" I tell ye what, Antwine," he said, drawing the first
full breath since leaving shore, " if I'm a-goin' tu persecute
fishin', I'm a goin' tu du it in suthin' diff'ent f'm these
'ere lawg and birch bark c'ntraptions. They hain't got
no stubility. I'm a goin' tu hev me a boat suthin' arter
the partern o' the one 'at that ol' gentleman fetched me
an' Jozeff an' t'other things daown here in, infactotum a
femaline or she boat, 'at is capacious o' kerryin' suthin'
right end up withaout oncessant discumbobberation."

" Well, seh ! Solem, 'f you can fan' dat kan' o' boats
Ah'll willin' you'll go in it ! Ah'll 'fred all a tam every
minutes you'll speel bose of it. Seet steel ! Dis can noe
don't fraid 'f you'll ant jomp an' weegly every tam he'll
top over leetly mites !" And Antoine swung his full
baited hook abroad and dropped it gently into the water.
Solon's splashing cast, made with an awkward motion, set
the canoe to rocking and his companion to swearing, and
reawakened his own fears. When quiet was restored he
got a bite, and after several ineffectual twitches hooked
and pulled up a broad sunfish, and as he swung it back
and forth, making futile snatches at it as it quivered past
and circled about him, always just out of reach, the danger
of a capsize became imminent, till the fish, by a twist, as

lucky for them as for it, unhooked itself and dropped into the edge of the weeds.

Antoine rejoiced aloud, while Solon gazed with a rueful countenance upon the spot where the fish had disappeared. " Ah'll tol' you, Solem, you'll ant goin' feesh some more 'less Ah'll go 'shore. Ah'll ant want no fun for be top over here, me !" Solon agreed to content himself with being only a looker-on, while Antoine fished. But the Canadian's skill and patience, faithfully exercised an hour longer, were rewarded by nothing better than a dozen perch and sunfish, which though he cursed, he saved for supper. " Yas, seh," as he drew out his hook and cleaned the fragments of worms off it, tossing them begrudgingly far away, and widely scattered, " Ah'll tol' you so de she bullpawt was all settin', an' he ant goin' stop for heat notin's. Wal, le's we'll go." And after winding up his line, he untied the canoe and paddled into the black shadows that had now fallen along the western shore. His labors faintly illumined by the last glimmers of departing daylight straggling through the willows, he scaled and cleaned the fish while Solon squatted near, assisting little but in the free offering of sage advice. Then they climbed the bluff, bearing the slender catch to camp, where, re-enforced by generous slices of pork, it furnished a bountiful supper. Smoking and chat filled the short hour between supper and early bedtime, when they fell into the sound sleep which blesses honest campers.

II.

JOSEPH HILL GOES FISHING.

Joseph Hill was the first to awake next morning, and deliberate in all things, he awoke slowly. While yet in the drowsy borders of dreamland he imagined himself at home, and began as usual to " tell M'ri" something of yesterday's performances or to-day's plans. Then the odor of the cedar bed beneath him and a glimpse of the canvas roof slanting close above him brought a dim realization of his unaccustomed surroundings, more forcibly impressed upon him when he crept forth through the tent flaps and saw between the tree trunks the channel of Little Otter shining through the film of mist that overspread it like a broad stripe of silver veiled with gauze, and heard a kingfisher clattering along it, and from far out on the lake the crazy laughter of a loon. Then he got out a new pipe, and filling it, began, since Uncle Tyler had taken his well-seasoned cutty, the old smoker's unpleasant task of mellowing the unripe clay of this.

The fiz of the damp tobacco or a mute demand of the inner Joseph reminded him of breakfast, and then arose the question of what that repast should be composed? Unlimited fish at all meals had been the alluring promise of this expedition, and now there was not one fish in camp to furnish even lenten fare. A noble ambition seized him to provide fish for breakfast, and with un-

wonted promptness he took a pole and bait and stole
away to the creek where above the Slab Hole the shore
and a patch of weedless water met.   He looped a great
tangle of worms on to the hook and cast it out with a
splash that troubled the quiet surface, but did not seem
to have frightened the fish beneath it, for presently there
came a slow, dogged pull upon the line, which then began to cut the water with a strong, deliberate sweep that
needed half of Joe's strength to check.   There was a short
but lusty struggle, and then the angler thought he must
be towing ashore all the bottom of the creek, but in the raft
of old and young water weeds that his steadfast pull
stranded he discovered the form of a great fish, which he
pounced upon and bore well back into the grassy field
before he loosened his hold upon it.   Then as it threshed
the sward with sullen strokes he gloated over it.   Dull in
color, small-eyed, and wide-mouthed, rimmed with a long
dorsal fin that met the round tail where it was marked with
a spot of black, its captor was obliged to admit that it was
not handsome, but its size made amends for all lack of
beauty.   Its weight could not be less than eight pounds,
and Joseph, with an angler's generosity, set it at three or
four pounds more.   What a grand breakfast it would
make, all the more to be appreciated for its unexpectedness.

The place offered conveniences for dressing it, a slab to
scale it on and water to wash it, so Joseph at once set
about preparing it for breakfast, having no desire to display it with its now useless adornments of head, scales, and
fins.   Possibly he thought there would be no loss of glory
in guessing at the undressed weight.   So he dressed and
cleaned it and bore it to camp.

He wondered a little, perhaps was rather disappointed

that none of his companions were astir to be astonished at
his luck, but the tent was silent except for the slow, regular
breathing of the sleepers, which he was sure he heard. It
would be an immense triumph to have the fish cooked
when they awoke and surprise them with a breakfast already
set which they had not dreamed of at all. He collected
some dry fallen limbs very silently, and started a fire, listening when it cracked loudest to assure himself that the
sleepers were not disturbed. He got a chunk of pork out
of the kit and cut some slices off it, which he soon had
sizzling in the pan, then took them out when they had
yielded fat enough, and filled their place with great cuts of
fish. The savor hardly answered his expectations, and
when he turned the pieces with a fork, unwashed since the
last meal, they crumbled in a way that reminded him of
frying frozen hasty pudding, but he was magnanimous
enough to blame his culinary skill more than the quality
of the fish. How could so great a fish be otherwise than
good ? Glancing frequently behind him in momentary
expectation of seeing some one overlooking the experi-
mental cookery that he was almost sorry for having undertaken, and even wishing that M'ri was in his place for a
little while, he urged the fire with frequent jabs of the
poker to do its best. " It beats Sam Hill," he whispered
to himself as he paused to wipe the sweat from his brow
and look at the quiet tent again, " 'at the' don't some
on 'em wake up !"

At last the fish was done beyond all doubt, for the fork
went through the thickest piece without resistance, which
he had heard M'ri say was a sure sign. And now he bethought him that he had forgotten the potatoes ! But if
there was fish, what did it matter if there were no potatoes,

nor bread, nor anything else? But there was bread enough, and so he pulled aside the tent flap and loudly announced breakfast. He was greatly surprised that no response came from it ; more so when, with a vague fear that some strange calamity had befallen his companions, he peered into the dim interior and found it empty. Joseph was not a superstitious man, but for a moment he wondered if some judgment of heaven had come upon them for such sacrilegious use of Brother Foot's old camp-meeting tent, sanctified as it must be by annual service in the religious picnics of the past twenty years. When he backed out on his hands and knees he noticed, as he had not before, that all the fish poles but his own were gone, and knew that his friends were out on the same errand that he had been. His loud shouts, or perhaps the voiceless calls of hunger, soon brought them back, when their admiration of his whole performance gave him all the reward he desired but the final one of gustatory approval, which he hoped would soon be given. The full frying pan was set out, the bread and pickles were brought forth, and while Joseph apologized for the lacking potatoes, as much missed at a Yankee feast as they would be at a banquet of the descendants of Irish kings, they gathered around the festive board, which was not a board, but a flat rock. As each took his first mouthful he looked about and saw the others furtively regarding him as they slowly and dubiously tasted their own morsels.

"Wal," said Sam, the first to break the silence, "this is turrible nice fish, but somehaow 'r nother it don't seem tu be ezackly the kind o' fish 'at I like."

"What kan' of feesh you'll call dat, Zhozeff?" Antoine demanded, with a grimace of disgust. "You'll fan' heem

dead on de water, or he'll got so hol he'll can' died an'
come for you for keel heem, hein ?''

"Wal, I guess you'd ha' thought he was live 'nough
an' spry 'nough 'f you'd a-hed a holt on him ! He pulled
like a yoke o' tew-ye'r-ol' stags —I d' know but three-
ye'r-ol's —an' flew 'raound like a nigger tu a quiltin'.
But, I swan ! it's a fact he don't taste so good 's I expected f'm his looks, for I called him ri' daown harnsome.
Anyways, he was big enough tu 'a' ben turrible harnsome
'f he'd ha' took a notiern tu run tu beauty. But I 'spect
the fault's in the cookin', er aour appetite t' eat, er
suthin'—the cookin', I guess, for I never could cook
nothin' wuth a snap, anyways. Naow, oncte when M'ri
was gone off vis'tin' her folks tew three days, I ondertook
tu make a johnny cake, I b'lieve it was—mebby 'twas a
short cake ; guess the' couldn't nob'dy tol' which 'twas
meant for—an' when 'twas done, I snum the young uns
turned up all the' noses at it, an' I'll be dum'd if Liern
'ould tech it ! I hove it in t' hawgs, an' they fin'ly wore
it aout rhuttin' on it 'raound. I wish 't I hedn't never
ondertook tu cook the tarnal fish ! I'd ort tu ben satisfied wi' ketchin' on it. But the's 'nough on 't left tu try
agin ; pitch in, Antwine, 'n' see what you c'n du with it.''

"Yes, du, Antwine," Solon urged ; " the's no knowin'
but what wi' your cumilary skill you c'ld make it quite
palatial.''

"Ah b'lieve,'' said Antwine, closely examining some
of the uncooked portion, " Ah'll know what kin' o' feesh
dat was be. Where hees head was ?''

"Why,'' Joseph answered, " on the for'a'd end on
him, jest the same as any fish's—an' his tail was on t'
other end on him, er most on 't was, 's nigh 's I c'n

rec'lect ; do' know but some on't was on his back, though, come tu think.''

" Ant you'll s'pose Ah'll know dat ?   Where you'll lef' hees head of it ?''

" Oh ! naow I begin tu onderstand ye, Antwine.   Over there where I ketched him.''

" Ah guess you'll on'stan' more better as you cook what Ah'll meant.   Where you'll t'row hees tail of it ?''

" Oh, I d' know.   It's layin' raound here some'er's, I guess,'' and he joined Antoine in the search for the missing link.

" Dah !'' cried Antoine, swooping down upon something and then holding aloft the rounded tail with its authentic black seal, " ant Ah'll guess what Ah'll tol' you ? Jes' same what Peltiet shoot dat tam he'll tink he do so big !   O Zhozeff, don't you shame mek us heat dat ?   Ant you'll see where de dev' put hees t'umb w'en he'll peek it an' t'row it 'way cause he so bad he won't have it hese'f ?''

Shamefaced with downfall of pride, Joseph said, as Pelatiah had on a similar occasion, " Wal, I hed fun a-ketchin' on him, an' some, I d' know but I did, a-cookin' on him—more, anyways, 'n we've hed a-eatin' on him.   I'm turrible sorry 't he ain't no better eatin', but I du think,'' he added, loath to relinquish the fish's claims to edible excellence, " 'at the fault is mostly in the cookin'.''

" Wal, seh, Zhozeff,'' cried Antoine, throwing his hands out from his breast and wide apart, as if in final banishment of the subject, " you'll ant wan' be sorry for dat. Ah tol' you, all de mans and all de hwomans was be de bes' cook in de worl', have it all de bur'r an' peppy an' salt was ever mek, can' mek dat bowfins fit for heat de dev'.''

Upon this assurance they attempted no further experiments with the despised fish, but made their breakfast of fried pork and bread.

Then they set about spending the day in accordance with the chief purpose of the expedition. Sam fitted up a trolling rig after the approved pattern of Uncle Tyler's, a bit of his flannel shirt furnishing the red rag unprovided by their kit, and trolled up and down the creek in the bark canoe. Antoine, intent on circumventing the bullpouts that would not bite, made a rude spear of a cedar pole and sharpened nails and prowled along the low shore of the creek in quest of spawning fish, while Solon and Joseph, unwilling to trust themselves in birch and dugout, wandered westward along the safe and stable shore of the bay.

III.

EXPLORATIONS.

Solon and Joseph fished off the rocks when they came to eligible places, and caught a few perch and rock bass, while they continually feasted their eyes with the wonderful sight of the lake, so immense a body of water that, it seemed to them, it gave a fair idea of the immensity of the ocean. This was more impressed upon them when they had strolled to Bluff Point, and looking beyond the promontory of Thompson's Point, saw the blue lake and the blue sky meet far to the northward, with bluer dots of distant islands hung between them, and the white wings of sloops whose hulls were beyond the horizon. And there was the tall white tower of Split Rock Lighthouse, newly built, and now a pillar of cloud by day, a star by night to warn mariners off its perilous rocks, and giving these mountaineers a vivid realization of the dangers besetting those who go down to the sea in ships ; perils and dangers that the waves seemed always whispering of as they hungrily lapped the rocks and chuckled wickedly in the water-worn caverns. By and by they saw a smoke arising from the watery horizon, and after it a speck, which at last grew till it became a steamboat, a leviathan which soon wallowed ponderously past, close to the farther shore, its gay flags and pennons flaunting bravely against the shadowed steeps of Split Rock Mountain, a wake of foam following the roaring paddle wheels. Some time after the majestic apparition had vanished behind the promontories to the west of them, the waves of its wake came in, beating the rocky shore with slow, sullen surges, like baffled foes retreating from the path of a conqueror. Strange woods set afloat far away came tossing ashore to the windrow of wave worn logs, slabs, chips, and bits of painted boats that lined the shores. An old shoe suggested thoughts of drowned men, and white-winged gulls hovered like spirits over the distant waves. It was all very new, and strange, and mysterious. These two anglers bore back to camp but few visible trophies, when in the afternoon they followed thither their shadows, elusive guides that were now distinctly seen leading the way across broad patches of clean forest floor, now dancing in vague outline and confused dismemberment on tree trunks and low branches, and now disappearing in a throng of other shadows or a mass of shade. But the sights they had seen better repaid the time and travel spent than much bigger strings of fish than they carried would have done, and they were content.

Antoine prowled along the shore from the Slab Hole to the South Slang and to the rotting and displaced abutment of the old bridge that had just given up the weary task of spanning so much marsh and so little channel. He transfixed many unlucky bullpouts wriggling slowly in and out of their spawning holes, and transferred them with great satisfaction from his rude spear to his string of elm bark ; battle scarred amazons, torn and stabbed by the horns of other amazons, and lean fathers of the race of bullpouts, as scarred and wounded as their warlike wives. To the Canadian a bullpout was a bullpout, to be taken at any time, by any means, and without regard to its condition. If he ever thought, as doubtless he never did, how the continuation of his most prized fish depended on procreation, doubtless he would not care, for what Canuck ever did? Apparently it is their belief that fish were created solely for them, and belong to them alone, and that they have a right to take in any manner, as they will if they can, the last one to-day, though there should be no fish for any one forever after.

Antoine discovered an old scow adrift in the marsh, water-logged, with red painted square prow, and stern, and gunwales just above the water and overlapped with clots of old weeds. By the help of a long pole, with a hook on the end of it, and by some wading, he succeeded in hauling it ashore, and after bailing it and overturning it found that with a little tinkering it would make a serviceable craft for those unsealegged mariners Solon and Joseph to go fishing in. A rusty fish hook, a bit of line with a hammered leaden sinker clasping its rotten strands, and a soggy pine float of a seine rope found lying in the bottom, the hole and step for a jack-staff, and the charred marks of fallen embers on the bow showed that it was a boat accustomed to fishing in various ways, so saturated with experience that it seemed as if it might impart something of it to those novices.

" Bah gosh !" said Antoine as he sidled around his prize, inspecting it with intense satisfaction and burning incense of rank tobacco at bow, and stern, and sides, " dat was jes' de sloop for Solem an' Zhozeff ! Dey ant worse notin' for go in can-noe, bose of it. Dey draownd evreebodee an' deysef dat go wid 'em in can-noe ! W'en Ah'll gat dis feex up wid some nail, an' rag, an' tuppy-time, dey can' teep it board over, dey can' speel hese'f off 'f he ant seet raght 'tween de middly of it. Dat was pooty good lucky for fan' dat boats, me ! He ant b'long for someboddee, Ah'll bet you head, an' 'f he was, he can' have it !''

So filled with the importance of great achievements he shouldered his spear and string of fish, and trudged proudly toward camp, but before reaching it he made his fish more presentable by stripping off their scarred skins.

As Sam with noiseless strokes paddled his canoe up the great bow of the channel where it winds through the lower end of the " wide ma'sh" and slowly trailed his lure of pork rind and red flannel along the border, marked by purple young lily pads, unwittingly he crossed it, and a grating succession of tugs at his hook reminded him that he had been too contemplative in his recreation and had gone astray into the shallow and weedy false channel that runs straight lakeward from near the mouth of the South Slang. He hauled in his line, cleaned his hook of its burden of weeds, and retraced his way to the true channel, which having regained, he paid more attention to his course, and was presently rewarded by a sturdy tug that had in it the unmistakable viciousness of a pickerel's bite. Yet as he hauled in the line, hand over hand, the resistance was so sullen and sluggish that he was half-inclined to think he was drawing in only another raft of weeds, till he saw the gaping jaws splitting the surface. He soon had a lusty pickerel boated, who beginning his fight too late to avail aught but annoyance of his captor, hammered the cedar lining of the canoe and snapped his jaws wickedly till he was knocked in the head with the paddle.

Moving forward again, Sam soon had a sharp bite that promised something better than the ambitious little perch that had attempted to gorge the alluring combination of pork and wool, and came skittering to hand with all the fight and conceit taken out of him. A little later the trolling bait was nibbled and then seized by a fish that proved to be of nobler metal. Swimming deep, he fought every inch of his unwilling way to the canoe, which when brought to he attempted to run under, but Sam foiled this device, got him alongside, and skilfully lifted and swung him aboard. He was of handsome form, and his small, firm set scales were golden green on his sides and silver white on his belly. In every way he looked gamy and good, a fish created to afford both sport and toothsome food. Sam had never seen his like, but rightly guessed him to be the " pike," whose excellence Uncle Tyler had extolled. So trolling up stream to the then well-defined mouth of the South Slang, now so disguised with mask of weeds that old voyagers may hardly recognize it, and a little way up the channel of this begrudging tributary, Sam got now and then a bite, and lost and saved some fish—another pike-perch and two or three pickerel. He had fish enough now, and paddled or drifted anywhere, hearing and seeing many things of interest to such a simple lover of nature. From far and near in the green expanse of marsh came strange outcries, laughter, yells, and more subdued jargon, converse of unseen waterfowl, strange voices of birds who were strangers to him. He recognized the voices of some old acquaintances when occasionally a bittern boomed, and the blackbirds grated and gurgled out their notes, and when some old choir leader of the bull-frogs sang his short prelude and his brethren struck in and bellowed a grand chorus that made all the wooded shores resound. Once an old wood-duck convoyed her newly-

launched fleet of callow ducklings out of the rushes into
the channel just before him, and then in sudden panic at
sight of his larger craft took wing for cover of the woods,
flying low and followed almost as swiftly by her brood,
simulating flight with ineffectual plumeless wings, but
actually making their way by running like water sprites
over the water after her. Now and then a dusky duck
would splash out of the weeds with a loud alarm of quacking, but her young always kept out of sight if they had yet
ventured so far as the channel's edge from their birthplace.
There were no signs of Sam's last spring's dear enemies,
the muskrats, but the floating crumbs of their midnight
feast, chips of the water-lily roots, and shreds of aquatic
weeds. Their winter huts had all been swept away by the
high water of spring, and only shapeless rafts of rubbish
grounded here and there among the rushes were left to
show how industriously these little water folk had builded
but a few months ago Their homes were now in burrows
in the banks, the occupancy of which was seldom indicated in day-time but by the roiling of the watery entrance
or the sluggish underwater wake of a silent incomer or
outgoer.

Great blue herons sentinelled the shallows, or fanned
their slow way from one to another, and now and then a
bittern made a startled, ungainly flight from the densest
beds of rushes, while kingfishers scolded and clattered along
their jerky course or hung over minnow-haunted shoals,
as if suspended by invisible threads, which presently were
severed, and let them fall into the brown water with a
splashing upburst of spray. The scraggy tangles of button
bushes were noisy and flashing with innumerable nesting
redwings, sunfish and perch were incessantly snapping at

the various insects resting on or hovering about the water plants, and great fish surged through the rushes in pursuit of prey or in swift retreat from the boat. The marshes were busy with the life of their thronging tenants in the happy summers of those days. Alas, that now they are so silent and deserted !

Over the tops of the rushes Sam caught occasional glimpses of Antoine stealing along the shore in his nefarious bullpout prodding, and mildly "dum'd him" in soliloquy "for a wus'n half Injin." In the afternoon he paddled to the mouth of the creek, and after looking at the dancing waves of the sunlit bay clasped in the arms of the green-clad June shores, and watching the majestic sweep of an eagle wheeling above the cliffs, he beached his canoe on the rushy shore of the landing and took his fare of fish to camp, whither his companions soon came. At nightfall they had their bountiful supper of fish, and then as they smoked their pipes about the dying embers each told the story of his day's outing.

IV.

A NIGHT ADVENTURE IN ANTOINE'S PRIZE.

NEXT morning, directly after an early breakfast, Antoine, with Solon and Joseph, set out to repair the scow and get her to the landing.

Meanwhile Sam kept camp for an hour or two, and then went out for a little trip on the bay, cruising across the shallow water of the northeast shore to the mouth of Lewis Creek, which till now he had not seen. Its beauty invited him upstream, and when at the first bend he turned and looked forth upon the lake, through the noble colonnade of ancient water maples and button-woods to the grim, un-shorn steeps of Split Rock Mountain, beyond the broad expanse of water, without a craft in sight upon it or any sign of human presence anywhere, he fancied that he felt something of the sense of complete isolation from all his fellows that the first white voyagers here must have experienced. But in those old days one could not have been so sure of having it safely to himself, as Sam was reminded by the sight of a flint arrow-head on a mud bank among the rushes. For many years after his visit to it this part of Sungahnetuk retained its primitive character, and was a place where one might easily imagine himself set back a couple of centuries to the times when New England was indeed new, when Petowbowk was the warpath of savage and civilized nations, and knew not the peaceful keel of commerce.

An inward yearning aroused Sam from his vague dreams of the past, and he plied his paddle lustily toward camp and dinner. He found his comrades at the landing, to which they had succeeded in floating the scow, its wounds almost healed by application of rags, turpentine, and grease, a medication for leaky boats imparted to Sam by his Indian friends and by him in turn to Antoine.

" Dah, seh, Sam !" said Antoine, standing with arms akimbo far enough away from his prize to take in all her proportions at one glance, "ant dat pooty good leetly sloops for de boy ? Ah'll sail heem wid a pole all de way from where Ah'll fan' of it, an' Solem and Zhozeff ant be some more 'fred of it as if he was in a middly of ten-acre lots. Dey can' feesh in de water naow, an' took some comfortubbly, ant it ?"

Sam admitted the perfect safety of the craft, but expressed some doubts as to the validity of its present ownership. " S'posin' some feller comes along some day, Antwine, an' ketches you or them a-usin' o' his boat, what ye goin' tu du then ?"

" Wal, seh, Ah'll goin' tol' it he can' have dat boats ! When Ah'll fan' dat, he ant no more boats as raf' was, an' Ah'll mek it into good boats aout of it ! Ah'll bail it wid rag an' tuppytime dat was ma hown, me ! Ant you'll see ?"

Sam was not convinced, but conceded that there could be no harm in using the scow till called for, and so it was planned that Solon, Joseph, and Antoine should go a-fishing in it that night at a stake just opposite the landing, whose age and marks of frequent use gave silent evidence of an approved fishing place.

" He was leek leetly mites naow," said Antoine, still

admiring his prize, as he scooped a few basins full of water out of it, "but he be all taght as one One' Lasha boot tam he gin soak up for we'll be ready. Yas, seh! jes' as taght an' gra' deal more comfortubbly as dat boots, Ah bet your head! Den when we gat t'rough of it, Ah do' know 'f he ant jes' well pull heem up in de rush for day-tam, so 'f some hole foolish tink he'll hown it he can' see heem. It was bes' kan' o' boats for use it in de naght, don't it, hein?"

"I notice," Solon remarked, as they took their way to the camp, "'at Antwine calls this boat o' hisn' *he*, which it seems tu me 'at it is a fac-smile of Uncle Tyler's boat, an' is intitled tu the respects due tu the femaline sect, an' my intentions is tu speak of it as she."

After they had eaten supper and in an unhousewifely manner washed their few dishes, Sam, under canvas, fell to dreaming open-eyed of Danvis's dearest inhabitant, and the others, well provided with tackle and worms, went fishing in the old scow.

The creek was almost as silent as the golden and black reflections of sky and wooded shore that rested on its bosom, and for awhile the silence was only broken by the whish of the intent anglers' lines and the splash of the heavy sinkers that sent segments of gleaming circles to break the ranks of brooding shadows along the shore. Then a bullfrog sang a solemn prelude, and all his brethren of the marshes bellowed forth a resounding chorus, which aroused a discordant cackle and gabble of some always invisible inhabitants of the rush-screened flats, whether beasts, birds, or reptiles, or all of these, one could only guess, and when the chorus ended and the clamor of the rude audience ceased, there came a hush as fully per-

vading the evening as had the previous uproar.   Then a
dreaming bird softly rehearsed his day-time love song, a
whippoorwill far away lightly whisked the air with his note,
one nearer lashed it with sharp strokes, the sound whereof
was presently almost overborne by the renewed bellowing
of the frogs, the trill of toads, and the weird outcry of the
unknown tenants of the marshes, only the last most insisted sibilant note of the whippoorwill being heard above
the pulsing waves of clamor.

"He'll leek dat poor leetly Williams pooty hard, ant
it?" Antoine remarked as he answered the regularly intermittent flashes of the lightning bugs signalling from marsh
and tree with the larger glow of his pipe, and then
announced with the sigh of relief that comes after long
waiting, "Dah, seh, sometings was bit. Ah do' know
mos' so well 'f Ah see it, but Ah guess it was heel."
After some moments of patient waiting he gave a twitch,
and the crooked pole writhed into more intense
crookedness, and after a brief struggle a tangled con-
tortion was torn from the water and dropped into the boat.
"Dah he was," cried Antoine, "ant Ah'll tol' you he
was heel? Dah he was." But where was he? Wriggling his way as swiftly as a snake from end to end of the
scow, he was felt here, heard there, almost at the same
moment, tangling the line about the feet of the excited
anglers, while Solon and Joseph madly stamped at him,
and Antoine as madly grasped for him in the gloom.

"Hit it wid you' boots, boy! Keek it wid a steck!"
he cried as he tried to pull toward him by the line the captured but unsubdued prize. "Zhozeff, strak it wid you'
boot!" And Joseph brought down his foot, clad in one of
the last and most solid pieces of Uncle 'Lisha's work, with

a crash that stunned the eel and started one of the bottom
boards of the scow. Their feet were getting wet before
Antoine had unhooked the eel, when he noticed the gurgle
of the incoming water and divined the cause. Hurriedly
unfastening the boat, he shouted frantically to his companions to pole and paddle ashore, while he wildly clawed
the water with his fish-pole. "Oh, Sacre! you'll bus' de
boats. Zhozeff! Pull! Push! Hoorah! All of it us be
draown 'f you ant hurry for git dar fiis' ! Aour hwomans
ant see us 'fore we was some corp 'f you ant be hurry!"
So Antoine urged them, as the old craft, fast becoming water-
logged, reeled and lurched toward the landing, to which
Sam was drawn by the alarming outcry, and reached just
in time to see the scow sink barely its length from shore
and Antoine plunge forward from the bow and wade hip
deep to the landing, while he roared, "Ah'll got de heel,
Sam! Go an' save it de boy!" Solon and Joseph came
floundering to land with no harm but fright and wetting,
and Sam, wading out a little way, hauled the boat to safe
beaching for the night. "Solon," Joseph asked as he
stood with bent body, legs wide apart, and dripping arms
slanting far from his sides, dismally regarding the craft he
had wrecked, "what sect du you call that ere cussed ol'
boat naow?"

"Wal," said Solon, after a little dripping consideration,
"she is sartinly most capericious, and consequentially I
shall continner tu call her a she."

"What on airth be you a-savin' that 'ere dum'd snake
for, Antwine?" Sam demanded, noticing the care the
Canadian took of the eel.

"Dat heels? Ah'll goin' saved hees skin of it, me.
You'll wore dat 'raoun' you backs, you'll ant never had

lame backaches !   An' it was de bes' flail strings you ant
never t'rach all you laftain !''

"Humph !   I've hearn tell o' folks wearin' snakes in
the' hats tu cure headache, an' I'd jest livs as tu hev that
pesky thing waound 'raound my body.   Ugh !''

"O Sam, you was fooler as a geese !'' and then to himself, as he tightened his grip on his prize, "Lak 'nough
you'll gat some dis snakes in you body 'fore you tink,
prob'ly !''

The camp-fire burned with unwonted fervor for a summer's night, while the drenched anglers dried themselves
in its warmth, and Antoine vaunted himself as the hero of
this latest adventure—"Ant Ah'll pooty good captins,
seh, to save all dat heel and de boat and de boy, hein ?''

V.

THE COOK FURTHER DISTINGUISHES HIMSELF.

THE young day was not out of its swaddling clothes of mist when Antoine began repairing the damages that the scow had suffered last night, and the spiteful whacks wherewith he drove home the nails were not more down-right and emphatic than the French and English curses which he bestowed on heavy boots and slippery eels. When the started plank was in place again, he drew the boat into its day-time rushy seclusion and set about getting breakfast.

He had privately made the eel ready for the pan and so divided it that its snake-like form was not easily recogniz-able. It was served up smoking hot, and relished and praised by all the hungry campers.

"You put in your best licks a-cookin' this 'ere fish, Antwine," said Joseph ; "it's turrible sweet an' rich, an' it seems 's 'ough you'd picked aout half the bones, or mebby more 'n half, for I hain't ben bothered scacely any sortin' on 'em aout. I've hearn tell o' some ol' fishin' critter 'at c'ld put his hunks o' fish int' one corner o' his maouth an' let the bones run aout o' t'other corner, an' keep right on fillin' up comf'able ; but I hain't no sech knack, an' git hungrier eatin' ri' deown bony fish—do' know 's I raly git hungrier, but it takes me a turrible spell tu git satified."

"That ol' feller's maouth must ha' ben built arter the fashion o' Sile Blakely's," Sam said. "They uster say the top of his head 'ould ha' ben an islan' if 't hedn't ben for his ears. One June trainin' tu Hamner's, that big John Dart sot nex' tu him tu dinner, an' arter dinner, when they was all settin' raound smokin' an' gabbin', Dart says, says he, ' I thought Sile was crazy the way I seen him eatin'.' ' What made ye think so, John ? ' says Sile. ' Why,' says Dart, ' I thought 't you was pokin' your victuals int' your ear, till I d watched you a spell 'n' see 't you was on'y stickin' 'em int' the corner o' your maouth.' But this is mighty good fish. What ye done tu them little parch tu make 'em so good ?"

"Bah gosh ! you'll s'pose Ah'll goin' tol' evreebodee all haow Ah'll cook ma feesh ? Wal, Ah guess no, me. Prob'ly 'f you an' Zhozeff an' Solem fan' aout all haow Ah'll make it ma cook, you'll ant want me some more 't all ! Den you'll said, ' Antoine, Ah guess dey wan' seen you up to Danvit pooty bad ; goo' bye.' No, seh ! Ah'll ant so fool lak dat for spile em up ma trades !"

"I du b'lieve, Antwine," said Joseph, casting a long-ing glance at the last savory morsel in the pan, "'at if you'd ha' tackled that 'ere bowfin you'd ha' made it cock r'yal, e'namost fit for President Van Buren t' eat."

"It was a dumn'd sight tu good for the ol' Locofoco cuss as you cooked it," said Sam, who was a stanch Whig ; "I wish t' he hadn't nothin' better 'n raw bowfin t' eat !"

"No, seh ! Ah'll can' mek dat kan' feesh fit for be good, Ah'll hown it up dat ! But you'll all gat done for heat 'ant it ? Den Ah'll goin' tol' you somet'ings mek you feel good of it in you stomach," and Antoine regarded his friends with a bland smile, while he ground between his palms a grist of tobacco. "You'll rembler haow you'll bruse me for heat mud turkey, ant it?"

"Antwine!" said Sam in a voice expressive of deep disgust, "you don't purtend to say 'at you've ben a-feedin' us on mud turkle?"

"Ant you'll rembler," said Antoine, waving away the question with the hand unencumbered with tobacco, "ant you'll rembler haow you'll mek me fooled Peltiet wid mash rrrabit, hein?" Sam nodded a reluctant assent.

"Wal, seh, was dat any more wus for me fid you mud turkey?" And Sam shook as slow and reluctant a negative, and added with a sigh of resignation, "Wal, it was good if 'twas mud turkle."

"Yas sah!" said Antoine, getting to the other side of the fireplace as he filled his pipe and scooped a coal from the ashes with the bowl, "it was a grea' deal more wusser as dat. It was snaikes!"

"Antwine!" said Sam, rising to his feet, while Joseph and Solon sat apart growing pale with qualms of their revolting interiors, "if I ever b'lieved a word t' you say, the' 'ld be a Canuck fun'al."

"What for ant Peltiet mek Yankee fumeral? You'll long 'nough Sam for mek it good one, prob'ly two of it. Cut you off, you'll mek fun for two day. Sermon so long you was evreebodee go sleep an' have it good tam, hein? Wal, seh, Sam, you'll ant goin' keel me for teached you snaike was good for heat, ant it? You wait Ah'll tol' you what kan' snaikes he was be. He'll ant striked snaikes, no, seh. He'll ant be addler snaikes, no, seh. He'll ant be common kan' watry snaikes, but he kan' watery snaikes, what you call snaikes. He was be heels! Dah, Sam, you'll ant wan' keel me naow for do you so good. Prob'ly you'll wan' kees me, but Ah'll ant let it, 'cause Ursule be mad 'f Ah'll have somebodee kees me 'cep' him."

" I'd ort tu kill you, Antwine, but the dum'd eel was good, an' I knowed 't you was lyin'--I allus know that whenever you speak, I hain't no more dependence on ye 'n ol' Amos Jones hed on his two boys when they was helpin' on him tend mill. ' Joab,' says he, ' hev ye tolled this grist ? ' ' Yes, sir,' says Joab. ' Jethro,' says he, ' hev ye tolled this grist ? ' ' Yes, sir,' says Jethro. ' You both lie so like thunder I can't b'lieve a word ye say, 'n' t' make sure on 't I'll toll it myself,' an' the ol' critter 'ld scoop aout another thirteenth."

" Lookin' at it phillysophicably," said Solon, " it hain't sartin 'at we hain't beholden tu Antwine for over-comin' our nat'ral antiquity tu eels, which they hes long been a populous food of human mankind. Aour bein' prejudicial tu 'em hain't exclusive proof 'at they hain't good. Hain't that so, Jozeff ?"

" I hain't quite settled on that p'int," said Joseph. " Not knowin' 'at I was eatin' eel, I liked it—wal, I could eat it. Naow 'at I know it is eel, I b'lieve I'll try that last lunsome piece in the pan, an' see 'f my stomach goes agin it," and so saying he began upon the remaining morsel, picking the few and easy bones with critical delib-eration. Then wiping his lips with the backs of alternate hands, and his hands on the legs of his trousers, while he regarded Antoine benignantly, " I do' know czactly whether it's in the eel or the cookin', but it is sartinly good, an' 'f you'll du the ketchin' an' the cookin', I'm willin' t' du what eatin' I can in my feeble way. The ketchin', mind ye, Antwine. Sam Hill ! haow the 'tarnal critter went

scootin' 'mongst aour laigs. Ugh ! I'd liveser handle a
snaike !''

" What dat nowse ?'' Antoine asked, turning an atten-
tive ear toward the creek.

The regular squeak and splash of approaching oars was
presently heard by all, and they went down to the landing
with the hope of getting some news of the upstream world,
or with a curiosity to know who was passing. In those days
the sluggish current of Little Otter often slept day in and
day out among its rushes, undisturbed by oar or paddle of
fisherman, and the infrequent boat that awoke it to a
ripple was worth looking at. Our friends had seen no
craft but their own since Uncle Tyler's departure till
now.

The dumpy figure now approaching in a scow propelled
by slow, laborious strokes, often withheld while the rower
turned his head to mark his course, had a familiar look
to Sam and Antoine, and when abreast of the landing he
became aware of them, and his gaping face was lighted up
with a grin of pleased recognition, they perceived it was
their last spring's adversary of the trapping grounds.

" Hello ! Danvis, who'd ever ha' thought o' seein' you
here ; 'n' here's Peasoup, tu ! Hello, Peasoup ! '

Antoine silently congratulated himself on his discretion
in not having disclosed to Solon and Joseph that this was
the antagonist whom he had vanquished in the great fight,
which he had more than once told them of, for the man
carried himself most unseemly for a conquered foe, and
Antoine was quite ashamed of him.

" Wal, I'm glad t' see ye,'' the new comer said, heading
his boat for the landing and bringing her into it with a
swash, " but I never thought o' seein' you this time o'

year, though I was a-thinkin' on ye when I come past the East Slang."

"Yes, we hed consid'able fun up there last spring," Sam said, "one way 'n' 'nother, a-spearin' an' a—" He was at a loss to name another sport without referring to possibly unpleasant topics.

"A-trappin' an' chawin' gum, an' bathin'," said the new-comer, helping Sam out and shutting the eye nearest him in a long tight wink that comically distorted that side of his face.

"Wal, yes, so we did, come tu think on't ;" and then, as if to think of it long might not be pleasant, and with a desire to change the subject, Sam asked : "Fishin' much nowadays ?"

"Fishin' ! Wal, I guess not much. Don't git no time." Sam remembering that this man's nickname was Time, thought he might find it difficult to induce himself to make so great an effort as to go a-fishing, for he looked the very personification of laziness.

"I hain't fishin'," he exclaimed, lifting his feet ashore while he sat on the broad bow of his boat. "I kinder thought I'd go daown t' the san'bar an' git me some sand tu make some mortar. Ben goin' t' patch my suller wall these ten year, but can't never git no time, an' I kinder thought I'd look along some for my scaow boat 'at went off in the high water last spring. Somebody er 'nother tol' a-seein' it daown this way in the ma'sh, but I p'sume likely some cuss has stole it 'fore naow. I ain't seen nothin' on 't ? Painted red oncte, an' fixed for a jack, an' burned some here for'ad where sparks fell on't. Not quite so big 's this one 't I borried, but a good sight better. I ain't seen no sech boat ?" His slow, inquiring look rested last and longest on Antoine, whose mind was now greatly perplexed, for he doubted not that the boat he had found was the one now desired and sought for by this man, and it lay within twenty feet of them, where if its owner arose to his feet he must see it, so evidently placed with intention of concealment that they would all be disgraced. Making the best of disagreeable necessity, he hastened to speak before one of his friends could :

"Yas seh!" he cried, grinning a well-simulated expression of pleased surprise, "Ah'll b'lieved Ah'll fan' dat boat, pruppus for you, seh! an' Ah'll rippair it all up so he was mos' better as he was new. 'F Ah'll had some paint Ah was paint it for you, but he was look pooty good, Ah tol' you. Jes' looked here!" leading the way to it and beating aside the rushes with both hands. "Ant dat heem ?"

"Her, Antwine," cried Solon, correcting him—"her is the properest sect to speak of a boat in."

"Oh, go to dev'! Dis boats ant dat man's waf, ant it? He'll gat no diffence what you'll call it heems or she, prob'ly."

"Wal, I'll be blest if that hain't my ol' scaow," said Father Time, after critically examining the craft and then sitting down on its cinder-scarred bow, with a satisfied and restful air, "I'm almighty obleeged tu ye, Mr. Peasoup, for takin' so much trouble to save it for me an' fix it up, tew."

"Bah gosh! Ah was glad of it, seh, an' de honly ting Ah'll was sorry for Zhozeff an' Solem. Dey can' bose of it sit up on ma can-noe! Dey can' git on Sam 't all! Ah do' know haow dey'll goin' to fishin's naow, 'less Ah'll buil' raf' for it."

" I p'sume likely you was cal'latin' tu fetch my scaow up tu me jest as soon's you faound aout who owned it, wa'n't ye ?" Time asked, casting a comical leer on Antoine.

" Dat was so !" Antoine said, emphasizing each word with a gesture. " Ah'll ask it prob'ly t'ree, prob'ly four mans 'f he'll b'long to it. Ant it t'ree, four, Sam ?" winking at his friend and beginning to count imaginary persons on his fingers. " Le' me see—yas, Ah b'lieve four, hein ?"

" You might 'f you happened tu see 'em," Sam said aloud, adding in an undertone to himself, " Dum'd 'f a Canuck hedn't druther lie 'n t' tell the truth, any time, an' 'f he c'ld make the hull toot on us lie for 'im he'd be happy."

" Hain't these fellers water faowl 'nough tu keep right side up in your cannews, Danvis ?" Time asked, indicating Joseph and Solon by a sidewise jerk of his head.

" Wal, they hain't much uster boatin' in anything but stun boats an' lumber waggins," Sam admitted.

" Wal, 'f 't 'll be any 'commodation tu ye, I'll leave that 'ere scaow for ye an' go hum in mine. It rows easier 'n that, an' I guess Gage won't want his'n for a spell. It won't tip over no easier 'n it rows, an' it'll du tol'able well for still-fishin'."

" Me an' Solon's a thaousan' times 'bleeged tu ye," said Joseph ; " we don't want to du no tippin' over ner not much oarin', an' it'll du us fustrate ; 'f the bottom hain't made tu come aout when you ketch eels, I'd a leetle druther hev' it 'n yourn. " And in reply to Time's inquiring look he related the mishap of last evening to the great amusement of that worthy. When he had had his long, lazy laugh out he arose, and looking awhile at the sandy point not far below said, with a yawn, " Wal, I b'lieve I won't go daown t' the san'bar t'day ; I'll git rowin' 'nough by the time 't I git hum. I can't stan' it t' row much—it makes me sweat. I c'n fix that suller wall arter hayin'. If you've got some good worms dug, le's g' wup t' the maouth o' the Slang an' ketch a mess o' pike. They'd orter bite t'day. We'll go in the two scaows. What d' ye say? Me and Peasoup in mine an' the rest on ye in t'other."

His proposal being accepted, they brought bait and tackle from camp and embarked. Antoine took the oars at the bidding of Time and pulled the smaller scow in the lead. The other followed, paddled by Sam with the awkward aid of Joseph and Solon. It required all Sam's strength and skill to keep her at all on her course, and even so they had ample opportunity to view the landscape on every side. When at last they reached the stakes at the South Slang and moored their boats there, they had no great luck in fishing, as Time and Antoine prophesied they would not when they remarked several villainous-looking gar pike swimming about just beneath the surface. Yet now and then a pike-perch was tempted to venture underneath and past these visible terrors and seize the greater danger hidden in the loops of fat worms, when if by the awkwardness of his captors he was not swung over-board to freedom, purchased with a torn lip or jaw, he presently found himself floundering in the bottom of the scow. Once Antoine hauled up an ugly ling, which Sam told Joseph was " one o' his bowfins 'at had forgot his scales," but Antoine oracularly informed them that this " was de mudder of de heel," for thus he had long since

settled to his own satisfaction the vexed question of the
generation of the eel.

" You're sartin 'at eels come f'm lings, be ye ?" Time
asked in a tone that plainly indicated his unbelief in this
theory.

" Yes, sah ! Ah'll seen it !" said Antoine.

" Wal, they don't ! Du ye want I sh'ld tell ye where
eels come from ?"

" Ah'll ant want you. Ah'll know all of it," Antoine
said, but the others signified their willingness to be informed.

" Wal, then," said Time, " eels comes f'm clams, them
fresh-water clams 'at you c'n see thaousan's on any day
daown yunder in the shaller water to the san'bar. I know
it, 'cause I've seen hunderds o' little eels in 'em, not
bigger 'n pin points."

" Haow you'll know he was heel 'f he ant more bigger
as pint pins ?" Antoine roared in the big voice the Canuck
assumes when he would make himself terrible.

" Where du eels come from, then ?" Time loudly demanded.

" L-l leeng, ant Ah'll tol' you ?" Antoine roared again,
lifting himself from his seat with a grip of both hands on
the seat of his trousers.

" Clams ! clams ! clams !" Time bellowed in a cres-
cendo so vociferous that it frightened the skimming swallows from their pretty sport in the neighborhood of the
boats.

" Say," Sam said in a lull of the storm of words, " 'f
you fellers don't stop hollerin' so, you'll hev ol' Uncle
Tyler comin' daown here tu see what the rumpus is, not
to say nothin' o' scarin' all the fish aouten the crik."

Indeed, the day was too pleasant to be disturbed by even the discussions of science.

Across the sunny blue sky drifted only silver shreds of clouds, too thin to cast a shadow on the sunlit marshes, and shores, and quiet waters ; throughout the rushy level the marsh wrens discordantly rejoiced over the building of their cunning nests ; in the woods the wood and hermit thrushes rang silver bells and breathed celestial flute notes, and the jangle of a thousand bobolinks came from the meadows.

The peaceful spirit of the scene presently took possession of our anglers again, and they plied the gentle art in such serenity of mind as its father might desire, till the conch shells of half a dozen farmhouses reminded them of dinner-time.

Then Antoine transferred himself to the larger craft, and Time, declining an invitation to return to camp and dine with them, took to his oars, though with much less stomach for rowing than for dinner.

" Oh, say !" Sam called to him as the lazy wake of his departure began to stir the rushes, " 'f you hev a chance tu send word tu a young feller o' the name o' Peltier Gove 'at's a-workin' for Mr. Bartlett up on the stage rhud, tell 'im 't we're here, an' tu come daown 'f he can."

" All right," Time answered, when his ears had thoroughly digested the message.

Long after he had passed out of sight they could hear the splash of his oars and his voice unmelodiously cheering his labors with the song of " Old King Cole."

The shadow of the bluff was creeping toward the northeast when they reached camp, and when the fish were dressed, cooked, and eaten, the day was too far spent for the undertaking of any further great affair, so they paddled the scow out of the creek on to the shallows of the bay, and there passed the remaining hours of the daylight in the comfort of perfect laziness. When the mountains loomed black against the afterglow of the sky, and the star of Split Rock light began to shed its crinkled ray across the darkening waters, they paddled into the gloom of the landing.

Presently the camp-fire lit up the tent front, the tree trunks, the canopy of leafy branches, and the little circle of mossy ground, frayed into the surrounding darkness : all of the world that they then cared to have illumined for them.

VI.

Soon after his visit to Sam and Antoine at their trapping camp, Pelatiah had returned to Lakefield and taken service for the season with Friend Bartlett. The smiles of the pretty hired girl, the memory of which had almost as great a share as the wages offered in luring him from his mountain home, had thus far continued to brighten his life and make his faithful toil light, since it was rewarded morning, noon, and night by the sight of the face that had become to him the most beautiful, by the sound of the voice that was the sweetest in all the world.

One Sunday morning in June the peace and quietness of the day seemed to have reached their fulness in and about the Quaker homestead. Pelatiah sat whittling on the platform of the well with his back against the pump, just breathing "Old Hundred" through his puckered lips. Near him stood the fat and sedate old horse which he had just harnessed to the "shay," and by his side lay the fat old dog, who, in semblance of sleep, was waiting to accompany his master and mistress to meeting. He could hear hardly a sound coming from the open doors and windows of the house. The buzz of a bumblebee imprisoned by the raised sash of the kitchen window was loud enough to well-nigh drown the almost noiseless footsteps of Friend Rebecca Bartlett as she moved to and fro in preparation for departure, though occasionally above these was heard the cautious, long-drawn clearing of Friend John Bartlett's throat, accomplished with care that it should be thoroughly though not too loudly done, partly as practice for the same performance during the stillness of meeting, and partly as a reminder to his wife that he was waiting for her. The hens in the dooryard clucked and crated in subdued tones, and the old red rooster, though his gay feathers were sadly " out of plainness," kept as decorously " in the quiet," as if he was a member of his owner's sect.   Two or three frivolous swallows twittered and swooped in pursuit of floating feathers, but the great body of the tenants of the eaves were holding a silent meeting on the barn roof. The bobolinks in the meadow, beyond the influence of the First Day atmosphere of the staid homestead, withheld not a note of their merry songs, meant, perhaps, only for world's people and naughty strawberry pickers, but the robins in the apple-trees were as voiceless as the unstirred leaves, and the catbird skulked in silence along the row of currant bushes.   Pelatiah wondered if the pump would utter its usual discordant shriek, and was almost tempted to raise the handle.   Then through forgetfulness or impatience he whistled aloud a few notes of the old Psalm tune, and Rebecca came to the door tying the strings of her " sugar scoop" bonnet.

" Peltiah," she said in a mildly severe tone, " thee needn't whistle for Bose, he's right there by thee !   Thee may bring up the horse now."

While Pelatiah pocketed his knife and arose, brushing the shavings from his trousers, she went back to free the bumblebee from its glass prison, brushing it down the lowered sash with a folded handkerchief which exhaled the faint odor of dried rose leaves. "Now, get off with thee, thee foolish thing!" she said, as the bee blundered away into its regained paradise of out-door June.

The chaise lumbered up to the horse-block, and the good couple got on board, Bose soberly wagging his tail as he superintended their embarkation.

"Don't thee think thee'd better go to meeting, Peltiah?" Rebecca asked, getting the young man within the narrow range of her deep bonnet. She asked him this question every First Day morning, and was regularly answered, "Wal, no, marm, I guess not this mornin'."

They slowly got under way, and when they were out of earshot of the hired man, Rebecca remarked: "Peltiah seems like a steady young man, but it is a pity he isn't more seriously inclined."

"He's a master hand with a hoe," her husband said, looking down the even rows of his young corn, where not a weed was to be seen among the green sprouts that regularly dotted the mellow soil, "and I do' know as I ever see a better milker."

Pelatiah was anticipating a day of perfect happiness, for the girl, whose name was spelled Louisa and pronounced Lowizy, had as good as asked him to go to the woods with her for young wintergreens. That morning when he brought in the milk and they were alone in the cheese room, she had said there were "lots of 'em up in the maounting"—the rocky hill which Lakefield folk honored with that name, for a mountain they must have, and this of all the hills in town came nearest being one—"lots an' sacks of 'em, an' anybody might git a snag of 'em if they was to go up there naow. She wish't she had some, but she dasn't go alone, for she knew she should git lost, an'

the' was an ugly toro in Austin's pastur'.'' Pelatiah felt
that he would brave all the bulls in Lakefield to gather a
handful of aromatic leaves for her, but he had not the
courage to tell her so, and only said he would get them
for her if he knew where to find them. Whereupon she
giggled and said that she would go and show him where
they grew, and that then, if there was time enough and she
could '' stan' it,'' they might go to the Pinnacle, where
they '' could see all creation an' part o' York State.'' So
it seemed settled that when chores were done and the old
folks had gone to meeting, they should go '' a-browsin',''
as Pelatiah inelegantly termed it.

Now he was waiting for her, while he conned gallant
phrases and neat compliments, and thought just how he
would tell her that he '' liked'' her. How easy it all was
now, as he rehearsed it to his heart, but he knew that opportunity would frighten away all utterance, and he reviled
himself for a bashful booby. Yet he felt himself brave
enough in the face of real danger, and if the terrible bull
that kept all the berry-pickers out of Austin's pasture would
but attack them he would show his devotion, how he
would defend her even at the cost of his life. If the bull
was put to flight then she would faint, as in such cases
young ladies always did in the stories he read, and he
would bear her in his arms to the nearest brook and bathe
her face till he brought her out of her swoon. He had
never carried a young lady in his arms ; Lowizy was a
buxom maiden, no light weight certainly, but he thought
he could manage such a precious burden, though it would
be more easily done if she could be induced to ride pick-
aback, which, however, would not be in accordance with
the established usage of the stories. When she was re-

stored to consciousness, opened her eyes and saw him
bending over her, what if he could not help pressing his
lips to her pale cheek? He blushed to think of it, and
wondered if she would ever forgive him. If he should be
badly hurt, who but she would nurse him; and if he died
how could she help but grieve for him? The thought of
it almost made him shed a tear for himself. But then it
was very likely that the bull was a harmless bugbear whose
viciousness was an invention of the owner of the field, and
would give Pelatiah no chance of heroic deeds. So he
drifted back to imaginary commonplace opportunities, till
Lowizy came to the door more bewitching than ever, in a
pink calico dress and a white apron with two little pockets
stuck upon it like swallows' nests made of snow, useless
but pretty.

Just then a young fellow, seated in a square-boxed wagon
of amazing height, drove up at a pace which seemed reck-
less, considering how far above the ground he was perched;
and as recklessly he sprang down to the ground, endanger-
ing the straps of his trousers, the long swallow tails of his
blue coat streaming upward and the brass buttons flashing.
He drew near to Lowizy, who greeted him too warmly and
with too great a display of her best manners, Pelatiah
thought, as he stood aloof glowering at the new-comer,
while the two conversed earnestly, though in a tone too
low for any word to reach his ear. Then she ran into the
house; and Pelatiah's heart grew sick with a foreboding
of disappointment. He tried to whistle in token of indifference, but his sullen pout wouldn't be utilized as a
pucker, and though defiant and attempting to fortify himself with the inward assurance that he was as good as the
finest dandy of the lowlands, he could not help feeling

mean and awkward as he contrasted his suit of sheep's
gray, new though it was, and as much too long for him as
all former clothes had been too short, with the gay and
fashionable apparel of his till now unsuspected rival. It
was exasperating to see the fellow take out a cigar, and
having decided which end to light, begin to puff it ; and
then with his thumbs in the arm-holes of his waistcoat
strut back and forth beside the wagon. " Tew high an'
mighty tu take a noticte on me, hain't ye ? For all, the top
o' your plegged shiny hat hain't so high as the seat o' yer
wagon box !" Pelatiah inwardly addressed him. " Oh !
you're a gol buster, hain't ye ? I'll bate a cooky I c'ld
heave ye ov' the top o' yer dum'd ol' waggin !''

All unconscious of such disparagement and of everything
but the fine figure he must be making, the rustic little
dandy strutted in his pride till Lowizy reappeared with
some new finery added to her attire and a useless little
parasol in her hand. When he had gallantly assisted her
to scale the steps of the wagon and the " boost," as
Pelatiah to himself termed the feat, had been accomplished, he climbed in. Not till the fine equipage began
to turn in perilous haste did Lowizy bestow a word or
glance on Pelatiah. Then as she spread her parasol she
looked back, and said : " Mr. Gove, when the folks return, tell 'em that my maw is quite sick an' I've got to go
hum—ahem—go home an' see her.''

" I guess her maw hain't turrible bad off," Pelatiah
said bitterly, when a few moments later he heard her laugh
ringing down the road as merry and care free as the song
of the bobolinks. So sick at heart that his knees were
weak, he leaned on the door-yard fence and watched them
out of sight. So the stories he had read of the fickleness

of women were not fictions, but simple truth, were they?
It was hard to learn it by actual experience, hard to lose
the simple faith that all things are as they seem, that affec-
tion may be no more than an outward show, and kind
words have no meaning. His honest heart was so sorely
hurt that the counter-irritant of anger could not cure it
now ; there was no present cure for it, but he bethought
him that there might be a balm for it in the sanctuary of
the woods, to which he had often fled when assailed by
lesser ills. He would not go to that contemptible little
mountain of Lakefield, to be continually reminded there
of the happy hours he had been cheated of, but to the
great woods westward, deep and dark enough to hide him
from the false, hateful, wicked world.

He cast the unaccustomed summer burden of his thick
sheep's gray coat on the nearest plum-tree of the door-
yard, and in the regained freedom of shirt-sleeves felt his
heart somewhat lighter as he pushed toward the Slang.
On a fallen tree he crossed its narrow upper channel where
the border of the green marsh was gay with the purple
blossoms of flags, where a lonely heron stalked in fancied
seclusion, and where a bittern, perhaps his last spring's
acquaintance, startled him almost off his balanced foot-
hold, with her affrighted squawk and sudden uprising to
her labored flight.

Breasting the undergrowth of the bank, he was soon in
the midday twilight of the ancient forest, where brooded
a solemnity greater than within any temple built by hands,
a silence deepened rather than broken by the summer note
of a chickadee, the chimes of a wood-thrush, and the sigh
of the unfelt breeze in the tops of the great pines and
hemlocks.

Pelatiah took his way along an old lumber road, where sled tracks and footprints of oxen, made in the latest of last spring's sledding, were almost overgrown with forest herbage, and every mossy cradle knoll was starred with the white flowers of dwarf cornel or glowed with the blood-red drops of the partridge berry.

It made his recent wound twinge again when he came upon a patch of wintergreen, the "young-come-ups" showing the tender tints of the first unfolded leaves among the rusty and dark-green leaves and plump crimson berries of the old plants. What happy moments he had thought to spend gathering the freshest and tenderest for the girl who had so cruelly forsaken him. He could not taste nor touch one now, and was sure he never could again, for even the sight of them made him sick.

On either side of the way stood old friends to welcome him—great hemlocks, maples, whose sweets only the Indians and squirrels had tasted, poplars shivering with the memory of a century's winters, towering elms and basswoods, and all the graceful birches. He saw also a few great pines which had thus far escaped the lumberman, hickories with sharded trunks, and noble white oaks, all strangers to him in the woods of Danvis; but he missed his familiars, the spruce and balsam firs, their songs and the odor of their breath. A shrewish jay came to scold him, a squirrel to scoff at him, a shy wood bird, some constant dweller in the forest's heart, flitted near and watched him with timid curiosity; a mother partridge made a fluttering pother almost at his feet, while her callow brood dispersed like a sudden spatter of fluffy yellow balls and magically disappeared.

With no purpose of reaching any particular point he

wandered on, holding his way along the dim woodland aisle till it led where sunlight and blue sky shone from the outer world through the green-gold leaves and netted branches of the marsh's palisade of water maples.

Passing under these he saw the creek, the bold bluff at its mouth, and beyond a broad blue strip of the lake. When his eyes became used to the sunshine he saw figures moving beneath the bluff on the farther shore, and heard voices that somehow seemed familiar. There was no mistaking Sam Lovel's voice when presently he loudly called Antoine's name, nor the Canadian's when he answered.

Pelatiah hastily mounted a huge fallen tree that reached well out into the marsh, and shouted lustily, " Hello, Sam ! Antwine ! whoop ! Come over here. It's me, Peltier."

The figures became motionless in attention, then drew together in brief consultation, then one detached itself from the group, a paddle banged against a boat's side, a canoe drew out from the landing, came swiftly up the channel and swished into the wide marsh in front of him.

" I never was so glad to see anybody in all this everlastin' world," said the heartsick and homesick big boy as his friend Sam stepped on shore and shook hands with him. " Of all folks I never hed no thought o' seein' you, an' me on'y shoolin' 'raound in the woods jest tu kill time."

" If you'd ha' come yist'd'y you 'ld hed a good chance tu kill Time, for he was a-fishin' with us. That feller, you know," he explained, answering Pelatiah's inquiring look, " 'at come a-spearin' in our camp las' spring. His real name is Joe suthin'-er-nuther, but his pardner called 'im Time 'cause he favors Time in the primer, an' so we

du, not tu git him mixed up wi' Joe Hill. He's a clever
cretur', but lazier 'n a fattin' hawg an' slower 'n col'
m'lasses. Wal, Peltier, haow be you gittin' along? Like
your place?" Sam asked, seating himself on a log and
making ready for a smoke, deferred since he left the camp
landing.

"Wal, yes," Pelatiah said, slowly considering his answer, "yes, I hev liked it fustrate."

"Hev liked it? You hain't hed no fallin' aout wi' the
folks, I hope."

"No, not no fallin' aout wi' them. Do' know haow
't I could, for they're the cleverest folks in all creation."

"Wal, that pretty gal hain't gigged back on ye?"

No answer but a look of woebegone sheepishness.

"Oh, shaw, Peltier, nev' mind a gal's tantrums. You
an' her 'll be thicker 'n tew hands in a mitten, t'
rights."

"No, sir! not never no more!" Pelatiah replied with
spirit. "I won't stan' bein' fooled by nob'ddy, if they
be harnsome."

"My!" said Sam, "she was harnsome as a pictur!"
and then, doubtful whether he was quite loyal to Huldah
in such admiration of another, qualified it by adding,
"but the's them 'ats jist as harnsome."

"If she's harnsome as a pictur, she's decaitful as a
snake, an' I won't stan' bein' fooled!"

"Oh, yes, you will, Peltier! They'll fool a feller agin
an' agin till he gits so's 'at he likes bein' fooled. She's
jest begun on you an' you hain't got use to 't, but you
will, see 'f you don't. But come, le's go over an' see the
rest on 'em. They ben a-talkin' an' surmisin' baout you
all the mornin'. Come, I'll git you 'raound by kyow

time." And Sam, leading the way to the canoe, shoved it afloat and stepped in.

Pelatiah took his place and was surprised at the little trepidation he felt on finding himself fairly embarked on the broad channel.

"Why, Peltier, you keep the tarve o' the canew lots better'n you did last spring," Sam said, approvingly. "Guess you ben a-practizin', hain't ye?"

"Hain't ben in a boat sence," Pelatiah said. "Guess it's 'cause I don't care 'f I be draounded."

"Oh, shaw, Peltier! 'F you was tu git spilt aout you'd claw fer shore an' holler like a loon. Folks 'at's got your ail is allus a-wantin' tu die, but they enj'y dyin' so much 'at they hain't in no hurry tu hev the job finished up. You'll wanter live forever when you git t' eatin' the fish Antwine's a-cookin'. Pike an' pick'ril 'at 'ould make a man's maouth water tu see, though the's more fun for me in the ketchin' 'an in the eatin'. But I du eat 'em to make a good excuse fur ketchin' more."

Pelatiah was warmly welcomed by his friends, and almost forgot his misery while he listened to the news they told of folks and affairs at Danvis. The fish were as good as freshly caught and nicely cooked fish could be. When they had eaten he was taken along the bluff to see something of the wonders and beauty of the lake, which impressed him even more than they had Solon and Joseph.

Antoine, with the air of its chief proprietor, expatiated on the immensity of its waters and its commerce, but more on the numbers, variety, and excellence of its fish.

"More as t'ree 'honded tousan of it, prob'ly, an' all de kan dat ever was hear of it, 'cep' whale an' dry cod-feesh, Ah guess. Ah'll lak dat lake, me, 'cause he'll gat so much feesh, an' 'cause one en' of it steek raght in Canada ! Yes, sah ! wen nort' win' blow he'll breeng wave from Canada, where Ah'll was baun, w'en Ah'll was leetly boy, where Ah'll married my Ursule an' where Ah'll faght w'en Ah'll growed up for be hugly !''

They urged Pelatiah to get a day off during their stay and spend it with them, which he promised to do, if possible, even though it cost him the glories of the Fourth of July at Vergennes.

In good season to get him home by chore time, Sam embarked with him in the log canoe and paddled up stream and into the East Slang. Such a change had summer wrought here that he hardly recognized the scene of last spring's exploits. Where then the wide water stretched from shore to shore, was now a green, rushy level, divided only by a narrow channel that crept with many turns on its sluggish way to the creek as if any other course or none at all might as well be taken. The scraggy clumps of button bushes were now green islands in the marsh and populous with gay and noisy communities of redwings. The western shore bristling with naked branches when he last had seen it, now was softly rounded with all the luxuriant leafage June could give it, and the old camp was just discernible embowered in leaves and shadows. A narrow boat-path leading to it and a clumsy log canoe drawn ashore there showed that the landing was yet in use.

Pelatiah was set on shore farther up stream on the east bank at an open place to which he guided Sam, informing him that it was known as the "John Clark place," and was a famous resort for bullpout fishing in May. Here it was agreed that Sam should meet him next morning, if the hoped-for day's leave of absence were obtained, and then he went his way and was soon heard "whaying" the cows home.

On his return voyage, Sam ran in at the landing, from which he noticed that a well-trodden path led away into the woods. Though the place showed disuse and wore the changes wrought by the season, the greenness and bloom of early summer where so lately had been the brown and naked gray of early spring, there was much to remind him of the pleasant weeks he had spent there. There were whitened piles of muskrat bones, picked clean by many a big and little scavenger of the woods, cast-away stretchers and tally sticks, scales, and mummied heads of fish, and Antoine's old fish poles. There were sticks of left-over firewood close by the ashes and brands of the last camp-fire. The shanty kept its form, though the slabs were losing the fresh hue of newly-rifted wood. The bedding of straw had grown musty and was pierced with pale sprouts of such unthreshed kernels of grain as its latest tenantry of wood mice had spared.

While Sam sat smoking a meditative pipe, his old acquaintance, the squirrel, became aware of his presence and gave him a characteristic welcome, snickering and jeering and making such an ado that his wife and children came to learn the cause of it.

"Hain't ye 'shamed to be sassin' your betters afore your young uns?" Sam addressed the bright-eyed native, "but I d'know 's I be your better, an' I'm glad to see ye fur all your sass."

Approaching footsteps drew his attention, and presently an old man came shuffling along the path bearing on his shoulder a long unwieldy contrivance of basket work. He was unmistakably Canadian, an older but less sophisticated

Antoine, who still wore the baggy homespun woollen trousers, red belt, and russet leather moccasins of his native land. When Sam accosted him, his startled halt was so sudden that he nearly dropped the long basket and uttered a prolonged and very emphatic "Saacré!" but, catching sight of him, seemed to consider the accident a good joke.

"Ah! Ha, ha, ha! you mek scare M'sieur! Bon jour, bon jour, M'sieur. You poot good, aujourd'hui, M'sieur! Parlez-vous Français, M'sieur? Non? Ha, ha, ha! me no parlez Anglais ver' good. Me come Canada las' printemps. Coupai le bois pour M'sieur Bartlette. Choppai de hwood. Onsten? Ha, ha, ha! Gat petit maison là, leet' haouse," pointing backward along the path and then beating his breast rapidly, "Jean Bisette, me. Me, ma femme, all 'lone, 'lone. Got garçon, boy, come here long tam, me can' fan', me sorry, oh! sorry, sorry. You no see it, prob'ly, M'sieur?"

"Whaty—you—cally—you gassaw's name?" Sam asked, in a tone so loud that he was confident his French must be understood.

"Hein? Oh! Oui, oui, oui! Son nom est An-toine, Antoine Bisette. You no see it, M'sieur?" he asked, anxiously.

"I'll bate a cooky 'at aour Antwine's his boy," Sam said to himself, "but 'f I tol' him so an' it turned aout he wan't it 'ld be awful disappintin' tu the ol' cretur'!" Then shaking his head, added aloud, "No, do' know 's I ever did. 'F I du I'll let ye know. What on airth be you agoin' tu git in sech a dum'd basket as that?"

Evidently his question was not comprehended, and he hastened to make it plainer with louder voice and simpler phrase, " Whaty for dat baskeet ?" which at last the old man understood and explained that his long basket was a fish trap.

Then he pushed off in his canoe and busied himself with setting it in a gap at the point made by two thickly set rows of stakes running obliquely across stream, and Sam went his way homeward.

Night was falling. The channel was strangely widened in the uncertain light ; its marshy borders far away vague and mysterious among the brooding shadows of the wooded shores, and the reflection of the first eastern star danced along his wake before he reached the landing.

VII.

CANADIANS ON THE SLANG.

THE camp was astir early next morning, so early that Antoine was prancing about the fire with a frying-pan of fish before the morning breeze had swept the cobwebs of mist off the marshes, and so early that, when breakfast was announced, Joseph Hill remarked :

"I never did set no gret on gittin' up in the night t' eat a meal o' victuals—that is, 'f I've hed supper in kinder decent season. Not to say but what I kin gin'ally eat hearty—that is, tol'able hearty—but mornin' naps, when you wake up jest 'nough tu sense 't you hain't got tu git up, is turrible comf'table, an' I hate bein' cheated aout on 'em. But I'll try tu rise tu the 'casion,'' and he crawled into place by the stone table.

"Some skeety talkin' was mek me gat up hairly dis mornin','' Antoine said, in explanation of his early rising.

"Skeeters talkin' !'' said Joseph. "I never heard 'em du nothin' but sing, an' dum'd poor singin' at that ; I d' know but it's good 'nough singin', but I don't like the tune.''

"Wal, seh, boy, Ah'll hear it talk dat tam, an' Ah hear all what he'll said. Fust w'en dat leetly nowse woked me up, Ah'll ant know what he was mek it. Den Ah'll fan' aout he was four skeety standlin' on top of

it me an' Sam, an' Solem, an' Zhozeff. Dat one standlin'
on Sam say, ' Dis man hide so tough Ah can' steek ma
beel in it.' De one standlin' on Zhozeff say, ' Ah can
push ma beel in dis one, but Ah can' tol' what Ah'll
get, bloods or water or sometings, an' guess he ant know
hese'f what he got hees inside of it.' De one bore Solem
say, ' Ah'll bore hole in dis mans an' de win' blowed
aout of it so he'll mos' knock ma head off ' Den de one
seet on me, he say, ' Ah'll bore in dis one very easy, an'
he gat more bloods as dey was water in de lake, an' it tase
more better as wines. Come here, boy, dey 'nough for all
of it.' ◆Den dey'll come on me an' Ah'll gat to jomp
ap pooty quick ! ''

" It's lucky they waked you," said Sam, " seein' 'at
I've got tu gwup betimes arter Peltier. An' come tu think
on 't, I forgot tu tell ye, Antwine, 'at I see a feller up t'
the Slang 'at come f'm the same place 't you did, I guess.
Like 'nough you know him.''

" He come f'm Saint Cesaire ?'' asked Antoine with
interest.

" No, he didn't give that name, but he come f'm Canady, erles he's strayed away f'm Uncle Lisha's Colchester
P'int. He looks ol' 'nough for that.''

" From Canada ! You'll s'pose Ah see evreebodee in
Canada ? Dat mos' bigger as Danvit prob'ly, an' you'll
ant know evreebodee lieve dar, ant it, hein ?''

" Wal, no, not quite all on 'em, an' the' 's some 't I
du know 'at I wish't I didn't. But I was a-tellin' on
him 'baout you,'' Sam continued, indulging in a white
lie, " an' he claimed 'at he knowed a man o' the name
o' Antwine Bisette. Like 'nough he lied, I've knowed
Canucks 'at did git a leetle mite off 'm the act'al facts

sometimes, but I guess you'd better gwup 'long wi' me an' see him.''

"Frenchmans ant never lie,'' Antoine protested with a great flourish of gestures, " 'fore he'll be here long 'nough for learn it of Yankee, 'cept once a while mebby he ketch it of Injin. Injin lie lak' a dev'.''

"Wal, they're turrible easy tu larn, some on 'em.''

"He'll gat good school mom fer dat w'en he'll gat Yankee !''

"Wal, nev' mind 'baout that naow, you'd better gwup an' see him, an' when you git through parly vooin'—you'd orter heard me an' him talkin' French !—you c'n come daown where Peltier did, an' some on us'll g' over 'n' git ye. Come on.''

"Wal, Ah guess Ah'll goin',' Antoine said, arising after relighting his pipe. "Ah'll wan' talk French wid somebody 'fore Ah'll fregit of it. An' it don't healt'y for Frenchman's talk so good Angleesh Ah do, all de tam.''

They were well on their way before the touch of the rising sun began to transmute their broad path of silver into one of gold, and it was just gilding the roots of the old hemlocks and patches of the forest floor when the canoe crushed through the rushes to the old camp landing. Antoine had no sentimentality to expend on the place which had given him all he could ever expect from it, and was at once ready to follow Sam.

They had not gone far along the path when the sunlight of a little clearing shone before them, and then they saw a small log-house with whitewashed sides and notched shingles along its eaves. Coming nearer, they saw an old woman at the door wearing a white cap and short white gown which Sam wondered at, whether meant for day or

night attire, and then an old man, on all fours, weeding
an onion bed close beside the house. When presently he
sat upright to fire with flint and steel a bit of punk to light
his pipe, his leathern old visage became plainly visible.

" There, du ye know him, Antwine?" Sam asked, in a
low tone.

The younger Canadian's face, which had till now
shown only amused curiosity, suddenly flashed into an
expression of recognition and strong emotion.

" Ah, mon Dieu!" he cried huskily, "c'est mon
poupa et ma mouman!" and he ran forward to the old
people.

" Huggin' an' kissin' on 'em julluk any little boy,"
said Sam with a quaver in his voice, and with tender
memories of his own mother who had been asleep under
the graveyard sumachs since he was a child, he retired before the rejoicing trio came fairly to their speech. As he
went his way back to the boat, the three voices broke forth
in such a confusion of incessant gabble that he could not
help laughing and remarking, " By the gre't horn spoon !
A flock o' blackbirds, no, nor all the noises in the ma'sh
put together, hain't a-primin'."

He was glad to find Pelatiah waiting at the " John Clark
place," his unhappiness somewhat lessened by the prospect of a day's outing.   Sam had had the forethought to
bring trolling tackle along, and as they fared slowly down
stream Pelatiah trailed the lure along the border of lily
pads and listened to the story of the discovery of Antoine's
parents, and thought it almost as wonderful as a story in
a book.

He struck a large pickerel, and had the luck, in spite of
his flurried awkwardness, to get it safely into the dugout,

and rejoiced exceedingly in its capture and in Sam's praise of his skill, as well as in anticipation of the display of such a trophy on his return to Friend Bartlett's. He would like, he thought, to see that little dandy spark of Lowizy's struggling with such a fish, almost as big as he, and as likely to haul him overboard as to be hauled inboard. Was it possible that Lowizy might feel a sympathetic pride in his achievement? He had fancied that his heart was steeled against her blandishments, some of which had been vainly expended on him last evening, succeeded by an air of injured innocence that proved as ineffectual. But now he began to feel a forgiving softness and some twinges of remorse. He began to frame excuses for her conduct, and accused himself of cruelty in answering her in monosyllables, and for not having filled the wash-boiler for her before he came away. Sam dispelled this silent mood by proposing plans for the spending of the day. "I ben kinder wantin' tu go aout tu Gardin' Islan' ever sen we ben here," he said as he sent the canoe on her way with slow strokes of the paddle, never changed from side to side, but steadily delivered on one side without a perceptible deviation of the bow from its direct course.

"The bay's as still as a mill-pawnd tu-day, an' s'posin' you 'n' me take a v'yage aout there in the scaow? We c'n git back afore noon an' then fish 'long wi' Sole an' Joe till it's time for you tu go hum."

The prospect of voyaging more than half a mile out into the immensity of the lake was rather appalling to Pelatiah, but his faith in Sam was unbounded, and the prospect of setting foot on a real solid island was as alluring as an adventure of discovery, and so after a little deliberation he fell in with the proposal.

Arriving at camp, the plan was broached to Solon and Joseph, who at once declared that they had no inclination for so perilous a voyage.

"It's still 'nough naow," said Joseph after a careful inspection of the cloudless sky, "but the's time 'nough for it tu up an' blow like all git aout 'fore we c'ld git aout there and back agin, an' the's no knowin' what dum'd caper that pleggid ol' she-boat 'ld take a notion tu cut up if the win' did blow. I b'lieve I'd druther look at the lake f'm one side 'an f'm the middle. You c'n see more on't tu oncte that way, an' I b'lieve that'll sati'fy me tol'able well, though 'f I felt julluk goin' I p'sume to say I'd go."

Solon advised keeping to the shore or near it, and gave it as his opinion that the contemplated visit to the island was "an attemptin' of improvidence." They were told of the meeting of Antoine and his parents, and Solon declared it was like the "return of the prodigy son, only proberbly the' wa'n't no calf infatuated for the o·casion."

"This was more as't orter ben 'cordin' tu my idee," said Joseph, "a sorter meetin' half way, an' nob'dy a·gittin' tuckered a trav'lin' as that ere Scriptur' young man did."

While Pelatiah tethered his precious pickerel safely in the shallow water, Sam got a lunch of bread and pork, some poles, lines, and bait from camp, and the two set forth in the scow. Sam took the oars, a rough pair of Antoine's fashioning, which Joseph Hill said "it wouldn't be no sin tu warship, for they wa'n't like nothin' in heaven or airth, erless the' was some more somewhere 'at Antoine hed made," and Pelatiah took his first lesson in steering with the paddle.

"Con-faound it!" he cried, when in spite of his best en-

deavors the boat had veered to half the points of the com-
pass, " I can't make the ol boat p'int nowheres ! I don't
b'lieve it's half broke !"

" Why, Peltier," Sam said, amused, though half-im-
patient with his awkwardness, " you haint no cause tu say
that, for you make it p'int most everywheres."

" I b'lieve," Pelatiah remarked, " 'at they call it steer-
in' 'cause the con-faounded thing acts so much like steers
'at hain't broke. It do' know gee f'm haw."

" Uncle Tyler, the ol' feller 'at fetched Sole an' Joe
an' to'ther duds daown in his scaow, says 't a boat don't
know gee an' haw, but it does starb'd and larb'd. My !
'f you'd a-heard him hollerin' at 'em you'ld a-thought 't
was Cap'n Peck a-trainin' his floodwood comp'ny."

Pelatiah improved rapidly under Sam's patient instruc-
tion, and was soon able to keep the scow quite closely
headed for the island, whose rocky shore, green trees, and
blossomy shrubs steadily loomed larger, nearer and more
distinct.

While they were on the shallows, frequent touches of the
paddle on the sandy bottom, assurances that connection
with the solid earth was not yet severed, had given Pelatiah
a feeling of safety. But now that the paddle could not
touch the bottom, the clams and their slowly traced tracks
faded out of sight in the deeper water, the ripples of sunshine no longer crinkled the sands with gold, and there
was nothing but water to be seen beneath the boat save
where some great rock dimly showed in the green depths,
like an ugly monster lying in wait for a victim, he wished
himself on land, and was glad enough when the scow
grated on the rocky slant of the island's southern shore.
He could hardly tell whether such isolation was quite

pleasant, but it was a new and strange sensation to have this little patch of rock and scant soil all to himself and Sam, but for its few inhabitants, the birds and reptiles, mice and perhaps a family of minks, for they saw one gliding along the shore, as lithe and silent as a snake.

They made the round of all its borders, the sheer wall of the north shore, where storm-bent cedars and birches clung along the brink, and the long incline of rock on the south shore, where thickets of flowering shrubs made a breastwork of bloom just behind the line of driftwood and pebbles thrown up by the high water of spring. They explored the interior, where a goodly growth of almost all the deciduous trees of the region was unaccountably nourished in the thin red soil. In one place they noticed that a pit deep enough for a grave had recently been dug, but for what purpose they could not imagine. They carved their names and the date of their visit on the largest white birch in characters which some later comer might possibly decipher. Then they fished off the eastern and western points of the island, catching perch whose armor of green and gold was darker and brighter than those of their brethren of the creek.

Once when Pelatiah cast his bait into a wide fissure of the submerged rocks it was seized in a sudden onset that reminded him of the biting of his familiars, the trout. But this was a lustier fellow than any denizen of Danvis' brooks, one that would not be jerked out overhead at the first stroke, but clung to the water tenaciously till, the line's length away, he broke the surface and sprang thrice his length above it, then regained his watery grasp almost as soon as the parted wavelets closed above his bristling dorsal fin. It was no exercise of skill, but only stout tackle and a strong pull that overcame him, yet Pelatiah was none the less exultant when at last he hauled his prize out on to the rocks and pounced sprawling upon him, as Sam said, "Julluk a boy ketchin' a frog."

"This must be a 'Swago, as they call 'em," he said when its captor ventured to quit hovering over the goodly three-pound bass, and gave him a chance to examine it. "Seems 's 'ough that feller speared one julluk this that night las' spring, an' him an' Time called it a 'Swago. They say they're the beaters of all the fish in these waters, on the hook or on the table, an' by the way this one skived an' flurrupped 'raound I jedge they've got the fust on't right. 'Cordin' tu their tell, Lewis Creek's chuck full on 'em, an' I wanter hev a slap at 'em one day 'fore we g' hum."

After awhile, when both had tired of trying to catch another bass, the pulsing rumble of a steamer's paddles was heard, and they hurried to the west point to see her pass. Compared with the little steamboat he had seen at Vergennes at the time of Uncle 'Lisha's departure, and the only one he had seen till now, this was a leviathan. Pelatiah thought he could never tire of watching her majestic progress as, with flags and pennons flaunting bravely in the sunlight, she spurned the vexed waters behind her in a long line of foam. Gayest and most conspicuous of her bunting shone the stars and stripes, and it made his heart swell with pride to see the flag of his country floating above so grand and beautiful a craft, and he was proudly thankful to be even the humblest of Yankees.

So intently did he and his companion regard the steamer that it was not till she had passed out of sight and the waves of her wake began to beat the rocks at their feet

with sullen surges that they noticed what a change had
come upon the sky, how silvery domes of thunder heads
had reared themselves above the mountains, shadowing
some in a blue black as sombre as the bases of the great
cloud temples had become, till mountain and cloud were
an undistinguishable, looming mass of blackness. The
south wind which had risen from a scarcely perceptible
waft of soft air to a breeze that ruffled the lake and briskly
stirred the leaves was now hushed, and no sound was
heard but the slow wash of the steamer's wake and some
voices of shore life, faint, occasional, and far away. It was
as if nature was holding her breath in expectation of some
outburst of her elements, presently voiced by a threatening
growl of distant thunder, rolling along the western horizon.

"Wal, naow," said Sam after a brief survey of the
storm signs, "I guess we'd better be pickin' up an'
pullin' foot for camp ; I d' know but we'll ketch it as
'tis."

Gathering their tackle and fish, they hastened to where
they had landed, but the boat was not there. She had
only been fastened by grounding her bow on a rock, and
the wash of the steamer had set her adrift. Standing at
the water's edge, with craned necks, they speechlessly
watched her drifting away, her oar handles bobbing up
and down and creaking and bumping with the swells as
if plied by some invisible mischievous water sprite.

"By the gre't horn spoon ! if we hain't in a boat
now," Sam said, as he exhaled his long-held breath.

"I wish tu Lord o' massy we was in a boat," Pelatiah
said dolefully, "erless we never'd a-ben anigh one. I
won't never git inter one o' the con-faounded things agin,
I snum !"

"You'll hafter 'f you ever git away f'm here, erless you wait till the lake freezes."

"I don't s'pose we will git away for a good spell 'f we ever du 'fore we starve tu death! Tew reg'lar Robi'son Crusoes we be, an' not a dum'd goat on this pleggid islan'! Oh, dear me suz!" Pelatiah wailed as a new and greater anxiety fell upon him. "What be I goin' tu du 'baout my chores? The' won't be nob'dy tu help milk, an' Mr. Bartlett an' the hull toot on 'em 'll think I'm the meanest, lyin' skunk in all creation."

"Wal," said Sam, "we can't help it naow and hev tu make the best on't. Joe and Sole won't dast tu come arter us, but when Antwine gits through parly vooin' with his ol' folks, 'f he ever does, he will. We c'n eat fish an' play 't we own the islan' till someb'dy comes. Le's go an' see haow it gits 'long stormin'," and he led the way to the west point.

VIII.

THE TREASURE-DIGGERS.

From the dark clouds a veil of rain had fallen, completely hiding the distant mountains and the farthest western shore, while it had begun to flatten the nearer crags of Split Rock into a sheer wall whose even tint of dull gray was broken only by the white shaft of the lighthouse and the dull flash of the waves which the coming wind hurled against the point of the rugged promontory. Beyond the advancing veil, whitecaps gleamed out of the obscurity, and out of it scudded a sloop with close-reefed sails and anchored in the shelter of Thompson's Point.

When the frequent flashes of lightning quivered down from the sky, it was as if the veil was torn with jagged rents that for an instant revealed a conflagration of the universe. Incessant peals of thunder rolled in repeated bursts and muttering growls, swelling, and dying in echoes from cloud, mountain, and headland, with a continuous undertone of the roar of wind and waves on distant woods and rock-bound shores. The wind, yet unfelt by the castaways, sent the hurrying clouds in a wide, majestic sweep across the sky till all the sunlit blue was blotted out and the landscape was overspread with a gloom more awful than the darkness of night, flashing into instants of distinctness when wind-swept waves, and clouds, and trees, for a pulse beat, stood still in the white fire of

the lightning. Then cat's-paws ruffled the black, still
waters near them, a brief patter of big drops fell like leaden
plummets on water, rocks, and leaves, and then all at once
the lake seethed at their feet, the lithe branches of the
birches streamed to leeward of their bending trunks, and
the sturdy cedars tossed in brief resistance as the long-
driven slant of the storm burst upon them.

Sam and Pelatiah were drenched before they could reach
the partial shelter of the nearest clump of cedars, which
only broke the force of the wind, while every branch and
twig seemed to become a conduit to pour, dribble, and
drip down their backs and upon their knees, every raindrop
the tree caught.

" I don't s'pose it's nothin' tu what they hed time o'
the flood," said Sam, wiping his wet face with a wetter
coat-sleeve, "but I du feel more'n I ever did afore for
the poor creeturs 'at was aouten the ark."

"I guess I've got tu the hayth o' wetness," Pelatiah
said, as with his chin on his knee he regarded the water
overflowing from the tops of his boots, into which his
trousers were tucked, "fer my boots is a-runnin' over.
Oh, con faound it, I'd ruther milk all aour caows in the rain
'an tu be squattin' here, like a draownded goslin', jes' fer
fun.   Dum sech fun !"

With such dolorous discourse and with watching the
storm they whiled away a half hour of discomfort.
Through the loop-holes of their poor shelter they could
see nothing but the blown and pelted trees and rocky
bounds of their island, and a little beyond these the seething, angry sweep of the waves, whose white crests and
black furrows faded into the gray downpour and fleeting
drift of the rain, and it was as if this patch of rocks and

earth was all that was left to them of the stable world whose blue mountains, green woods, and fields and sunlit waters an hour ago had shone about them. Then the fury of the wind abated somewhat, the rain hissed less angrily upon the hurrying waves, the torn clots of black clouds swept more slowly across the sky, grew more infrequent, then had all passed by ; the nearest headland was dimly revealed, vaguely defined shores reappeared and again clasped the bay, a distant field was lighted by a gleam of sunshine and shone through the vapor in golden green, the leaden hue of the waves turned to living blue and green, and as the last growl of the retreating storm was muttered among the eastern mountains, the sunlight came sweeping over all the landscape.

Sam and his companion crept from under their roof of dripping branches and stretched their cramped limbs in the genial warmth of the rekindled sunlight, while they scanned the lake in hope of seeing some friendly craft that might come to their rescue. But no vessel of any sort was in sight, save the sloop that had taken shelter inside Thompson's Point, and which, if not beyond their hail, was unmindful of it, for it now spread its white wings to the fresh northern breeze and sailed away to the southward.

Her captain and crew they had never had speech with nor seen, but at such a distance that they were unrecognizable specks, presumably men, who might be white or black, brother Yankees, Yorkers, or Canadians, for all they could make out concerning them, but they, too, had suffered the fury of the storm, and as the bellying sails bore them away, passing out of sight behind the cliffs, a heavier sense of loneliness fell upon Sam and Pelatiah.

Sam comforted himself with a pipe, a solace which

was denied Pelatiah, as was also the rumination of his cud, for which he vainly searched his pockets, remembering at last that he had given his only remaining piece of gum to the faithless Louisa. Far better, he thought, than if he had it, if she was now chewing it and was reminded by it of him. Would she feel any anxiety concerning him if he did not return that night, as it now seemed probable he could not, and be sorry that she had been unkind? Or would she and all of them think that he was careless of his word or had deliberately broken it? This seemed the likelier chance, and again he groaned aloud, "Oh, con-faound sech fun!"

Standing on the south shore and looking toward the mouth of Little Otter, they saw two figures on the beach to the westward of it which they made out to be Solon and Joseph. They were moving excitedly about in the neighborhood of an object which Sam presently guessed to be the scow, stranded on the shallows. The favoring wind bore Sam's hail to them, and though their answer could not be heard, they could be seen frantically swinging their hats, delighted at the assurance of the safety of their friends, and Sam laughed to think of what he could not quite see, how Joseph was prancing about like an upreared mud turtle, and of the big words he knew Solon must be uttering.

Then they were seen to wade out to the scow, bail out the water it had shipped, board it, shove it into deeper water, and then, with a heroic endeavor to practise the lessons of Uncle Tyler, attempt to row to the island. It soon became evident that they might as well have undertaken so to voyage to the moon, for they clawed the air more than the water with the oars, making no progress, but in irregular circles, which, if they should become wide enough, were as likely to take them out into the broad lake as to the island.

Sam became more alarmed for them than for himself and Pelatiah, and roared to them to get back to the shore if they could. When they comprehended his instructions they were fortunately in shoal water, and more effectually using the oars as setting poles, they happily succeeded in beaching the scow on the sands at the foot of the bluff. Then Sam shouted to them in well-separated words, slowly delivered between his hollowed hands :

"When—An—twine—gits—back (if he ever does an' hain't parlyvooed hisself to death," taking his hands down and also taking breath as he addressed this aside to Pelatiah), " hev—him—come—over—arter—us—with—the—scaow ! Du—you—hear ?"

When they had taken time to ponder the message, Sam caught their faint " yes" making its way against the buffets of the wind.

"Naow, Peltier," he said, " le's dress aour parch—you wanter save that 'Swago—right here where the sun 'li dry us, an' make us a fire an' hev us a hot dinner. The punk in my wa'scut pocket's dry's bone spite o' all this 'ere flood, 'n we c'n git a fire aout o' suthin, I guess."

In the lee of the blooming thicket they set about scaling their fish. So absorbed in their occupation or with far-away thoughts they took no note of the unobtrusive sounds about them, the wash of the subsiding waves, the rustle of the leaves, and the songs of the vireos among them. Once they thought they heard mixed with these the thump of oars, but listening they heard no more.

Presently they were startled by the tramp of stumbling,

heavy feet, the noise of spades and a crowbar thrown down, and then as one pair of feet came to a halt quite near them, a loud nasal voice broke out :

"Oh, look a-here ! John-ah, Job-ah, here's seas an' oceans an' thaousan's o' Seneky snake rhut, I vaow !"

A voice that greatly resembled that of the first speaker, though it sounded more familiar to Pelatiah, answered impatiently :

"Oh, dum your Seneky snake rhut ah ! We got suthin' 'at's more 'caount 'an or'nary rhuts tu tend tu ; what the Bible calls the rhut of all evil is what we're arter ah. Come here an' le's git tu diggin' right stret off, 'fore some darn fool comes shoolin' raound. I ruther guess, Jethro, 'at you an' Job, Junior, hed better dig, an' I'll keep watch, bein' 'at I'm the sharpest sightedest an' t' the spine o' my back's kinder lame-ah."

Peeping under the bushes, Sam and Pelatiah saw, standing quite near them, a tall, awkward lout, who with a face expressive of green conceit and low cunning regarded the patch of medicinal herbs that spread their broad leaves before him, and just beyond him, above the undergrowth, the heads and shoulders of two others of the same unfinished strong build, the same expression of conceit and cunning, with a little drying of the greenness that more years had given, unmistakably elder brothers of the one who had spoken first.

"I hain't a-goin' tu dig a dum'd inch-ah," said this one, still gloating over his discovery of herbs, an aromatic root of which he had pulled and was crunching with swinish voracity, "erless I'm a-goin' tu hev a third o' all the money we git ; so there."

"Naow, con-faound it all, Jethro-ah," said the oldest

brother, coming nearer and halting, while the swing of
his arms gradually abated like the subsiding beats of a
pendulum, " what's the use o' your bein' a nat'ral born
fool, if you know anything ? Who tol' us where we was
a goin' tu find all the money 'at Bennydick Amil hid
here, when he was a-retreatin'-ah ? Wa'n't it Sairy,
Sleepin' Sairy, when Job Junior hed gin her the inflewernce-ah ?''

Evidently Jethro could not gainsay this, and maintained
a sullen silence. " Wal, then,'' his brother continued,
" 't wouldn't be no more 'n fair fer her tu hev half on't,
for haow'ld we ever ha' faound it 'f 't hedn't been for
her-ah ? Say, you darned off ox-ah !''

" Wal, we hain't faound it, hev we-ah ? We've got tu
dig for 't, hain't we-ah ?'' Jethro demanded with a sar-
castic grin.

" Gol dum ye !'' cried John, " we would ha' hed it 'f
you'd hel' your plegged gab-ah. A speakin' jest 's the
crowbar hit the chist, an' then of course it moved, jest 's
any tarnal fool might ha' knowed it would-ah. But we're
a goin' tu git it naow 'f you c'n keep yer hed shet a spell,
an' all 't we ast is a quarter on 't for Sairy, jest a ekal
divided quarter, 'n one fur me 'n' one fur you, 'n' one
fur Job Junior ah. An' that's more 'n fair. Neow,
hain't it, Job-ah ?''

" Wal,'' answered Job, " I 'low 't is—that is to say fur
you, bein' 'at Sairy's your womern, which it jest in fac'
gives you half—a hull half-ah ! I wanter ast, naow, who
give Sairy the mess miricle inflewernce-ah ? 'Twan't
you, not by a jug full.''

" Jest so,'' said Jethro.

" Ah, wal-ah, strickly speakin', it wa'n't exakly me,''

the eldest reluctantly admitted, "but I furnished the womern, which she is the mess miricle subjeck."

"I'm goin' tu hev a third on't," Jethro emphatically reasserted, "erless I'll go an' tell Annernius, an' break up the trade for the islan', which I can, bein' 'at the' hain't no writin' 's drawed yit. So there-ah."

This threat seemed to strike dumb him whom they called John, but after swelling and choking with rage for a little, speech returned.

"Job an' me hed ort tu kill ye an' heave ye int' the lake, so we hed ah !" but Job did not assent to this simple method of settling Jethro's claim, and John went on somewhat less angrily. "Wal, condum ye, take a third, take it, you tarnal hawg, an' be dum'd, 'f you wanter take the bread aouten your brother's maouth 'at's allers bin your guardeen an' the mainstay o' the fam'ly sence the ol' man yer father, Job Senior, died ! Take it, but go to diggin' 'fore some fool comes gawpin' raound. An' keep yer head shet when ye git tu diggin' !"

Sam now whispered to Pelatiah that if they were to get these men to help them to return to the mainland it would be best to enter upon negotiations at once, before the treasure seeking was begun, and of which they must pretend complete ignorance.

Crouching low, they stole silently away to some little distance and then noisily made their way toward the money-diggers, who were now gathered about the pit, which Sam and Pelatiah had noticed in their survey of the island.

"Haow are ye ? I'm turrible glad to see ye !" Sam said heartily.

"Where in thunder an' chain lightnin' did you come from-ah ?" demanded the eldest of the brothers, surprised,

shamefaced, yet half defiant. "What ye duin' here?
Clear aout! This is aour islan'! we jest bought it, an'
we hain't a goin' tu 'low anybody on it stealin' cedar pos's
an' raisin' Cain-ah. We'll sue 'em fur trespuss—yes, sir,
we will, an' you'd better put 'er."

Sam hastened to explain that he and his comrade had
come there fishing, that their boat had gone adrift in the
storm, and that all they wanted of the island was to rid it
of themselves; now how much would they ask to set them
ashore at the mouth of Little Otter?

"Wal-ah," said the self-constituted mouthpiece of the
three, "we come here a-fishin' tew, got aout o' worms,
an' come ashore tu dig some here," indicating the pit with
a sweep of his arm. "We allus carry tools for diggin'
worms," with another sweep in the direction of the spade
and crowbar. "A man orter be prepared for everything
when he goes a fishin', but the' hain't many 'at knows
'nough tu be. Naow, 'f you'd ha' ben prepared-ah, you
wouldn't ha' got ketched so."

"Wal, no," said Sam. "If we'd ha' fetched lumber
an' tools to build another boat, we'd ha' ben all right,
but seein' 'at we didn't think on't, haow much be you
goin' tu charge tu take us over t' the crik? We got some
fellers over there 'at 's expectin' of us, an' we're willin'
tu pay you reasonable tu take us over."

"What be you a-duin' on here so many on ye-ah? I
don't like the looks on't. Don't ye tech nothin' on this
islan', not a cedar pos' nor not one stun-ah, nor dig
none, for we cal'late tu pastur' sheep on't, an' we don't
want it all tore up-ah. It's all aour'n tu hev an' tu hol',
we, aour heirs an' 'signs forever, et cetery un' so forth-ah."

Sam reasserted that he and his friend coveted nothing

that the island contained and repeated his query as to the
sum demanded for taking Pelatiah and himself away from
it, to which John did not at once reply, but continued to
ask questions, for his inquisitiveness was as craving as his
acquisitiveness. " Where du ye live when you're 't hum?
I don't remember seein' ye afore tu taown meetin', nor
trainin', an' I don't b'lieve you b'long in Lakefield ah.
You've got a kinder furrin aspeck, so to speak-ah. Oh,
you live in Danvis, du ye, an' come a-fishin', hey? Come
to think on't this young man does look kinder familler,
an' I b'lieve I see him a-sloshin' raound arter pickril up t'
the East Slang las' spring. Wan't ye? Say-ah?"

Pelatiah nodded an affirmative.

" Wal," he continued, while he meditatively pawed the
earth with his big boot, " it'll hender us consid'able, but
we wanter be 'commerdatin', an' seein' it's you, we'll
take ye over fur, le' me see, wal, tew dollars in money,
seein' it's you-ah." He announced his terms as if a sudden burst of generosity had overcome his better judgment.

" Seein' it's us," said Sam, with calm indignation,
" we'll stay here till the lake freezes over an' Tophet teu,
'fore we'll pay you tew dollars for a half hour's rowin'!"
and without further words he and Pelatiah turned away.

They had gone some distance and Pelatiah was suggesting that they should take the boat without leave, or, as he
put it, " kinder borrer it for a spell," and make their
escape, and then, towing it back with their own, restore it
to the owners; when they heard some one hastily following them in a clumsy attempt to do so stealthily. Looking back they saw Jethro struggling through the undergrowth, his arms at full swing where there was space for them.

" Say-ah! Hol' on-ah!" he half-grunted, half-whispered, and coming up to them, continued in the same tone, " I'll take ye over for seventy-five cents in money-ah, 'f you'll give it tu me right in my own fist. Will ye, say-ah ?"

" I'll give ye fifty cents," said Sam, " an' pay ye soon as you start."

" Wal, gol dum it, fifty cents, then. The ol' capt'in wouldn't gi' me a cent 'f he'd got tew dollars. You shy raound tu the boat in the cove on the north side, an' I'll come in less 'n no time. Naow, don't ye let 'em see ye, an' I'll fix it slicker 'n goose grease." And he retreated while Sam and Pelatiah, gathering up their tackle and fish silently, made a wide detour and gained the rendezvous. As silently they got on board the scow of the money-diggers and, ready to shove it off if discovered by the two elder brothers, awaited the coming of the younger. Him they heard saying loudly, " I guess 'at I'd better go an' see 'f them critters don't hook the scaow," and then come threshing his way through the brush to them. He clattered over the stony beach, shoved the boat off, floundered on board, took the oars, and after a few back strokes which sent the craft well away from the shore, addressed his brothers in a tone which was not intended to reach them, " There, consarn ye !"

But their suspicions had been in some way aroused, and they came hammering down to the shore in hot haste while Sam was handing over a Spanish half dollar to the exultant Jethro.

" Come back here, you old heap, you," shouted the irate mainstay of his family, as he stooped and picked up a stone so big that his big hand could hardly grasp it ; " Come back here or I'll—" Jethro jeered at him a derisive guffaw, and the missile was thrown at the retreating boat with a cast strong enough to reach it, but it fell to one side and only splashed the occupants. A few more strokes took them beyond the reach of anything more harmful than angry words, which John and Job continued to hurl at them as, with Sam at the steering paddle, they swept around the west point of the island and headed toward the mouth of Little Otter, defined by the light green of its willowy gateway.

Jethro's brothers followed the shore, keeping the boat in sight and continually pouring after it a volley of threats, opprobrious names, and words that came as near curses as church members might venture to use.

" You'd better save your breath and keep your temper," Sam advised, " an' go tu diggin' your worms. An' when you git tu diggin' don't ye speak. 'F you du they'll move, an' you won't git 'em."

This hint that their secret was known was enough to silence them without the threat thrown after it by Jethro, whose patience was becoming exhausted. " 'F you don't shet up and stop yer sass," he shouted, resting on his oars, " I'll go right stret an' tell Annernius the hull o'— you know what, dum ye. So, there naow-ah !"

Then the island became so quiet that a party of crows faring across the bay ventured to alight there, while Jethro, whose strength was as ox-like as his motions, sent the scow surging onward with strong, slow strokes.

When with a long swash, like a restful sigh, she came to the landing, Solon and Joseph were there to welcome their friends, undemonstratively, but heartily, and to comfort them with that balm which we are ever ready to give but never to receive—" I told you so. "

The day was now too far spent for Pelatiah to get back to his evening chores, so he was easily persuaded to wait for the supper for which some hours of Crusoe life had given him a sharp appetite. Jethro was hospitably invited to remain and partake of it, and was nothing loath, improving the opportunity as one to whom such generous fare seldom came. "Dum 'em," he said, when, uncomfortably full fed, he arose from the stone table, "they'd be madder yit 'f they knowed haow much I'd hed t' eat. But they dassent kill me, an' they can't lick me, so there ah." With this fraternal comment and without a word of thanks or good-by, he departed.

"Perlite 's a pig," said Sam as the sound of their guest's departure changed from clumsy footfalls to as clumsy oar-beats. "Wal, I don't want tu say nothin' agin my breed, but it's all in the fam'ly, here, an' I will say that of all mean critters a mean Yankee is the meanest."

While Sam was making ready to transport Pelatiah on his homeward way, Antoine was heard lustily hailing the camp from the eastern shore, and Pelatiah proposed to cross the stream to that point with Sam and make his way thence through the woods, thus saving his friend the long voyage up the creek and Slang. Sam thought this inhospitable and a non-fulfilment of his promise, but Pelatiah insisted that he had had quite enough of boating for one day, and would much rather feel the solid earth under his feet. So he was landed where Antoine was waiting with a load of Canadian news that he at once began to unburden himself of.

Breaking loose from the thread of a story just begun, Pelatiah went his way into the gathering twilight of the woods.

IX.

RECONCILIATION.

PELATIAH had not been brought up in the woods to be scared by owls, as he had more than once assured himself as he stumbled along the darkening wood road, half-carrying, half trailing his big pickerel and bass, but he fancied that their hollow hoots had never sounded so like derisive laughter, "Ho! ho! ho! Ho! ho!—ho! ho!" repeated by one another till the echoes joined in the dolorous mirth. A whippoorwill, far away on the border of the forest, was not insisting on the summary chastisement of poor Will, but repeating this new culprit's name with sharp reproachful reiteration, "Pel-a-tier, Pel-a-tier, Pel-a-tier!" The trill of a toad rang in his ears like a long-drawn jeer, and the bellowing of the bull-frogs along the Slang was shaped by his fancy into solemn words of rebuke, advice, and warning, "Didn't go hum! No, no! Go hum! Go hum! Don't du it agin, agin, never agin!" Not a word of comfort for the poor fellow among all these voices of the night, that followed him out of the gloom of the woods, and, looking up to the sky, he saw the stars blinking at him with unpitying eyes.

Shellhouse Mountain, which but yesterday he had despised as a hillock that would be but a pimple on the face of old Tater Hill, now uplifted on a vague foundation of shadows and asserting itself as a bound of the visible

world, stood before him and frowned upon him like a
dark, scowling brow. The lights that dotted the highway
went out one by one, as the farm folks went to bed but a
little later than their poultry. The living world was forgetting him, or cared nothing for him, the good-for nothing
fellow who had broken his word, and Bose was barking
as if he scented a stranger. Yet it heartened him a little
when, prompted by his faint shadow, he looked over his
right shoulder and saw the thin crescent of the new moon.
In confirmation of this lucky sign, he presently discovered
a light shining from an upper window of the big white
house, Lowizy's window, he was sure, and, perhaps too
anxious to sleep, she was waiting for him. Yes, now he
saw her form, a lovely silhouette set in the frame of the
casement. She was looking for him, and he was only
restrained from calling to her for fear of arousing the
household. He would have ventured to whistle just once
if his tremulous lips had not refused to pucker. Then
the silhouette faded to a shadow and the light was put
out. As he entered the door-yard Bose ceased barking,
and came whining and panting to welcome him, and
assure him that he had, at least, one friend there, and
who, following close at his heels, superintended the hanging of the precious fish in the cool, safe corner of the
woodshed. In those happy times when tramps were unknown, farmhouse doors were never fastened at night, and
in summer were often left open, as Friend Bartlett's
kitchen door was now. So pulling off his boots at the
threshold, Pelatiah silently went in and made his way to
his bed in the kitchen chamber.

The blithe chorus of the robins had not long been ringing in the dewy freshness of the early morning, when

Pelatiah was astir an hour before any other member of the family. First he cleaned the fish so nicely that Antoine could have found no fault, and then he drove up the cows from the night pasture. He was milking his second cow when Friend Bartlett appeared with his pail and stool, and he was glad to see no shadow of displeasure on his employer's kindly face, to detect no tone of reproof in his cheery voice when he addressed him.

"Well, Peltier, thee didn't get back quite so airly as thee expected, did thee? I didn't hardly think thee would, for when I was a boy an' uster go a-fishin', if they bit, I hated ter go off an' leave 'em, an' if they didn't bite, I wanted ter wait till they did."

"Oh, I'm awf'l sorry, Mr. Bartlett, an' shameder'n I c'n live, but I couldn't help it!" and he went on explaining his mischance, forgetting to milk old Spot till she thought he had done with her and moved on. When he went to the cheese-room with two filled pails, by some lucky chance, Lowizy was there, blushing like a June rose and never handsomer than now.

"O, Peltier!" she cried, coming toward him, radiant with a pleasure that surely could not be feigned, and so shone upon him that the last icy corner of his heart melted at once. "O, Peltier! I'm dreffle glad ter see ye! I was afeared 'at you was draownded an' I never slep' one wink all night a-thinkin' on 't!"

"Would you ha' cared 'f I was draownded, Lowizy?" he asked, trembling so that his unsteady hands poured half the milk outside the strainer and a little on the floor.

"Don't ye slop!" she said, sharply, and then in a tenderer tone, "Don't ye think I would? But you never

thought o' me onct a-worryin' while you was hevin' high
jinks wi' your frien's !''

" I swan tu man !'' swore Pelatiah, as he set down his
last-emptied pail, " the' wa'n't a minute 'at I wa'n't
a thinkin' 'baout you while I was a-fishin', an' when we
was hove away on a deserlate islan', an' a wishin' 'at I
hedn't ben cross an' 'at I'd filled the wash biler for ye.
O, Lowizy, I was mean, an' I'm sorry, an' I won't never
du so agin, an' I wish't you c'ld forgive me, but I don't
s'pose you ever can.''

She could not withhold forgiveness so humbly asked.
She rushed to him with upturned face and put her arms
astride his neck, one cream-bedaubed hand holding the
dripping skimmer, the other the half filled basin, and as
the tins clashed behind his head he held her in his arms
and kissed her.

" Peltier ! Hey, Peltier ! Bring back them pails !''
Friend Bartlett shouted from the cowyard gate.

As the heavenward-soaring lark, pierced by the cruel
shot of the gunner, falls fluttering down to earth, so at
Friend Bartlett's impatient call Pelatiah dropped from the
rose-tinted clouds whereunto in delicious affright he had
been upborne, and went stumbling through the dooryard
knot-grass, while a still, small voice repeated Sam's words,
" They'll fool a feller agin an' agin.'' But his heart
whispered that this could not be fooling, and then, as he
sat down to his cow, sang inwardly to him this sweet assurance, while the dancing streams of milk kept rhythmic
time to the song that no one else in all the wide world
could hear.

At breakfast, Rebecca Bartlett's placid face beamed
kindly upon him as she said : " Thank thee, for the nice

mess o' fish thee brought, Peltier, but I'm sorry thee had such a tryin' time. We see it stormin' on the lake and felt a good deal concerned about thee, thinkin' thee might be out in a boat, and more so when thee didn't come back, for we knew thee would if thee could.''

The gloom of night was gone, its dolorous voices hushed. Sunlight flooded the earth, and the soft air was full of the joyous songs of birds. Could this world, now so full of light and joy, and warm with love and kindness, be the same that so lately frowned upon him ? He would never doubt the signs of the moon again, and never Lowizy.

When the next Sunday came, Pelatiah again declined to follow Rebecca Bartlett's suggestion that he should attend Friends' meeting. Yet he heard something of the simple service, for he was wandering with Lowizy along the western rocky slopes of Shellhouse, where, hidden by the leafy screen of the woodside, they could look forth across the pasture to the gray and brown shingled sides of the old meeting house, through whose open doors and windows came the voice of the preacher, whose spirit was moved most audibly. To-day, certainly, the green and flowery aisles of the woods were pleasanter than that barren interior, and distance softened to tunefulness the doleful cadence of the sermon.

The "young-come-ups," though a week older, had lost nothing of their pungent sweetness. In fact he, who, a week ago had thought he never could touch one again, now was sure they never tasted so good. If at times the low song of the pines seemed to voice solemnly the words, "They'll fool a feller agin an' agin," he shut his ears to it, it was not sung for him.

X.

SEINING.

THE night after Pelatiah left them, Sam, Solon, and Joseph were not lulled but tired to sleep by Antoine's interminable rehearsal of Canadian news, in which their chief interest was that it might come to an end. It was very confusing to hear that " Ma brudder-law, he'll come dead wid some small poxes," and then, " Ma brudder-law, he'll goin' bought it farm in T"ree River," and " Ma brudder-law gone work in mill in Mass'chusin," " Ma brudder-law, he'll want it ma fader an' mudder come leeve 'long wid it in Ogdenburg, where he'll go las' fall." But when some question was asked concerning the resurrection and ubiquity of this remarkable person, Antoine cried :

" O sacré ton sac' ! Ant you'll s'pose Ah'll gat more as one brudder-law. Ah'll gat more of it as Ah'll got chillens !" Poor, indeed, would be the Canuck of mature age who had not at least a dozen such relatives.

Antoine's recital of the various fortunes of his brothers-in-law was by no means finished when sleep closed the ears of his unwilling listeners, and he abruptly ended the first chapter.

The camp was hardly astir next morning, nor Antoine well out of his nest, where incubation of long stories had silently progressed, when he began to cackle over the lives and adventures of his sisters' husbands and his wife's brothers. Even the long-enduring patience of Joseph Hill could not keep that kindly man from uttering a sound that might be taken either as a groan or as a grunt caused by the exertion of stooping to light his pipe.

"I du most wish—I do' know, but I du quite," he said, as he arose and fostered with his fingers and attentively regarded the kindling spark, " 'at your sisters hedn't never merried or your womern hedn't hed no brothers, an' then you wouldn't ha' ben pestered a-tellin' 'baout 'em nor we a-listenin' !"

"It would be conjugal tu my feelin's if they wa'n't quite so numerical," Solon remarked, and when Antoine, quite unabashed by these hints, began to tell of his fifteenth " brudder-law, he'll gettin' 'long fus-rate, he'll gat two twin, t'ree tam," Sam broke out :

" Dum yer brother-in-laws ! You'll starve us tu death on 'em. We can't live on 'em. Hurry up an' cook the breakfas', an' let them set a spell !"

Whereupon Antoine fell into a fit of sulks which silenced his tongue while it increased the unnecessary banging of the frying-pan and the clattering of the tin dishes. But these were sounds which his companions had long been accustomed to and had learned to philosophically endure. Joseph Hill remarked that " it make him feel 'sif he was tu hum, an' hed tol' M'ri 'at she couldn't go tu see her mother, er go tu a fun'al ten mild off."

" Did you ever da'st tu ?" Sam asked.

" Wal, I da'st tu, but I do' know's I ra'ly ever did," Joseph replied after due consideration, while he poked the fire with a stick that might serve to relight his pipe ; " but if I hed, I know th' 'ld ha' ben jes' sech a clatteration, the stove an' things 'ould ha' ketched it."

And Solon, as one having had experience, assented. "Yes, it is the nat'ral natur of most all created creturs tu make a audible noise someway when they're mad—women, Canucks, babies, bulls, and the hull toot ; if they can't du it vocabulary, they'll hammer an' kick an' carummux. A mud turkle, naow, 'at hain't got no visible voice, 'ill cuss jest as wicked, a-snappin' his onspeechless jaws. It seems as 'ough the' wa'n't nothin' denied the comfort o' cussin', somehow."

Though Antoine vented his ill humor on his utensils, no flavor of it was imparted to the food he prepared, but on the contrary a quality that restored his good-nature before the breakfast was half eaten, and its effect on the others was such that they would have listened with patience, if not absorbed interest, to a further account of his Canadian relatives and friends.

This was to be a busy day, for to morrow they were to break camp and go at least as far as the Falls on their homeward way. For their credit as fishermen and for the pleasure of their friends at home, they must take with them fish enough to give each neighbor a mess. Danvis would expect every man of them to do his duty and bring it—a pickerel.

If the angle alone was depended on, this expectation was unlikely to be realized, for the moods of fish were uncertain. Solon and Joseph had not the acquired skill nor the gift of luck with hook and line, and Sam and Antoine could not fish for all Danvis nor the half of it. Therefore, it was decided that they should this day put their trust in the greater certainties of the silver hook and employ the fishermen who were hauling their nets every day near the mouth of Lewis Creek. Then Sam hoped he might run up that stream and try titles with some of its abundant bass, as he had more than ever wished to do since witnessing the fighting qualities of Pelatiah's Garden Island prize.

As he looked eastward from the top of the bluff beyond the broad creek and above the wall of woods, the first object that met his eye was Shellhouse Mountain, and it struck him that the outline of its long crest, rising from the north end with one short curve and another longer one to the rounded highest point, thence sloping away to the south, greatly resembled a huge fish. Not far away a kingfisher hung steadfast for a moment on vibrant wings above the shallows, then dropping like a plummet, arose almost with the upbursting splash of his plunge, and presently proclaimed his good luck with a metallic clatter of his castanets. A fishhawk, cruising vigilantly above the channel, suddenly swooped and tore from the water a prize so heavy that, in labored retreat, he barely gained the cover of the woods in time to escape the swift onslaught of an eagle, lord paramount of all air, water, and earth hereabout.

"S'posin' you tackle Shellhaouse naow," Sam said as the baffled tyrant wheeled sullenly from pursuit, "I ha' no doubt you feel big enough t' think it wouldn't be more'n your sheer if 't was a fish."

Sam accepted these omens as auspicious of a good day's fishing, verifying what he had already felt in his bones, and was in haste to be off.

He embarked in his canoe, the others in the scow. Going out of Little Otter and rounding the willowy sandpoint, the two craft fared across the bar toward the seining ground. Near them on the right curved the flat shore, marked here by willows, farther on by a pale of rushes, the border of a great marsh that was walled south and east by the ancient forest on the north, by the great water maples and button-woods of Lewis Creek, a bay of rank marsh herbage, with islands of button-bush dotting its fresh verdure with clumps of darker green. The water was so shallow, that oars and paddle often touched the bottom, crinkled with a golden net knit by sunlight and the light northern breeze.

Such voyaging was much enjoyed by Solon and Joseph, who had a wholesome dread of deep water. As the latter watched the swarms of minnows flashing their silvery sides and attended by the shadows that swam in a darker school beneath them, slipping through the tangled meshes of sunshine threads, he said : " Wal, naow, I call this a sorter sensible place for ridin' in a boat, where you c'n see what's a-goin' on onderneath of you, an' if you take a notion tu, er git tired o' ridin', er your boat gits tu cuttin' up, you c'n jest git right aout anywheres an' go afoot an' go off an' let your ol' boat cut its carlicues, or if you're a min' tu, take a holt o' the rope an' halter break it till it gits waywise, er lead it ashore. Ef I was a-goin' ter hev me a lake made a puppus, I don't b'lieve I'd hev it no deeper nowheres an' this is right here. Ye see, the' couldn't nob'dy git draownded in 't 'thaout they wanted tu bad 'nough tu lay daown, an' the' 'ld be water 'nough fer fish 'at wa'n't tu big, an' 'nough tu drink, 'thaout 'twas better'n this is."

" O, bah gosh ! Zhozeff, what you talk so foolish ?" cried Antoine, " what kan' o' lake you s'posed dat was be you'll have it ? De feesh be so scare for see you, he ain't bit. He cook hees back wid de sun in de summer, in de winter he be freeze wid de ice. Haow you'll s'pose stimboat goin' travelled, if de water so thin he was here?

Haow you'll s'pose ma brudder-law comin' from Canada in hees bateau nex' fall for git happle? Hein? He'll comin' 'f he can git ma nudder brudder-law come long of it. Ma fader hees tol' me."

"O, wal, Antwine, the fish 'ould git tame arter a spell an' when the' backs git tew hot they c'ld turn over, an' they 'ld keep good in the ice an' be 's good 's new in the spring. An' I hain't got no steamboats nor bateaux, I like tu know the airth is under me an' the water not so deep 'at like 'nough it's Chiny water on t'other side. But you c'n hev this lake jist czackly as it is."

"Yes, sah! jes' as he was, dis pooty good lake, Ah tol' you. An', seh," swelling with the pride of proprietor-ship, "ant you'll know de fus' man dat fan' dis lake was Ferrenchman! An' it gat hees name too-day! Champlain! Dat ant Yankee name, don't it?"

"Was he a brother in-law o' yourn?" Sam asked, being within short earshot.

"No, seh, 'cause he'll ant, 'cause he'll dead great many while 'go. But prob'ly 'f he'll leeve two t'ree honded year an' see ma seester Marie, he'll was be; O, she'll han'somes, more han'somes as Ursule! More han'somes Ah was."

"The contower of her complexion an' featur's must be most superguberous," Solon remarked.

"What I'm a wonderin' is," said Sam, "if the' is anybody in Canady 'at hain't your brother-in law, Antwine. Seem's 'ough we'd hear'd of 'nough on 'em tu fill it chuck full, an' some on 'em has got craowded aout int' the States."

"Wal, sah, boy," Antoine answered, dropping his oars and making a pretended computation on his fingers,

"Ah'll b'lieve dey was two, prob'ly t'ree. Dere was de priest in Saint Cesare an' ma aunt, an'—Ah'll freegit who was tudder one. But prob'ly you'll ant b'lieved Ah'll gat some brudder law! You'll come to Canada 'long to me Ah'll showed you, boy."

"Them 'ere clams," said Joseph, still contemplating the bottom, "must be turrible happy creturs. Never in no hurry, never wantin' to go nowhere, knowin' 't they couldn't git there 'f they did. Tu hum, wherever they git hove tu, all alone an' never gittin' scolded. I do' know, but it don't seem 's 'ough they could cuss, Solon, 'f they hed 'casion tu."

"You protrude your finger int' the' maouth an' see 'f they don't profane with a audible feelin'. The masculine paower o' their jaws is astonishin'."

"I wonder if the tarnal things is good t' eat," said Joseph, yet interested in the unio with which the sands were populous, and everywhere marked with the tracks of their slow and apparently purposeless travel, "er whether they wasn't made for nothin' only enjyin' life."

"Ah'll try for heat it, but Ah'll ant never heat it," said Antoine. "He'll tender lak jim-rubbit,* an' ta'se mos' so good. Ah'll bile one of it two nhour, then Ah'll chaw it two nhour, an' he'll ant got no difference Ah can feel of it! Moosrat heat it an' tink dey can' be no better, an' dey'll said sheephead feesh heat it, but Ah do' know 'f he can brek hees shuck, me. He can have it he'll want it. Ah'll ant quarly for heem wid it. Here we'll was:"

The scow swept prostrate the rushes and made a landing that it might feel at home in, the canoe was beached

---

* India-rubber.

alongside and the party landed. Before them a long in-
curved beach stretched away to the north, ending at a
rocky point. The waves of immemorial years had thrown
up the sand into a low breastwork that resisted now their
own assaults on the marsh behind it, wherein flourished
a rank growth of rushes, sedges, and other aquatic plants,
nourished by the undisturbed muck of their own decay.
So close along the waterline that their wave-washed roots
were spread like a tangled net upon the sand stood an
irregular row of great water maples with tower-like trunks,
buttressed, loop-holed, mossed, and lichened by age,
scarred by the battering rams of ice that the lake had hurled
against them, with tops wind-torn and decaying, but yet
sending up new smooth trunks and abroad with youthful
vigor a graceful ramage of branches and fresh leafage as if
they might endure for a thousand years. They are gone,
now, and their ancient sites are marked only by rotting
stumps on the barren unshaded shore. A meaner and
deadlier foe than time, or wind, or waves has sapped their
foundations, and years ago they were peddled out at so
much a cord by their avaricious owner, who begrudged
even the sands the shadow of a tree.

There were two gangs of seiners on the beach. The
three men composing one gang were Canadians, those of
the other Sam at once recognized as his unpleasant Garden
Island acquaintances, who it would seem had not yet
unearthed Arnold's hidden treasure or were masking their
new opulence with this humble avocation. However it
might be, he had no desire for further intercourse with
them, and he and his party at once began negotiations
with Antoine's compatriots.

Their chief was an old fellow of large build, of greatest

dimensions at the hips, tapering thence upward to his ears
and downward to his bare feet. It was from the interior
of this widest region, apparently, that his broken English
was laboriously upheaved to the surface with intermittent
guttural grunts. His face bore a grim expression of good-
nature and also a pock-marked red nose that much resembled in shape and color an immense strawberry. His
younger assistants, who were clearing the net of sticks,
weeds, and clams, and folding it on the broad stern of
their scow, appeared to be his nephews, for they frequently
addressed him as Onc' Theophile.

"Haow de du?" Sam saluted him.

"Ough! How do," Uncle Theophile grunted in
labored response, and then glibly gave in French an order
to one of his nephews.

"Hevin' any luck tu-day?" Sam inquired with an assumed languor of interest.

"Make, ough, one haul, ough; gat dat," Uncle Theophile answered, pointing to a bushel basket half full of
pike-perch and pickerel.

"Wal, that'll du tol'lable well," Sam said after tilting
the basket till some of the bottom fish were exposed and
critically examining the gaping mass, "haow much be
you goin' tu tax us for, wal, say four haul?"

"Ough, twanty-fav cen' haul," Theophile answered,
coiling the elm-bark seine ropes on the beach, "fo' haul,
ough, dollar."

"Prehaps," said Solon, "'at them other angulars aout
yunder hain't so pecuniary in the' charges. Le's go an'
see them."

Theophile comprehended the spirit, if not the matter of
the proposal.

glittered on the gray sand in a great heap of mother-of-pearl, emerald, silver, and gold.

" Dah, seh !" said Antoine, proudly, when the net was emptied, " ant Ah'll mek it pooty good hauls? Ah'll de boy can ketch de feesh ev'ree way Ah'll man to ketched it ! De hookanline, de spear, de nets, Ah'll gat no different of it me !"

Though no one else claimed the credit or even a share of it, all were much gratified by the successful haul except the Canadians who had really made it. They seemed to feel no pride in it, but rather to begrudge having given their patrons so much for their money, and went sullenly about clearing and making ready the net.

" What's the matter ails your friends, Antwine?" Sam asked, noticing their sour looks.

" Wal, seh, Sam, Ah do' know 'f prob'ly it ant mad 'cause Ah'll ketched more feesh he was. "

" Like 'nough ; I never thought on't, though."

" But Ah'll ant to blem 'f Ah'll know more as he was, ant it? Dat was way Ah'll was be mek, 'sides leetly maght Ah'll was larn."

A lumber wagon, whose jolting course across the fields had for some time been heard, now appeared, grinding its slow way over the sand to them. It was freighted with half a dozen back-countrymen eager for fish, who, seeing this seine employed, halted near the treasure-seekers and began negotiations with them. These were presently seen preparing to make a haul, while the new comers unhitched their horses and fastened them to the hinder end of the wagon to eat their bait of hay in the shadow of the maples. This acquisition of patronage by their rivals further increased the ill-humor of the Canadians, and the sight of a big jug taken from the wagon and passed around, added bitterness to their feelings.

"I tell ye what," said Joseph, thirstily watching the passage of the social stoneware, "them ere fellers knows haow tu go a-fishin'."

"Shaw!" said Sam, "nob'dy never fished no better nor hunted no better for bein' full o' sperrits."

"But," argued Joseph, "if they don't hev no luck, they c'n hev some fun, an' they're kinder prepared to stan' disapp'intment, seems 's 'ough they wus. An' jes' look at that ere feller 'at's got a holt on't naow, the one 'at fetched you an' Peltier f'm the islan', hain't he? Sam Hill! won't he never le' go on't? I'll bate his mother never licked him for a-holdin' his breath. I don't b'lieve she ever did, not so much as she'd ortu anyway. It's a pity to waste good sperrits a wettin' sech mean sile. I c'n smell it clearn here an' it's ol' Medfo'd!" he said, sorrowfully, as he sniffed the favoring north breeze.

"Oh! don't feel so bad, Joseph," said Sam, "like 'nough 't ain't nothin' but water arter all or mebby cider."

"The' hain't nob'dy dum'd fool 'nough tu fetch water tu the lake, I don't b'lieve, an' if it's cider thet's better'n water, the bes' way o' keepin' apples the' is. But 't ain't, it smells julluck a mad bumblebee."

"An' it's wus 'n a nest full o' mad bumblebees when it gits top on ye," said Sam, whose poor father had suffered much from the touch of that which biteth like a serpent and stingeth like an adder.

"Ah'll bet you head!" cried Antoine, who had been intently scrutinizing the new arrival, "dat was Onc' Lasha hol' Bob hawse! Yes, seh! An' dat beeg feller was dat long John Dark dat bought it w'en Ah'll want bought it.

Hoorah, Zhozeff, le's we'll go visit dat hol' hawse. Ah do' know 'f he'll ant give us introuduce of dat jawg prob'ly, hein !''

" Wal, ta' keer 'at you don't get tu well 'quainted. An' naow you c'n go ahead an' git your tother hauls, an' I'll gwup this ere crik an' see 'f I c'n ketch a bass. I'm spilin' for a tussle wi' one on 'em.''

" Wal, naow, Samwell,'' said Joseph, "seems 's 'ough you was foolish tu go off an' leave sech fishin' 's this for the onsartinty o' not ketchin' nothin'. It don't seem 's 'ough you c'ld find no better fun 'n this.''

" It's a good 'nough way tu get fish, but 't ain't no gre't fun fur me. The best part o' fishin' is lackin'. The' hain't no fair play 'baout it, an' it makes me feel kinder mean.''

" Wal, naow, Samwell,'' said Joseph, pondering, while he searched for his pipe in every pocket but the one it was in, "seems 's 'ough 'f I was a fish, an' it mos' seems 's 'ough I was a-drinkin' nothin' but water, 'at I'd livser be swep' up kinder easy in a net wi' a hull lot for comp'ny in misery 'an tu be fooled wi' a worm or suthin' wi' a hook inside on't, an' then hev my jaw half tore off, julluck ol' Darkter Wood pullin' a back tooth.''

" I wa'n't considerin' on't f'm the fish side,'' said Sam, " but fish does hev jes' much fun a-foolin' us as we du them. Why I've seen an ol' Beav' Medder traout laugh clean tu the end of his tail when he'd peeled my hook bare naked, an' I b'lieve them 'ere 'Swagos is up tu jes' 's much fun 's a traout is.''

" Oh, wal,'' said Joseph, who, having found his pipe and got it between his teeth, was now exploring his pockets with both hands for his tobacco, " if you're only a-goin'

—where in Sam Hill is my terbarker?—goin' to give the fish some fun, go ahead ; I guess they'll hev more'n you will, but I d' know, mebby they won't be there. They never be when I go a-fishin' erless they stan' off an' gawp like a fif' calf 't hain't got no te't."

XI.

SUNGAHNEE-TUK.

WHILE his friends' attention was divided in watching the progress of their own haul and that of their neighbors, Sam departed in his canoe, paddling up the lower reaches of the stream, where the dipping willow-tips scarcely bent to or rippled the slow current, and the reflections of trunks and leaves stood motionless on the glassy stream till the boat's wake set them a-quiver, as its slanted bars of golden light climbed rushes, ferny shores, and gray tree-trunks and then dissolved in green and gold among the sunlit leaves, or a gar-pike, watching with wicked eyes the advancing prow, stirred them with the slow ripple of his sullen retreat. Then a muskrat voyaged from one shore with a freight of weeds trailing from his jaws and undulating with his wake, then sank with it to the underwater doorway of his home and left his wake fading in slow pulsations above him. A green heron, startled from an overhanging branch, went flapping awkwardly along the narrow lane of sky while his distorted double flapped more awkwardly along the lane of water.

There was no sign nor sight of the outer world but the frayed stripe of blue sky overhead, one glimpse of Camel's Hump set in darker blue against it, and, seen for an instant through a break in the green and gray wall of trees, Mt. Philo's crown of pines and shorn sunlit slopes.

The solitude was very pleasant to this simple lover of nature who in certain moods was happiest when alone, yet not alone, for he felt a perfect companionship with the woods and their inhabitants close about him. There were other fishers than he but for whose busier plying of their craft he might have forgotten why he had come, so satisfied was he with the lazy voyaging. A heron stood with poised spear in an outlet of the marsh waiting for luck with an angler's patience. An alert mink slid from the bank, cleaving the water with an almost noiseless plunge as if he were a brown arrow shot into it. Not so a kingfisher, who proclaimed from afar his coming, just swerved from his jerky course for the boat, then hung for a moment in quivering poise and dashed down so close that the spray of his noisy plunge fell in splashing drops not twice the canoe's length from her prow, then flew to a raft of driftwood and perching upon its topmost stick bragged as loudly of his minnow as Antoine might of an eel.

Sam had passed one landing which showed in its forked rests for poles, brands, and ashes of fires, heads and scales of fish, much use as a fishing place. Now he came to another where the stream bent from north to west, just above a little islet, whose willows, great elms, water maples, and one noble button-wood were bound in a tangled cordage of grape-vines. Here were the same signs of frequent fishing. An old boat that had long since made its last fishing and trapping trips lay rotting at the bank, with fish at home under its sunken stern and remnants of muskrats' recent feasts on its mossy thwarts. Landing here he fished from the shore, and having no bait but worms, for a while caught only perch. These bit vigorously enough to raise high expectations, sadly disappointed when the brief spurt

of resistance was over and the fish came swinging ashore.
But when such trivial warfare ceased for a while and there
came at last, after a brief toying with the bait, a downright
tug and then a strong up-stream sweep of the line that
made it sing and the cedar pole trembled to the shrill song
as it bent in his grasp, Sam felt assured that he was con-
tending with a bass without the proof presently given.
The water was smitten underneath, shivered into crystal
drops as the gallant fish shot thrice its length above the
surface, raining crystals from every fin till the circling
wavelets of upburst and plunge met. Though Sam's
weapons were of clumsy strength, he fought his antagonist
fairly as he often had large trout with lighter tackle, not
heaving him out overhead as boys do sunfish, but tiring
him out with the long, uncertain struggle which, if we are
to believe the only testimony that we ever hear, is as much
enjoyed by the fish as by the scientific angler.

"There," said he, when he had gently lifted the exhausted bass ashore, "you didn't git away, did ye? It
mos' seems as if you'd orter, but I guess I'm glad you
didn't. By the gre't horn spoon ! You're harnsome as
a pictur' an' you fit like a coon !" If there were other
bass here they scorned such humble fare as worms, and
after offering in vain the finest in his box, Sam re-em-
barked and voyaged farther up stream. There was a
stronger current to make way against, running between
higher banks, overhanging in a fringed network of roots
of old trees that shaded them, elms with great buttressed
trunks, water maples so nearly like them in form that it
needed a second glance to assure one that they were not
elms ; oaks that had showered down mast to feed wood-
ducks in a hundred autumns, clumps of basswood, lusty

sons of the dead giant whose mouldering stump they stood around, and here and there towering button-woods, shining spectre like among the shadows, more like ghosts of other departed giants of the forest than like living trees.

Stream and banks beautified each other with shadow, with mirrored greenness of leaves, graceful bend of trunks and limbs, with quivering rebound of sunbeams from ripples again and again repeated till they flickered out in the translucence of pools or the gilded green of leaves. Every reach disclosed new beauty and promised more beyond when the glitter of the stream flashed forth from the shadows of a bend.

One who sees it now for the first time, can hardly imagine how beautiful Sungahneetuk was then. One who saw it then and now beholds its abomination of desolation, the shrunken current crawling between banks avariciously shorn of all their trees, of their last green fleece of willows, worthless dead, but priceless to him who loves the beauty that the hand of God has wrought, can but wonder why some awful retribution has not fallen upon the spoilers, nor can he withhold his own feeble curse, wishing that he had the power of God to enforce it.

A railroad in Vermont was almost undreamed of then, and there was no shadow of coming destruction brooding over the peaceful woods and waters, nor did the thought enter Sam's mind to mar his enjoyment of the sylvan scene, that it ever would be changed but by growing older, nor lose anything but by the natural decay that in some way compensates for all it takes.

Now and then, where the bottom faded out of sight in a swirl of dull green under tangled threads of sunshine, he invited the bass to taste his worms, but they would not, though he frequently saw them hanging near his bait on waving fins, then moving away in leisurely disdain.

Presently he descried on the bank above him another angler who was just slipping a fine bass on to the withe that already held a dozen or more. When he had again tethered them in the edge of the stream, he took up his pole and stole cautiously along, carefully scanning the water. Sam landed and followed, watching him in the hope of learning something from one so successful, if he were not so by sheer luck. As Sam drew near the man saluted him with a nod given over his shoulder, showing a face beaming with good humor, for how could a man who had caught a dozen bass wear a sour visage ?

"I kinder wanter see haow you du it," Sam said in a low voice. "I never ketched but one 'Swago in my life."

The fisherman looked at him in pitying wonder, then laughed a little and beckoned him nearer. He pointed to a little basin scooped in the sandy bottom and cleared of every large pebble and water-logged weed and stick. A bass hovered always near it and sometimes over it, and now charged furiously upon a perch that had intruded on the sacred precincts, pursued it out of sight, and in an instant returned. When a sodden water weed drifted into the precious basin, she seized it before it could lodge there, and, carrying it beyond the down-stream rim, dropped it where it was borne away by the current.

"That ere 's a bed," said Sam's new acquaintance. "Naow, see here," and sheathing his hook with an un-looped worm, he dropped it quietly a little above the bed and let it drift down on it. The fish rushed at it, seized it, and darted away with it, but before she had time to drop it the angler struck sharply, and almost in the same instant landed her on the grass behind him.

"Thet's the way tu du it," the fisherman said, as he unhooked the fish.

"Wal, it does take the rag off'm the bush for quick work," said Sam ; "but I don't ezackly git a holt on 't. Does these here 'Swagos live in them places all the time ?"

"Laws a massy, no ! Them's the spawnin' beds, where they lays the' aigs. Don't you see this one's just ready tu lay her'n ?" and Sam now noticed that the bass was profusely voiding spawn in her struggles.

"She'd stick tu it like teazles till they was hatched an' a spell arter, an' not 'low nothin' on 't. Then they clear aout, an' arter the middle o' July you won't see a 'Swago bass in the crik till 'long airly in the fall. Then the' 'll be some little fellers not bigger'n rock bass."

"Wal," said Sam, with a sigh of disappointment, "I allers thought it was a pleggid mean trick tu ketch traout on the' beds, an' I guess this hain't no better."

"But it ketches 'em, an' that's what a feller wants," argued his companion. "Come along an' we'll find another bed, an' you try it once, jest for greens."

"Wal, I do' know but I will jest once to see 'f I can," and they went slowly along the bank till another bed and its guardian were discovered.

Sam did exactly as he had seen his instructor do, and soon was fast to a good three-pounder. This, however, was not torn from the water as the other had been — though the guide shouted, "Slat 'er aout ! You got 'er hooked good. Slat 'er aout !"—but was vanquished in a fair fight and then drawn gently to the shore. Sam un- hooked her tenderly without taking her from the water, then watched her as, lying on her side, she feebly waved her fins, then stood still a moment as if dazed by the recovery of freedom, and then, as she surged away and vanished in a flash, he addressed her :

"Good-by, marm. Nex' time you see a worm in your nest you poke it aout wi' your nose."

"What in thunder d'd ye let 'er go for?" his companion demanded in a vexed tone, when his astonishment found other expression than a blank stare.

"That's the way t' du it," Sam answered quietly ; "I jist wanted tu show you haow."

"Wal, I swan ! you mus' be a dum'd fool !"

"That's what I've tol' myself a hunderd times," Sam replied rather sadly, but with good nature, "but I can't help it, an' so I hain't tu blame for it. Wal, I guess I'll be goin'. I'm 'bleeged tu ye for what you've showed me an' tol' me. Good-by."

Looking back as he turned the first bend he saw the bass-catcher still staring after him in motionless amazement, but could not hear him saying to himself, "Some poor crazy creetur 'at orter be in Brattleburrer ! Nex' thing he'll be draowndin' hisself !"

Past landing, island and quiet shores the canoe slid down stream in greater solitude than it had voyaged upward. The kingfisher had ceased his clatter, the full-fed mink fished no more, the heron had flown to his mate in the tall pines, and the muskrat was asleep in his burrow. There was a sluggish stir of life when the turtles slid off the logs with a clump and an unctuous splash, and in the lazy float of myriad insects drifting against the sunlight like a veil of gauze in the unfelt wafts—a suggestion of life somewhere in the boom of a bittern far away in the marshes, in bird songs sung in distant meadows. Smooth, even swells from the lake barred the channel of the last reach with glassy undulations, that slowly heaved up and down the broken reflections of clouds and trees and stirred the rushes with a whispering rustle. Now an azure band of the lake was disclosed, and Garden Island, shining against the shadowed steeps of Split Rock Mountain. Then the talk and laughter of the seining party was heard faintly, then louder as he drew nearer, and presently Sam landed and was with them.

The later draughts of the net had not been quite so successful as the first, and this giving of less for what they received had had a happy effect on Uncle Theophile and his nephews, and as Solon, Joseph, and Antoine were quite satisfied with what they had got for their money, the utmost good humor prevailed. Sam was derided for the small visible result of his expedition, but he had brought back much that his companions could not see, nor would have cared for could they see, wherewith he was too well content to mind their jeers.

Dart and his friends had good luck with the money-diggers' seine, which was yet being hauled for them, while they took their ease on a log of driftwood eating their late dinner of fried fish.

" Hello, Lovel ! haow du you taller * these days?" Dart accosted Sam, as he sauntered over to their wagon to have a closer look at old Bob. "Come an' ha' some grub with us, won't ye? Lots on 't—sech as 't is."

" No, thank ye, I hain't no 'casion. I jest wanter see the ol' hoss a minute. Him and his'n 's ol' frien's o'

---

* Tallow.

mine. The ol' feller 's slick as an auter,'' Sam said, patting the shining black side of the venerable beast, who gave him a low whinny of recognition.

'' Wal, he hain't starvin', an' I guess he hain't turrible sorry 'at he lives 'long wi' Dart stiddy your Canuck over there. Say, Lovel, the's a jug of O-be-joyf'l under the buff'lo, pull it aout an' take a snort ; I ess it chippers yit. 'Tain't none o' Hamner's hoss medicine an' 't won't kill ye in yer tracks ; take a holt.''

'' No, thank ye, I hain't dry,'' Sam said.

'' Hain't ? Wal, it allers makes me dry tu go fishin', kinder sympathizin' wi' the poor critters I've ketched, I s'pose,'' Dart said as he got upon his feet, brushing the crumbs from his broad breast and wiping his mouth. '' But I don't go often. 'F I did, an' eat 's many 's I hev tu-day, the' wouldn't be no fish. If you won't take nothin' solid nor wet, hev a little smoke,'' and opening a big blue paper of tobacco, he offered it to Sam.

'' Ben here a week hevin' fun alive, Briggs an' mongst 'em tells me. Wish 't I'd knowed it afore. Didn't know ye wa'n't t' hum till I seen ye, but I hain't seen nob'dy f'm your way in a fortnit,'' Dart went on when they had lighted their pipes and seated themselves on the wagon-tongue. '' Got fish-hungry an' thought we'd come daown an' fill up 'fore hoein'. That 'ere's Putnam ; mebby you do' know him wi' ol' close on. Do' know why he didn't put on his Sunday-go-tu-meetin's tu come fishin', but he's got his thirty-five-dollar rifle in the waggin, the Lord knows what for, wropped up in tew blankets. Oh, say, hain't that 'ere young Gove livin' somewhere 'raound here ? Thunder in the winter ! 'F you didn't make the all-firedest shot 'at ever I see. Seventy-five rod if 't was a foot !''

"You mean tu Hamner's shootin' match?" said Sam, trying to wear a look of innocence; "I didn't shoot no turkey, it was Peltier."

"Oh, beeswax! You go tu grass!" cried the giant, giving Sam a gentle whack on the shoulders that nearly knocked him off the wagon-tongue. "Don't ye s'pose I c'n tell the mark o' the Ol' Ore Bed? Beeswax!" Then he arose and dragged the jug from its seclusion. "Come! Take suthin'; I ben wantin' tu treat ye ever sence, for that shot done me more good 'n a quart."

"Thank ye jest as much as if I drinked a quart, but I don't never drink nothin'."

"Ye don't never? Wal, the least mite in the world won't hurt ye. If you live 's long 's I hope ye will, you'll git awf'l dry," said Dart, pulling out the corn-cob stopple and swinging the jug to his lips over his arm. "An' here's a-hopesin' 'at you will. I don't see," reseating himself after tucking the jug in its nest, "haow on airth you c'n stan' it wi' that Canuck o' your'n. He knows so much he makes a feller feel like a tarnal fool. This ere ol' puke 'at's a-haulin' for us knows more 'n he orter. Ben tellin' me 'tween hauls haow 't he'd a spellin' book —bate he can't spell baker—all planned aout, an' fust he knowed aout come Webster's, julluk what his'n was goin' tu be! Then he said to wait a spell till the steamboat went 'long an' it 'ould scare all the fish in the lake in here an' we'd get the almightydest haul! But your Mister Antwine come over an' sot aout tu tell this old dickshinary more 'baout fishin' 'an he'd ever dreamed on, and both of 'em got madder 'n settin' hens. It was fun for us, only the bilin'·over consait made us feel smaller 'n was comf'table, I du b'lieve 'at these Yankeefied Ca-

nucks thinks 'at the Almighty has tu ask some one on 'em
every mornin' what He'd orter du that day. An' each
one on 'em thinks he'll be the nex' one ast, an' cal'lates
tu be a leetle might ahead in tellin'. Blast 'em ! I wish 't
the' was a wall 'twixt the States an' Canady so high 'at
nothin' but angels could fly over it ! Mighty few o' these
creeturs we'd see then.''

" Wal, Antwine ain't no angel, do' know 's he ever will
be much o' one,'' Sam admitted, but loyal to his comrade, added in his behalf, " Arter all, I druther hev a
dozen sech Canucks as him, or that ol' Duffy, 'an tu hev
one sech Yankee as them 'at 's haulin' for you, jest as full
o' ign'ance an' consait as any Canuck wi'aont no fun nor
no humern streak in 'em but what a hawg's got. They
be dum'd hawgs, they eat like 'em an' act like 'em an'
I'll bate they got brussles on the' backs longer 'n your
finger.''

"Oh, I don't dote on 'em,'' said Dart, "they ain't
mine. I'm only usin' on 'em. But we've got them an'
tew many sech an' can't help it. But it seems 'ough we
hedn't orter ketch the slops o' all creation as we du.''

So they drifted into talk concerning national affairs ; but
belonging to the same political party, there was not difference enough in their views to create an interesting warmth.
In town politics, too, they found each other holding the
same opinion, that their last year's representative "hedn't
ortu die a ye'rlin','' but should be re-elected this year.
Then the seine came in, and less important matters gave
way to the excitement of this event.

There was a heavy job of fish-cleaning and packing to
be disposed of before the morrow's departure, and time
and tide and Uncle Tyler would wait for no man, so Sam

and his comrades bade farewell to their townsmen and voyaged across the bay to camp.

There on the flat shore, under the willows, jack-knives were plied till the sands were silvered with the incessant shower of scales that only ceased falling when the grounded star of Split Rock shed its ray across the darkening lake, mingling its steadfast beam with the fading reflections of the sky's afterglow.

XII.

BREAKING CAMP.

The cobwebs of mist on the marshes had not caught a sunbeam when the camp was astir next morning, for the smoke of its fire arose earlier than the sun, that had only gilded the tree-tops above it when breakfast was ready. The meal was eaten in unwonted silence. There were no plans proposed for the day's sport, for there was to be no sport, and no one attempted to joke, for though the prospect of getting home was pleasant to men who had seldom been so long away from it, there was some heaviness of spirit attending the last of these days of care-free life, days without beginnings and endings of chores, nor filled with worry nor weary toil, days of hand-to-mouth living and such primitive unthought of to-morrow as the heart of the best-tamed man loves and yearns for when its last drop of old, wild blood awakes as it sometimes will, and tingles through his civilized veins. This uneliminated atom still holds us to kinship with nature, and though it may not be the best part of us, without it we should be worse than we are. He who loses all love for our common mother is, indeed, a wretched being, poorer than the beasts.

When breakfast was eaten, the frying-pan, kettle, and tin plates were cleaned as they had not been before since leaving the home cupboards, for they were soon to undergo the inspection of housewifely eyes, which the glamour of a hundred pickerel would not blind to the imperfections of man's careless or unskilful scullionry.

"I tell ye what," said Joseph Hill, as he scraped away with a clam-shell at the bottom layer of a week's accumulation of burned grease, "I'm a-goin' tu tell M'ri 'at we hedn't got no soap, an' the water here is hard, 'nough on't an' tew much, but it's hard an' won't take a holt o' grease, no mor'n it does yer stomerk."

"The way 'at oliogernous grease conjoles in a dish when it ketches it away f'm hum is suthin' beyond my misapprehension," said Solon, while he swabbed a plate with a stick of firewood. "It's suthin' 'at nothin' but the female mind o' womern c'n rassle with. Consarn the dishes! Let's sink 'em in the crik, accidental."

"Then we'd ketch it wus," said Joseph, as he began scouring his frying-pan with a stone. "I druther send this an' stay myself, 'an tu go hum wi'eout it. M'ri's allers tellin' how 't her gran'ther, I don't know but 't was her gran'mother, fetched it from C'nnect'cut an' cooked basswood leaves in 't in the scase year.* Sam Hill, you take it, grease an' sut an' all, an' leave me here!'

Antoine, on his knees scouring knives and forks by thrusting them into the earth, said :

"Wal, Ah don' care for me, 'cause you see, boy, Ah'll was be de cook an' Ah'll ant risponsibilitee for de clean, hein, Solem, ant it?"

"Wal," said Sam, wiping out the kettle with a handful of leaves and packing a dirty shirt and a pair of socks in it, "I hain't responsible tu nob'd'y."

---

* A season when all crops failed, and the early settlers of Vermont were reduced to pitiable straits, was long remembered as the Scarce year.

"But your time's a-comin', young man, an' you wanter be gittin' ready for 't. H. P. is the fust letters of her name, an' she hain't thick under the nail an' won't be when the's a L. sot tu 'em. You'll see!" said Joseph, and his words had a portentous ring as he delivered them into the frying-pan held close before his face while he anxiously inspected its interior. "I r'aly du b'lieve 'at I c'n see iron, leastways I've got daown tu signs o' the fust breakfus. If folks only hed sense 'nough tu du the cookin' on sticks an' coals an' hot stuns an' eat off'm chips an' birch bark, they 'ld take more comfort in livin', seems 'ough they would. If they didn't hev quite so much present enj'yment, they wouldn't hev so much dread o' the futur'. Anyways, I wish 't this dum'd ol' fryin'-pan hed stayed in C'nnect'cut if M'ri's gran'ther an' gran'-mother 'd hed tu eat the' browse raw. Seems 'ough I did, most."

To Sam occurred the happy thought of taking the dishes down to the lake shore. There, with the abundance of sand and water, the labor of cleansing went on more satisfactorily to the men, but greatly to the discomfort of as many sandpipers. These flitted back and forth past them on down-curved wings or stood astilt in the shallow verge, jerking out cries of alarm with every beat of their wings or tilt of their slender bodies.

About the middle of the forenoon, Sam looking upstream from the camp, where he was busy packing blankets and outfit and more odds and ends than he remembered bringing, descried a boat in the farthest bend. At first it seemed stationary, with oars rising and falling in purposeless strokes, like a great waterbug waving its antennæ for the mere sake of motion. But it was drawing nearer; the red flannel back of the rower's vest could now be made out, and the rise and fall of his straw hat, and the thump, squeak, and splash of his oars could be heard, and the surge of the water before the broad bow of the scow. And then forsaking the long curve of the channel and striking right across the marshy cape, that is half water and half weeds, it headed for the mouth of the creek. Sam was certain enough of the rower's identity to shout to his comrades that Uncle Tyler was coming.

They went to meet him at the landing, when gaping with his deaf stare at his course, though he who is known as Time was steering for him, he sent the scow ashore with a final stroke. Time's salutation shouted at the top of his voice was, " Any of you fellers got any terbarker fer this ol' critter? He begged the last mossel 't I hed an hour ago."

Uncle Tyler took his pipe from the seat beside him, knocked the ashes out on the gunwale, and came rheumatically ashore with his left hand extended.

" Massy sakes alive ! I sent up tu the store for some by Sargent's boy, but he forgot it ! That tarnal boy can't never remember nothin', an' I'd orter knowed better'n tu sent by him."

" I'm glad it wa'n't you 'at forgot for oncte," said Joseph, who by a lucky chance had at the first attempt hit upon the right pocket and handed over his last depleted paper of long-cut. Uncle Tyler was soon comforting himself with what most mitigated his chronic unhappiness, a pipeful of what it pleased him to call " borrered terbarker."

" Naow hurry up an' be spry," he said, " for I'd orter be tu hum a-workin' in my gardin."

Time explained that he had come to steer for Uncle Tyler, and to get Gage's boat, which he was willing to steer up the creek, if some one would row it. As for his rowing that was out of the question, for it made him sweat to row. Sam freely offered him the services of Solon or Joseph, either of whom would certainly do their share of sweating at the oars.

"Them fellers?" asked Uncle Tyler, who could hear some things much better than he could others, and now glared balefully on his companions in the previous voyage hither, "Massy sakes! They'll row ye int' the woods, or cross lots, wi' the' hawin' an' geein'! Do' know one eend of a bwut f'm t'other!"

"Haow is anybody tu, special in the case o' one o' these 'ere femaline boats which one end 's the fact smile o' t'other?" Solon demanded, for he would rather suffer the pains of rowing than such disparagement of his skill and knowledge. But Joseph did not resent it, and only said, regretfully:

"I'm 'feared you're right, Uncle Tyler. We can't row. We wantu awf'l bad, but we can't; leastways, I can't wi'aout studyin' on 't more. Ha' some more ter-barker, won't ye?"

It has not been told who rowed that boat up the Little River of Otters, nor whether it ever reached its home port.

Brother Foot's camp-meeting tent had been taken down and packed, and with all their other effects and the box of salted fish put on board the scow, and they were ready to depart; but Sam had forgotten something, which obliged him to revisit the site of the camp. He was ashamed to tell it was only for a last look.

The downfall of noontide sunlight splashed the floor of

the woods with gold around silhouettes of branches, twigs, and leaves, bent over the rocks and crinkled along the last year's leaves they were laid upon. Between leaves, branches, and tree-trunks, were shown, in fantastic shapes, patches of sky and lake, and all the sunlit outer world. Birds sang blithely of their happy life, and mingled with their songs came from far away sounds of the life and stir of the world, and yet this place seemed lifeless.

How lonesome and forsaken it was ! The carpet of old brown leaves worn by frequent footsteps down to the black mould of dead years, strewn with tobacco paper, broken pipes, and fish-bones, the castaway ridge-pole of the tent lying like a fallen roof-tree athwart the matted bed of cedar twigs whereon they had dreamed dreams pleasanter than life, so deserted now that a chipmonk ventured to explore it. It seemed to Sam almost like the ruins of a house wherein he had dwelt for years.

For old acquaintance' sake he tried to light his pipe in the ashes of the fireplace, but the last ember was dead and only exhaled a faintly pungent odor of smoke.

" But I'm comin' agin !" he said, and as he hurried down the steep footpath, a vireo sang behind him as if to call him back.

XIII.

AT THE FORGE VILLAGE.

On the afternoon of the next day, the wagon bearing the fishermen and their camping outfit made its lumbering entry into the street of the straggling hamlet known to all Danvis folk as The Village, when the horses halted in front of the store, more in obedience to the custom of their lives than to the long-drawn persuasive "whoa!" that Joseph Hill uttered. When they had almost come to a stand-still, most of the inhabitants had become aware of the arrival, and hastened forth to welcome their townsmen, now safely returned from adventure in foreign parts. The storekeeper, atilt on the hinder legs of his chair, absorbed in the latest New York paper but little more than a week from the press, came down with a resounding bump of his boots and the forelegs of the chair when, glancing over the top of his sheet, he saw who the newcomers were, and descended to greet them, carefully folding and pocketing his precious paper as he went down the steps. His clerk deserted a customer, a boy who was endeavoring to negotiate the exchange of an egg for a fish-hook, and hurried out to the edge of the stoop to look at the fishermen and their fish, whither his customer followed him, and being a born angler as well as a boy, could not forbear climbing the wagon to feast his eyes upon the monsters of Champlain. Observing him, Sam at once recognized a younger brother of the gentle craft and the only son of Widow Wiggins.

" Here, bub," he said, taking a goodly pickerel from the box, " take a holt o' this an' kerry it hum tu yer marm ;" and the boy departed in a daze, so thankful for the gift that he forgot to utter his thanks, forgot to take egg or fish-hook, and forgot even his own identity as he ran homeward with eyes on nothing but the biggest fish he had ever had in hand, till he stubbed his bare toes on a stone, got a " stun biv" on his heel in trying to recover himself, and then went sprawling in the dusty road. But his prize had suffered no injury but a little griminess, and he forebore even a whimper as he limped home with it almost as proud as if he had caught it himself.

One and another tended toward the centre of interest, some sauntering thither with assumed indifference, others with no attempt to disguise their haste to be first to see and hear. A brawny, red-shirted bloomer, clean and off duty for the day, slowly detached himself from the attractive precincts of Hamner's Hotel and strolled toward the store, stopping half-way up the street to light his pipe with one of the newly introduced friction matches. The little shoemaker whose business had increased since Uncle Lisha's departure to such a degree as to seriously interfere with his favorite occupation of fishing, arose from his bench at the first glimpse of the returning anglers, spilled an almost finished boot off his lap, and rushed forth bareheaded to have his heart torn in twain by envy and admiration. Every boy of the neighborhood ran thither at top speed, while every woman looking out of window or door wished that she might as decorously do so rather than poorly content herself with no nearer approach

than to her own or her neighbor's door yard gate. Two
or three bethought them of some twopenny article, never
so much needed as now, and making themselves seemly
with a hasty stroke of the hair, donned their log-cabin sun-
bonnets and clean aprons and hastened to the store. A
farmer riding along the street in his ox-cart hawed his slow
team to the side of the wagon, and clambered out to get
a closer view of fish that were almost as strange to him as
the wonderful fishes of the sea whereof he had heard or
read. Indeed such an interest was aroused by this arrival
that every one within sight who might on any pretext
leave his affairs did so and drew near, and for a while all
sounds of labor ceased, except the heavy thud of the forge-
hammer. Even that seemed to slow and hush its ponderous
throbbing for a little, as if the forge, too, was listening to
the stories of the capture of the fish, drawn in laconic answers from Sam, more fully from Solon in words that his
hearers had never found in their spelling-books, and from
Antoine with an embellishment of facts and an invention
that set his hearers agog and abashed his comrades.

"Wal! If these 'ere men folks don't beat all natur'!"
said one goodwife to another, to whose gate she had come
for companionship and case of mind. "Jest a-runnin'
crazy arter some fellers 'at's ben tu the lake a-fishin'.
Your man's gone an' my man's gone, an' they're all gone,
an' there's Sally Goodwin a-scootin' over, purtendin' 'at
she's got tu git some sallyratus! 'Mongst all them men!
Oh, my sakes!"

"Hain't that 'ere that Sam Lovel?" the other asked,
without relaxing the intentness and severity of her frown fixed
upon the wagon across the way. "I sh'd think he'd better
be tu hum with his folks stiddy loafin' 'raound here!"

" Why, du you s'pose he's heard ? I don't b'lieve he
has, for they say 'at he's a real good-hearted feller, 'f he
does fish an' hunt. You know it was him 'at faound the
little Pur'n't'n gal."

" Hmp !" snorted the other, " course he's heard !
But what does he keer for anythin' but fishin' an' huntin' ?
It's my 'pinion 'at he lost that Pur'n't'n gal hisself a puppus tu find her an' make up with Huldy, an' the's others
'sides me 'at thinks so. An' if she hain't ben through the
woods an' took up wi' a crooked stick ! An' oh, dear,
tu think 'at poor Mis Lovel's troubles is over ! I s'pose
she's hed 'baout as tough a time on 't as most on us with
tew sech goo'-for-nothin' creeters as ol' Tim Lovel and
that 'ere Sam. It's bad 'nough tu raise a body's own
child'un, 'thaout takin' on 'em secont han'."

" Wal," said her neighbor, " I kinder guess 'at
S'manthy kep' up her eend o' the row wi' 'em, an' didn't
make it none tew pleasant for 'em. She had a tongue,
hung in th' middle an' sharp both eends. Why, 'f there
hain't my man comin' wi' a fish ! An' there's yourn
comin' wi' one, tew. Why, my sakes ! An' I ben hank-
erin' for fish."

" Yis, fish, tu be sure ! An' I'll bet they paid twicte
what they wus wuth ! Say, you," addressing her husband, as he drew near and proudly held forth a big pickerel for expected admiration. " You ben a payin' them
scallywags more'n the price o' good broadside pork for
that 'ere fish ?"

" No, sir !" her husband replied stoutly, " not a red
cent ! They gin it tu me ; er Sam Lovel did. They're
a givin' on 'em away tu ev'ybody 'at'll take 'em, an'
hain't much trouble fin'in' customers."

"Wal," his wife admitted, "that hain't so bad 's I expected, but you might ha' got more."

"Has he heared what's happened tu his haouse?" the other woman asked, when, after admiring the fish her husband had brought, her thoughts reverted to what had been uppermost in the minds of the gossips.

"My goodness gracious!" the good man ejaculated, and his face grew blank with the shock of suddenly remembered propriety and neglected opportunity.

"I don't b'lieve nob'dy ever thought tu tell him! Here, 'Lizy, take a holt o' this fish, an' I'll go an' tell him." But when he returned to the store he saw that his news was forestalled.

Sam's face had become decorously serious, though showing no sign of grief, and he and his companions were silently making haste to depart. For when the tide of excitement had ebbed and almost every one had borne away his present of fish, the storekeeper, slowly ascending the steps and considering what cheapest return he might make for his two great pike perch, bethought him of news that might cancel his obligation. He was almost certain, as he recalled the unconscious air of the late comers, that they had heard nothing remarkable.

"Oh, say, Lovel," he said, returning and putting one hand on Sam's arm, as he reached over the wagon box, "hev you heard f'm hum to day? Hev you met Tom Hamlin 'tween here an' V'gennes?"

"Heard f'm hum? Met Tom Hamlin?" Sam repeated with a puzzled air. "We hain't heard nothin', nor met nob'dy but three four forge teams;" and then anxiously, "the' hain't nothin' happened tu father, hes the'?"

"Wal," said Clapham, considering, "the' hain't tu your father, an' then, agin, the' hes—not egzakly tu him, but tu his wife." Then after a little pause, "Not tu break the sad news tew suddingly, she died and departed this life at twenty minutes arter nine this mornin'. She come daown here," he continued, while Sam stared at him in dumb amazement, "yist'd'y arternoon in her usuil state o' health an' vig'rous intellects an' in her own waggin, a drivin' her own hoss, an' arter purchasin' some neces-sary articles, started humerds in c'nsid'able of a hurry, bein' it was a gittin' towards night, an' abaout a half a mild this side o' your haouse she eyther run onter a hawg a-wallerin' in the rhud an' upsot, or the hoss got skeered of the hawg suddingly uprisin' an' a woof! woofin' an' upsot the waggin, which it broke the spine of her back or neck, causin' instantaneous death in a few hours. When the hoss come runnin' hum with the empty waggin, your father went in sarch of her an' found her layin' unconscious with a paound o' my best young hyson an' five paound o' white sugar scattered an' spilt promiscous in the rhud, all completely spilte, sir. It's a turrible thing for your father, sir. He sent Thomas Hamlin off this mornin' tu tell ye the sad news, an' it's sing'lar 't you never met him. He must ha' went the turnpike, an' you come the shun-pike, or maybe you missed one other in V'gennes."

"It's more sing'lar 'at some on ye didn't tell me fust thing," Sam said with some bitterness; "stiddy lettin' me stan' 'raound here 's 'f nothin' 'd happened! Jozeff, 'f you 'n' Solon 'n' 'mongst ye'll go 'long wi' the team 'n' leave my duds tu your haouses, I'll put for hum the nighest way. Give the fish where you're a minter, only leave a few good ones tu Uncle Amos Pur'n't'n's. I'm dreffle sorry for father." And he swiftly took the shortest homeward way.

His tall figure was a speck against the sky on the shorn crest of a hill, when his companions, resuming their journey, looked to see what progress he had made.

" Goes 's if he was pintin' fur a runway," said Joseph. " Wal, I s'pose it's kinder upsot Timothy Lovel a losin' his wife so onexpected. Proberbly it hes, if she wa'n't none tew clever an' even-tempered. I do' know but she was even-tempered, allus mad, an' I s'pose he'd got wonted tu her. I've knowed a sheep an' a hawg tu get wonted, runnin' in the same lot jest one summer, an' the sheep 'ould blaat, an' the hawg 'ould squeel whence ever they got sep'rit."

" Yes," Solon said, heaving a sympathetic sigh ; " it is sartingly tough indeed tu be called tu mourn the loss of a secont pardner, an' she took away so simultaneous ; momentarily as it ware. Oh, dear ! the' hain't nothin' sartain about the humern life o' man but its onsartinty."

" Yas, sah ! it was pooty bad lucky for mans los' hees waf sometam," said Antoine. " But Ah dunno for Timaty, me. Hees waf pooty hugly w'en he man to mos' always. Ah dunno 'f he be too sorry. Naow Ah dunno 'f Sam an' Hudly ant be marree raght off an' kep de haouse for hol' man ! Hein, boy ? Bah gosh ! Ant dat de bes' way of it, seh ?"

Very likely the others were thinking of the same thing, but Joseph did not word his thoughts, and Solon, slowly shaking his head, said :

" Not in no onseemless haste, they do' want tu."

XIV.

REST.

Sam drew near his home ; its outward discomfort never more impressing him than now, as, coming across lots, he approached the rear of the house where litter and make-shifts were most displayed. There was a clutter of broken crockery and useless tinware pitched from the back door into the vigorous growth of weeds ; a cart-wheel with half its felloes gone, set upon a sagging post and bearing some dishcloths and a couple of milk-pails ; two or three barrels laid upon their sides with pales driven in front served as hen-coops, wherein as many unhappy hens were in a con-stant worry concerning their wandering chicks, a worry intensified when a cat prowled past toward the house with so much more than ordinary uncanny feline stealth that Sam's flesh crept as he watched her creeping, halting, listening, always intent on something unseen within the house. When he hurled half a broken earthen milk-pan at her, she crouched and glared wickedly at him an instant before she scurried away through the weedy cover.

One of the half dozen neighboring women who had come to help, coming to the door caught sight of him, and crying out :

" Why of all this worl' ! If here ain't Samwill !" at once retreated to inform the others of his arrival.

He hastened toward the front of the house in search of his

father, his footsteps brushing the rank mat of mallows that
had almost crowded out the fox lilies his mother had
planted. As he was recalling the time of year and marking the very spot where he sat when he watched her at her
toilsome recreation, he caught sight of some one among
the currant-bushes just beyond the cherry-trees and half-
tamed wild plum-trees of the garden. A finer if not a
keener sense than the cultivated instinct of the hunter informed him that it was Huldah, though he could not see
the face nor even the outlines of the figure. He was close
to her the next moment, only the sprawling hedge of currant-bushes between them, and when she turned her
blushing face toward him it expressed more gladness than
surprise, for her thoughts were just now so fixed upon him
that she knew he could not be far away. When some
things had been said that need not be written, Huldah,
picking at the half-grown stems of currants in her pail,
said, with downcast face, "I don't s'pose it looks jest
right for me tu come here, Sam, but it did seem 's if some
women folks ort tu come f'm aour haouse, an' mother sot
ri' daown an' said 'at she could n't du no more'n come
tu the fun'al, an' so I come, an' I can't help what folks
says. I hed tu. An' them women in there hes ben tryin'
tu joke me ! a-jokin' sech a time ! I would n't stay with
'em, an' come aout tu pick some currants for sass. The'
hain't half growed, but the' hain't no rhubub. I wisht I'd
fetched some ; we've got sights, but I never thought."
Then, starting suddenly, "Why, you hain't seen you'
father. Jes' tu think o' you stan'in' here talkin' tu me an'
you hain't never seen him yit !"

Going to the front of the house, Sam found his father,
where he was almost sure he should, leaning forlornly on

the sagging gate-post, gazing abstractedly at nothing when
not casting a casual glance up or down the road.

"Wal, father, haow be ye?" he asked, putting his
hand on the old man's shoulder.

"Why, Samwil!" turning with a little start, and taking
his son's hand, "I wa'n't 'spectin' on ye so soon. You
must ha' started 'fore Tawmus got tu ye? I'm awf'l glad
you've come, for this 'ere's knocked me gally west. You
never liked her none too well, I know, an' I know 't the'
wa'n't no love lost, but won't ye go in an' see her? She
looks turrible peaceable— more so'n I most ever seen her."

Sam could not refuse this common mark of respect expected of all who came to the house of mourning, and
followed his father into the house, stopping on his way
through the kitchen to greet the women whose tongues
had been busy with the gossip which was the chief com-
pensation of their labors. When the two men entered the
room they suddenly ceased conversation, which was always
carried on in low tones and whispers, as if they feared they
might awaken her who had fallen into eternal sleep. The
wives of Solon and Joseph were of the number, and they
asked some questions concerning the welfare of their
husbands.

Sam remarked they met him with rather an air of reproof. Whether they blamed him for not being at home
at the time of the accident, or for having inveigled their
husbands from their homes, or for having met Huldah in
the garden, he could not guess. "Ary one 's 'nough tu
raise the' quills," he said to himself, in resentment of their
coldness. "Womern fashion, but the' 's one womern 't
ain't that way," and he went with his father into the mysterious presence.

When he saw into what serenity the hand of death had
moulded the face that he had always seen so fretfully un-
restful, he marvelled at the undreamed-of kindly possibil-
ities of the harsh features, and all resentment of past injuries
was swept out of his heart. He forgave her and wished
he might ask her to forgive him for hard and angry words
that now could never be recalled. It came upon him suddenly how repentance may come too late for the soul's
perfect comfort.

When the father and son came out of the " square
room" some of the women had already gone, and two
were putting on their bonnets in the first preparation for
departure.

" I b'lieve the' hain't nothin' more 't we c'n du naow,
Mr. Lovel," said Solon Briggs's wife, as, holding her chin
aloft, she carefully knotted the strings of her log-cabin
sunbonnet. " We've got ev'ything fixed up f' the watchers.
Mis Gove and her man 's a-goin' tu set up tu-night, an'
we'll stop 's we go 'long an' tell her where 't she c'n find
ev'ything f' the' luncheon. There's the last pie 't poor
Mis Lovel ever made onderneath a pan on the top shelf in
the butt'ry. You an' Samwil 'd orter eat a piece, each
on ye, an' the' 's nut-cakes 't we fried tu-day—oh, dear
me suz ! who knows 't they hain't the last ones 't we'll
ever fry ! an' who knows which one ?—in a stun jar on
the floor. An' the' 's some o' them plums 'at poor
Mis Lovel put up—poor woman, she'll never put up no
more, an' the trees is jest loaded this year ! why couldn't
she ha' ben spared ? but like 's not they'll all blast 'fore
fall—settin' by the butt'ry winder. We'd stay an' git
supper f' you an' Samwil, but we got tu g' hum, me an'
Mis Hill hes, tu tend tu aour men. Jemimer Bartlett 'll

stay an' git it, an' like 's not,'' casting a sidelong glance at
Sam, '' she'll hev help f'm younger han's.   Wal, M'rier,
we mus' be a-goin', but I guess 't we'd orter go int' the
square room a minute fust;'' and they let themselves in,
opening the door just wide enough to squeeze themselves
through, '' Cats does act so!'' Mrs. Briggs apologized in
a loud whisper.

Presently they came forth, with awed faces, from the
room whose solemn stillness their hushed voices and light
footfalls had scarcely broken, and without many more
words went their way.

'' Such a muss as the' 'll be wi' them men's dirty clo's
an' dirty dishes jest makes me sick tu think on!   Don't
it you, M'rier?'' said Mrs. Briggs to her friend with a
tone more cheery than such a prospect seemed to warrant,
when they were fairly out upon the highway.   '' It ort tu
be a comfort tu S'manthy 'at she hain't got tu clean up
arter Sam, but tain't likely she realizes.   Oh, dear, them
things!''

'' If Mr. Hill 's only fetched hum that fryin'-pan, I
sh'll be setisfied,'' Mrs. Hill said.

Friend Jemima Bartlett and Huldah got supper ready,
and the four sat down to it, the three world's people in-
voluntarily joining the sedate Friend in her silent grace
before meat.   When in almost equal silence the meal was
eaten, and the dishes washed and put away, it was time
for Huldah to go home, and so late that Sam could not
but offer to go with her.   When he came home, the night
had deepened into all the darkness that night can when a
starlit sky overarches the world, but the world had never
looked brighter to him, nor had his path through it ever
lain so pleasantly before him.   After going to the barn to

quiet Drive's doleful howling, he entered the kitchen and
found there Pelatiah's father and mother, who were to
" set up" to night, and Joel Bartlett, who had come to
settle the arrangements for the funeral and then accompany his wife home.

The visitors made transparent attempts at cheerful discourse, while decorously avoiding lightness of conversation, and discussed crop prospects and forecast the weather
from the moon's signs and the last days of the past month.
The Goves had many questions to ask concerning their
son's welfare, and listened with intense interest to Sam's
account of the Garden Island adventure, with a feeling
that they had almost become famous as the parents of a
new Crusoe.

Sam told Joel and his wife something of their lowland
relatives, for whom they felt a kindly regard, but had had
no unity with nor had ever visited since the memorable
" separation," when good Quakers first began to hate one
another for difference of religious opinion. When the
" Uncle Lisher clock," which since the " vandew" had
stood in the corner of the Lovel kitchen, warned for nine
with a solemn clank of its machinery, the two arose as if
moved at once by the spirit, and made ready to depart, but
still Joel had something on his mind, as was shown by the
tighter pucker of his lips.

" 'Thee 'll halfter make pervision for a haouse-keeper,
Timerthy, thee an' thy son, an' it's a-goin' tu be a trial,
I tell thee as it hes ben a trial tu thee tu hev thy com-
paniern took from thee. An' I feel a consarn tu advise
thee tu not be hasty. It's better for thee an' thy son tu
endure privations, discomforts, yea, an' triberlatierns for
a spell 'an for thee tu make a hasty ch'ice of some on-

worthy womern kind tu minister tu your temporal wants.
It has ben a weighty matter in my mind, an' I wa'n't
clear till I laid it afore thee.''

" I hev hed sech a consarn," his wife said when he had
done, " but all this arternoon I've felt easy in my mind, for
it hes ben bore in upon me that the' 'll be a way pervided,
an' I'm clear that Samwil 'll provide the way at a proper
time," and her quiet face beamed benignantly on Sam for
a moment.

They went their way, and Sam and his father betaking
themselves to bed, the watchers were left to their vigil.
The house became silent but for the ghostly sounds that
always pervade old houses in the night time, and were now
so much more awful and mysterious in this one that Ashbel
Gove and his wife felt more comfortable when their chairs
were drawn quite close together.

" It's a turrible long time sence me an' you sot up
tugether, Hanner; an' arter all it don't seem so dreff'l
long nuther," he whispered, and surprised the good
woman by taking her hand.

On the third day after Mrs. Lovel's death, the Lovel
house was filled with Danvis folks who met " at ten
o'clock at the house," to pay the last tribute of respect to
their deceased neighbor.

Timothy Lovel was appalled at the greatness of his loss
when he heard the minister recount the virtues of his departed wife. Indeed, no one of the company breathed a
word against her, if there was none to be said for her.
One good soul, casting about for something to say in
praise of the dead without doing violence to her own con-
science, whispered to her neighbor :

" S'manthy was 'baout the spryest womern 't ever I see !"

Some of the sumacs that grew at will in the uncared-for burying-ground were displaced to make room for her, and she was laid beside Sam's mother on the hillside, a pleasant and restful place, for all its loneliness, where longest the birds sang and the bees delved above the silent sleepers, and where latest the sunlight fell upon the peaceful graves.

XV.

NEW LIFE IN THE OLD HOME.

The Lovel house, which for many years had not been a very cheerful one, was now more lonesome than ever. The two men, the hound and the cat were its sole inmates for many weeks, except when a neighborly housewife came to wash, iron, and bake for them, and Sam realized as never before how different were the "good lonesome" of a solitary camp-fire and the dreariness of a womanless hearthstone.

When the good people of Danvis had been for some time expecting it, it happened of a Sunday that the intended marriage of Samuel Lovel and Huldah Purington was "published" at the town house, in which, for lack of a church, all religious meetings but those of the Quakers were held.

A week later there was a quiet wedding at the Purington homestead. Not more than twoscore guests were present, mostly relatives of the bride and groom, but quite enough the groom thought when he stood up before them and 'Squire Bascom. He went bravely through the ordeal, though in such trepidation as had never before assailed him. He also stood manfully at his post, while a dozen young men enjoyed their first and last opportunity of saluting his bride, and more girls offered him their lips than he had ever kissed before.

"I couldn't never ha' went through sech a job fur nob'dy but you, Huldy," he told her at the first chance of a word in private. "Never! An' by the gret horn spoon, I won't never agin fur nob'dy!"

There was no display of gifts, for there were none but the silver spoons given by the bride's parents, for in those days wedding guests were invited for their presence, not for their presents.

There were white bride's cake and black groom's cake, and no end of more substantial good cheer for all.

Later in the evening, by some chance a fiddle and fiddler came in conjunction, and those so disposed had an opportunity to prance with some regard to the time and tunes of "Money Musk," "Hull's Victory," the "Backside of Albany," and many another tune that has outlived its dancers of those days. The inspiring voice of the fiddle soon rid Sam of his bashfulness, and when he was as well rid of his coat he cut the pigeon-wing in a fashion worthy of legs so used to nimbly climbing Danvis hills, and Huldah tripped as nimbly with him.

Much pains had been taken that an invitation should reach Pelatiah Gove, and he had taken no less to be present. As he went home from the wedding with his mother, he stammered out a confession that he was engaged to a "gal as harnsome as a pictur' an' smartern a steel-trap, an' her name was Lowizy."

"Why, Peltier!" cried the good woman, stopping short and facing him in almost breathless amazement. "Why, my sakes! You're tew young tu think o' sech a thing! Y'r father an' me was much as ten year older'n you be when we was merried."

"Wal, what on't? You tew lost ten year o' good

times 'at you'd ha' hed, an' we hain't a-goin' tu be fools 'cause you was—not by a jugfull, maw.''

Wedding journeys were not the fashion in Danvis in those days, and that of Sam and Huldah was only from her father's house to that of his, and was quite uneventful. Perhaps it was made on foot across lots, or on top of one of the lumber wagon loads of the bride's '' settin' aout,'' of quilts, blankets, and linen, all home-made ; feather beds, each with its thirty pounds of good live-geese feathers ; the big and little wheels and the reel and many other articles that had long been set apart as Huldah's.

She was duly installed as mistress of her new home, and now Timothy Lovel could smoke his pipe in peace in his own kitchen, or in the square room if he chose, and Drive might take his ease undisturbed in the best patch of sunlight that fell upon the floor.

A great deal of the Purington thrift seemed to have been transplanted with its new mistress to the tumble-down place, which out-doors as well as in began to brighten into a pleasanter home than its old inmates had known for many a year.

Huldah was intently counting the stitches on her needle, held close to the candle that faintly illumined the close of the short summer evening. Sam had succeeded in the discovery of a sheet of foolscap whereon the flies of more than one season had recorded their summer's sojourn, and he was now rummaging the top shelf of the cupboard in quest of a pen.

'' The' hain't no pen in this hull haouse, I du b'lieve,'' he acknowledged at last, '' but here's a quill, an' when you an' me went tu school you was a master hand at makin' pens, an' s'posin' you try agin. My knife 's big

for a leetle han', but the leetle blade's keener 'n a brier,
an' you c'n whittle aout suthin' ; I c'n write 'baout as well
wi' one thing 's another.''

"Why, Sam Lovel, I can't make a pen," said Huldah.
"What be you in sech a tew to write ?''

"I've put it off tew long a'ready," he answered, "an'
naow I'm a-goin' tu set ri' daown an' write a letter tu
Uncle Lisher tu come. Him an' Aunt Jerushy c'n hev
the back bedr'm as we talked, an' he c'n hev the linter
for a shop.''

"An' they'll be most welcom's fur 's I c'n make 'em,"
said his wife, "an' I shan't never take no comfort 's long
's I'm a-thinkin' o' them poor ol' lunsome folks a-dyin' o'
humsickness in that hatef'l West. We won't never go there,
Sam," rocking forward, with knitting dropped in her lap,
and putting both hands on her husband's flaxen poll, while
she looked straight into his gray eyes.

"Not, never, Huldy," he answered. "If you was
with me I d' know but I c'ld stan' it a month or tew
aouter sight o' these maountains," as looking out of the
window his eyes dwelt fondly on the western mountains,
a looming mass of blackness against the darkening sky,
and in whose jagged crest the evening star lingered for a
moment more of shining ; "but not for long, noways. A
Green Maountain boy I be an' a Green Maountain boy
I'll die, an' take pride in't.''

With a sigh of satisfaction, Huldah rocked back into
the fuller light of the candle, and after some intent examination of quill and knife began a careful whittling of the
goose-feather. While Sam watched the fashioning of the
pen, and in his mind framed the words it should write, he
pictured to himself a renewal in the "lean to" of the old

comradeship that had existed in Uncle Lisha's shop. For he was too young to know that old times can never return in all their fulness, and that the happy, care-free days of youth, once spent, are gone forever.